"All the warm fuzzies from this book! Hope Bolinger delivers a heartfelt, laugh-out-loud romance. She's one to watch."

—**Caroline George**, author of *Dearest Josephine* (HarperCollins)

"*A Country of Their Own* celebrates love with twists and turns sure to delight readers through a journey of discovery. Bolinger's altered reality sweeps readers away through vivid scenes that will have you smiling, sighing and reaching for the kleenex. A must read for all the young at heart."

—**Melony Teague**, Author of *A Promise to Keep*

A COUNTRY of their OWN

HOPE BOLINGER

A Country of Their Own

End Game Press books may be purchased in bulk at special discounts for sales promotion, corporate gifts, ministry, fund-raising, or educational purposes. Special editions can also be created to specifications. For details, contact Special Sales Dept., End Game Press, P.O. Box 206, Nesbit, MS 38651 or info@endgamepress.com.

Visit our website at www.endgamepress.com.

Library of Congress Control Number: 2022939886
ISBN: 978-1-63797-043-0
eBook ISBN: 978-1-63797-049-2

Cover by Greg Jackson, Thinkpen Design
Interior design by Greg Jackson, Thinkpen Design

Printed in the United States
10 9 8 7 6 5 4 3 2 1

Chapter One
PRISCILLA

THE HOUSE SMELLED OLD. Priscilla loved it.

She slid off her flats by the shaggy carpet at the front door and inhaled the aroma of must and lavender. Home sweet summer home.

"Where's my granddaughter?" Grandpa Silas tipped off his Gators baseball cap and grinned at her, a tooth or two in the front a charcoal black. He'd sometimes complained about toothaches—literal ones. Grandpa did like his sweets.

Priscilla unlatched her fingertips from the suitcase handle and buried herself into a hug. Her grandpa giggled and bounced his fingers against her hair. "It's huge."

Instinctually she reached to detangle some of the dark curls. "Florida's made it all frizzy. Now I look like Kerry Washington." Hair a little longer and skin a little darker, but the humidity did help with mirroring the natural look her favorite celebrity sported from time to time.

It wasn't all that often that she liked *modern* celebrities, compared with the classic movies. But who didn't love a strong Black woman who got the job done?

"Well, I like it relaxed. Didn't even know you were capable of doing that." Laughter bounced at the back of his throat again. "Relaxing."

Grandpa released her from the hug and shuffled toward the suitcase. She dodged around him and reached the door first. Couldn't have him carrying it up all those stairs, not after he had that lung scare this last year that landed him in the hospital. She hoped to God they wouldn't have a repeat this summer.

He slumped as he watched her fingers grip around the handle again.

"Then again, we might need to work on the relaxing bit." He sighed and lifted a shaking arm in the direction of the stairs. "Don't be too long up there. Maria prepared snacks in the kitchen. I hope you like sangria."

Of course Maria had. Even though she spent time here as a caregiver, the woman had a tendency to go above and beyond the call of duty. Within months, she'd incorporated herself well into Priscilla's family.

"Grandpa, you know I'm not old enough to drink." Even in the safety of his home ... alcohol tended to run a bad history with her family.

A dark, wrinkled finger raised to his lips, eyes a-twinkle. "You're seventeen, right? Eh, close enough. It's Florida, Prisca." He winked at her nickname. "Age doesn't matter here. Now show me those dimples."

She held back an eye roll. Didn't want to show any disrespect in front of him, not that he would care. Mom sure would.

Speaking of her mother, and Priscilla's dimples ... her mother used to poke fun and say she could dip a bucket in them and draw out water, they tunneled so deep. Mom didn't have dimples. Must've gotten it from ... she didn't want to think about him.

Not now in the Paradise State.

Still, she smiled, and Grandpa returned the expression, albeit without the dimples on him.

"That's my girl. Sangria in five minutes." He gave a slow wave as if churning his hand underwater, turned, and shuffled down the hallway.

Love you, Grandpa. But you're such a bad influence. I wonder how much trouble you got into as a teen.

Her knees cracked as she stooped to grab the bag and let the thick carpet tickle her feet as she marched up the stairs, around the corner, and into the guest bedroom. Good, Grandpa put the vintage-looking comforter on the bed.

Maroon and with golden detailing, she loved the feel of the velvet swirls.

Running her fingertips up and down the bed, she grinned at the "Vasquez Family Portrait" that hung directly across from a seahorse ornament Mom had given Grandpa last Christmas. She unhooked the picture from the wall and placed it on a side table near the queen-sized mattress. A quick scan of the photo shifted her thoughts. Maybe Maria was right. Memories flickered back to a FaceTime call Priscilla had with Grandpa and his caretaker, Maria. Besides the glasses she now wore and the extra inch she grew sophomore year, she hadn't aged a day.

She hated it.

Priscilla spun around and hoisted the suitcase on the bed, making quick work of unloading her baggage. Smallest pocket first, as she wound the blue zipper open, her phone slid out onto her sheets.

Whoops, she'd almost forgotten about that.

She clicked off the Airplane mode and listened to the device buzz on the comforter as she folded some shorts. Fourteen or so buzzes later, she relented and decided to see who had messaged.

MOM: Text me when you arrive.

MOM: Hope you have a great time with Grandpa. I know it was last-minute, but I'm out too much at conferences this summer. And I couldn't have you throwing parties at the house ;)

Priscilla sniggered and fought a lip twitch. *Ha, nice joke.* She didn't hang out with anyone under the age of fifty, and their idea of a good time was knitting club at the library on Wednesdays.

Sometimes they got really wild and would knit stuffed animals. The hooligans ...

She would've packed the swan she made back in March, but limited space on the airline prevented this. And she doubted the scarf she made would do much help here in the one-hundred-degree June weather.

MOM: But seriously, it just isn't safe to leave a teenager at home all summer, no matter how responsible she is.

Priscilla knew the rest of the text Mom was leaving out. With her mom posting on social about going to writing conferences as staff ... that left the apartment empty.

"Yeah, Mom, I know you mean well." She smirked and pulled on a seashell string dangling from the ceiling fan. The blades whirled to life.

As an acquisitions editor, her mother enjoyed her job for the most part. But a few writing stalkers too many validated the extra need for sending her daughter from New York to Florida for the summer months. Not that Priscilla minded. That meant a slower pace of life plus plenty of porch space to read books and curl up with Grandpa's cat Ambrosia.

Her phone buzzed again, this time in a phone call. Mom knew her too well. Priscilla swiped open on the second ring.

"Hey."

"Hey, you weren't answering texts."

Priscilla chewed on her lip. "Sorry."

A pause.

"I need to prepare for a session I'm teaching, so I don't have much time to talk." Her mother's voice came out breathy on the other end. "Now I know spending time in a state populated by mostly retirees sounds like heaven, but I am worried about you and your antisocial habits."

Priscilla chewed on her tongue. Much as she wanted to argue ... when did that ever work?

Mom continued. "I took the liberty of contacting the pastor at the church right by Grandpa's house. I told them you'd go to their youth group on Wednesdays."

Priscilla's thumbs itched to tap the hang-up button.

Ugh, Mom, no. She knew Priscilla's weakness. She always followed through on commitments, even if someone else signed her up for them. She even stuck through ballet for nine years straight until, at long last, she managed to sprain her ankle before one of the performances. No more dance classes for Ms. Vasquez.

Good, she hated dancing.

And it looked like her mom booked her for youth group, *tonight*.

Priscilla blew out a long breath and forced a smile. Mom could often hear facial expressions across phone calls. "Okay, thanks for telling me."

"Love you. Stay safe. Make friends." Three beeps followed. Her mom hadn't lied about needing to talk fast.

Inhale, hold the breath, release. At least six other days during the week she didn't have to spend time with teenagers.

Buzz, buzz, buzz, the phone and fan attempted to outdo each other in noise levels in the room. Priscilla huffed, slumped on the bed, and slid a sweaty finger onto her phone until she managed to click the Do Not Disturb button.

"Time for some snacks." She'd get back to folding clothes later. *Here's to hoping Grandpa has something without alcohol in it.*

Chapter Two
CARTER

"CARTER, GET OFF YOUR PHONE."

He glanced up from the TikTok feed in time to catch his mother glare across the table. She'd just set down a plate of pulled pork on the table and swabbed a greasy hand through her auburn bangs.

"You could at least stay off it for five minutes the first night your grandma is here."

Right next to her, a pale woman in a flowery sundress shrank into the wooden chair. Hints of red showed through the white in her hair. They all looked like perfect Weasleys—at least Carter determined so when he devoured *Harry Potter* at the bright age of ten. The curved top and arms of the chair looked as though they wanted to swallow the old woman whole.

If Grandma minded, she didn't let on. She just pushed her glasses up her long nose and adjusted the napkin on her lap.

She almost never said anything. If she didn't prefer to live with his family, would she let on? Did she hate the fact the family decided to have her stay with them after she broke her leg tripping on her staircase?

When she broke her leg, Carter had suggested that they check her into that nice assisted living center a few miles away ... what was it called? Country Homes? Country Living? Something like that? ... his mother had to clench her yellow oven mitts to keep from slapping him.

"Carter Michael Irvin, you think I would check my own mom into a nursing home? My own lifeblood?"

"It's not a nursing home; it's an assisted living center. There's a difference. And the youth pastor says it's very nice there." Better than living with two parents who just divorced but hadn't figured out new housing yet.

"Youth pastor, youth smchastor. When was the last time you'd even been to youth group?"

Easy. Since they grounded him for the incident in the school parking lot last April that almost prevented his graduation. Grounding included sending Carter to youth group for an intervention, which involved the pink-faced youth pastor keeping him afterward, pacing the floor in skinny jeans, and yelling at Carter for "purpling."

Youth pastor liked to use a lot of Christian-ese. Purpling, of course, meaning mixing pink and blue. Doing the do. The forbidden sideways samba.

At first, Carter had wanted to fight the fact that his school tried to withhold his diploma for his ... illicit activities. But private Christian schools did make their students sign a waiver at the beginning of the year stating something along the lines of, "I will not bring drugs to school." "I will not send no-no pictures across DMs to fellow classmates." "I will not purple." Infractions could lead to punishments such as the school threatening to withhold privileges, including a diploma.

Heck, one student almost didn't graduate because of a library fine. *Gotta love private schools.*

And even if it was illegal, Mom didn't care. She would force her son to do youth group and who knew what to atone for his crimes.

Lucky for him, he'd dodged youth group a couple of times afterward until his parents finally gave up on the matter.

"Sorry." He placed the phone on his lap and scrolled as his mom wiped some broccoli juice that had spilled on Grandma's plate. With a nervous tug on the collar of his shirt, his finger brushed the sunglasses he always kept hooked over the fabric: hurricane or shine.

Grandma croaked something about shaky hands, and Mom told her not to worry about it in a voice that sounded worried.

He watched the video he'd posted an hour ago on silent. Yikes, his hair looked awful. A tangerine mess of a mop against freckles and sunburnt skin. Carter braced himself for his mother's lecture on sunscreen usage.

At least the video had a few thousand views, small consolation.

Rookie numbers, but he'd gotten inconsistent in posting after his parents took away his phone. Part of the grounding, since he ...

His thumb stopped scrolling. Of course, Mia Patel's video would appear right after his. Why hadn't he unfollowed Patels' yet?

Right, because he felt his throat go dry and stomach tighten any time he saw her at Bean Juice, a local coffee shop. That gorgeous short dark hair, her short, small frame he could hug for minutes on end. He still loved her, even after everything.

He stole a glance at his mom as she prayed grace over the table and slid into his last DM with Mia over Instagram. She'd sent it in May, a month after the purpling incident in the school parking lot.

@MiaPatel'23

Heyyy, listen, sorry about you stumbling into me and Marcus on a date at Bean Juice the other day. I know you and I had dated, but I figured we went on a break after Principal Velez threw you into detention and almost prevented you from graduating when he discovered us, umm, discovering us in the parking lot. I guess you getting off with doing service hours at that nursing home was some dumb luck, huh? Although they're having me do mulching for people in my neighborhood, apparently that wasn't good enough for Mom. Had to get a quieter job at a library instead of at the ice cream shop at the pier. She's worried I would get too carried away with the boys at the beach, so now I'm surrounded by a bunch of middle-aged ladies. I guess with her job in Planning and Development, she has an in with most of the government employees. Pulled a few strings and got me a job at the good ol' library.

@MiaPatel'23
Plus you went all quiet and stopped texting me, so I figured we were done.

Thanks, parents, for taking away that phone for a month.

@MiaPatel'23
Aaaand, I just realized the dozen roses sent to my house came from you. I was wondering why Marcus would put "Happy Anniversary," since he and I have only been together for three weeks. Almost forgot it was our one-year.

Grandma dropped a spoon off the table. Their dog Sadie raced to grab it.

@MiaPatel'23
What we had was amazing, don't get me wrong. But you can be a little forward. I mean, you sent me a DOZEN ROSES. Which would be sweet for most girls, but ... it was intense.

@MiaPatel'23

Anyway, I wish you the best. Maybe you'll find a girl who is into hopeless romantics.

@MiaPatel'23

And even though it was your first time, you purpled well. If it's any consolation.

It wasn't.

He glanced up in time before his mother craned her neck in his direction. His eyes flicked away from her stare and landed on the empty wooden chair across from Mom. Right next to a puddle on the hardwood floor from where the spoon had landed. Dad probably wouldn't get back until his mom headed to bed.

"Where's Justin?" Grandma spoke this through a napkin she'd pressed on her mouth. Probably to catch some of the pulled pork.

"Remember, Mom?" Carter's mother spoke in slow, irritating tones, as though to Sadie the dog. "He's doing an internship at Biola. He and some other juniors have to do their practicum credit to graduate."

"Oh."

Grandma stewed in silence, the sound of chewing pork disrupting the quiet. She swallowed. Carter retreated to the TikTok app to refresh the number of views.

"What's your youngest doing over the summer?"

Youngest apparently wasn't allowed to have a conversation with the oldest person in the room. Which didn't seem like Grandma. Whenever she did talk, she seemed interested in having conversations *with Carter*. Maybe Mom had let Grandma in on the school parking lot purpling, and it scandalized the "eldest" in the room.

"Carter? Well, for starters, he's going to youth group tonight."

His neck snapped up in time to watch his mother perch, back straight and triumphant in her chair. One eyebrow shot up so high, it disappeared into her bangs.

He opened his mouth, closed it, and grit his teeth. "That so?"

"Yes, unless you want to spend time with Grandma tonight. She and I want to watch *The Notebook* together and peruse through some old photo books."

Fine, he'd go to youth group.

Maybe he could meet some cute girls there tonight. Madison, that pretty girl with the deep brown eyes, did like to go. No wait, he saw something on her Insta feed earlier about a trip to Spain.

Oh, there was Bri with the green hair, great figure, and nose ring. Hold up, she said something about working nights at an ice cream shop. No luck there. Huh, if God worked in *mysterious* ways, maybe He'd have some *mysteriously* good-looking girl walk into church tonight.

Carter shoveled the briny pulled pork down his throat and sent it on a journey with a swig of sweet tea.

Mom's other eyebrow blasted off. "You're moving awfully fast."

"Gotta spend time with God."

"Funny, you got the word 'God' and 'girls' mixed up, son."

Bitterness from the tea leaves lingered on his tongue for a moment before he swallowed.

He felt his face pinch together.

"Speaking of," his mother swabbed her bangs with a greasy hand, "you best be heading to youth group now. Youth Pastor changed the time from last summer to an hour earlier, at least that's what it seemed from his email. Doesn't it start in ten minutes?"

The clock behind her blared in orange numbers: 6:51 p.m.

Wow, Mom, way to wait till the last minute to tell me. Made sense. If she'd told him any sooner, he may have bolted.

"I can leave in five."

"It's a seven-minute walk."

Walk?

They locked gazes as he rubbed his thumb on a groove in the plate. Ay, yi, yi—she wouldn't let him take her car again. Not after his last video stunt where he accidentally got green spray paint on the license plate. A curved verdigris line still covered the AEG.

With a sigh, he shoved his chair back, scooped up his plate, and shoved it in the sink. He rushed toward the door and caught the words "Dishwasher's empty," in the door slam.

He'd put them in the dishwasher when he got back. Oof, the sun was blinding today.

A slender silhouette blocked the tangerine sun in the driveway. He shielded his eyes to absorb the large hair, dark skin, dark brown eyes, high-cut cheekbones, and ... wow, hideous white socks that almost went up to her calves.

This girl didn't hail from Florida, no doubt. Everyone here wore no-shows if they even had the audacity to put socks on in the summer.

But most striking, he noticed the dimples. Even though she was frowning, they showed on her side profile. Warmth filled his chest, summer heat excluded. Socks or no socks, this girl was hot.

"New to the neighborhood?"

She jumped and clutched something heavy to her chest. He squinted at a gold ESV emblazoned into the spine of the book she held. A Bible. "I'm not here for long."

Her tone came out short, low, like a warning. Too bad he liked low and vaguely threatening voices.

Did he like red flags or what? Might as well have beamed at him with those eyes shining like a lighthouse. Come hither, and crash thy ship, Carter.

"You off to youth group too?"

Shoulders, up to her ears, relaxed an inch. "Yeah." She winced and brushed her lip with the back of her palm. The girl probably came from someplace with less humidity.

"You sound hesitant."

She passed him a withering glare. Measuring him, calculating her next words. "Mom's making me go."

His lips twitched. Maybe he could forget about Mia Patel for a minute, two minutes.

"Mine too."

Through watery eyes he swore he spotted her lips curve up her cheek. Ice cream with this girl sounded real nice right now.

"What do you say we ditch and grab some ice cream at the pier? It's about a mile away."

Lips formed a thin line. Those beautiful brown eyes flicked from him, to the Bible cradled in her arms, and to the church stationed on a slope in the distance. Inch by inch, her shoulders hiked up again. Yikes, he'd lost ground.

"So you're deliberately going against what she told you to do?" She chewed on her lip again. "And do what exactly?"

He shrugged. "Sometimes I like to round up some kids at the pier. One of their moms makes a great margarita. Doesn't ask for ages. I don't think she cares."

"You're asking me, a girl who clearly doesn't look like the partying type, if she wants to ditch an activity she promised she would go to, to do underage drinking?"

Throat tight, he tugged at the sunglasses strapped to his chest. Didn't he say that when Mia had invited him out for drinks the first time? And what did she say in reply?

You're young once.

So they had a mango margarita that night. Maybe the same wording would work on this girl? After all, he used to carry a brick-shaped Bible up the same winding sidewalk. People could change.

"You're young once, right?"

Shoot, she could block her ears with those bony shoulders now. "Thanks, but I think I'll be heading over to church." She paused, glancing at the sunglasses clipped onto his shirt. No eye contact. "Alone."

He clenched his fists and let the jagged nails dig into his palms.

Relax, my dude. Mia played a little hard to get before you went on a first date with her.

"I didn't catch your name."

She'd already begun walking down the sidewalk, palm tree leaf shadows covering the gauche socks.

"Hey, I'm sorry if I said something to offend you. Start over? Start with names?" He nearly had to shout this now. His shoes somehow melted into the white cement of his driveway.

"Not interested."

A honk blared down the street, and a jeep whooshed past the girl who had found security for a moment underneath the shadow of a palm tree in someone's front yard. In a red flash, the car skidded to a stop at the base of his drive. In the passenger seat, a guy with an ear piercing and blond beard flashed a grin. The car was full of neighborhood kids Carter sometimes would hang with at the ice cream shop by the pier. Not as many flavors as that one 50s diner downtown, but a good, cheap cone to grab while watching waves somersault over each other. Orange from the glow of the sunset.

"Cartie, where you heading?"

Carter gave a curt nod to the passenger as his heart sank from his chest into his gut. The girl had disappeared around the corner of a house at the end of the street. "Depends. Where do y'all want to take me in your jeep?"

Two passengers, the driver, and a girl with dark curly hair in the back, gave a whoop.

The girl in the back glossed her lips with her tongue. "Skipping church again?"

He glanced back at the robin's egg blue house, at the church in the distance, and then at her. Then, he clicked open the door to the back, sliding onto the smooth leather seats.

After all, he was only young once.

Chapter Three
PRISCILLA

"THE GAME IS SIMPLE ENOUGH. Everyone hold out your right hand." The youth pastor's jeans coiled so tightly around his leg that he had to waddle back to his place in the circle. All the teens held up their right hands, Priscilla's an inch shorter than the rest.

She didn't like where this was going.

"Now grab hold of someone else's hand in the circle, preferably someone not next to you."

She reached for a hand with a silver dolphin bracelet wrapped around the wrist. Dry skin met her sweaty palm.

Ugh, I'm already regretting this. She wished she could wipe her fingers once more on her shorts to trim some of the sweat. The AC blasted from the vents from above. But when she walked into youth group, she did hear a girl say, over a bowl of Cheetos at the snack table, "They only turn it on for this." The church hadn't cooled down completely yet.

"Everyone hold up your left hand."

Hers grappled with another that dangled a few inches short of an orb light fixture swinging above the circle. Was that a purple lantern? She'd seen some like that at Target.

"Now, I'll give you ten minutes to untangle the knot. You may not release your grip for any reason. Ready? Go."

A girl in a floor-length denim skirt and Priscilla matched expressions: pinched eyebrows and winces. They knew exactly how this would go.

Sure enough, one boy standing next to the youth pastor, with the shadow of a beard and an orange tank, tried to instruct members of the circle which arms to duck under or hurdle over, landing Priscilla dead center with her arms hugging her ribs like a makeshift snake hold.

Ten minutes passed, and they'd tangled themselves more than how they'd started.

And this is why I don't hang out with people my age.

"Time's up. Release your grip."

Priscilla's fingers recoiled. She snaked through the crowd until she found a pocket of space to breathe at last. Of all the youth group games to start the night.

The youth leader snapped his fingers, and a group of boys rolled in a rack of tan chairs they began to unfold. Priscilla stationed herself at one, with the most berth between seats, and waited for her heart to stop tearing at her rib cage. How she missed knitting club back at home with the ladies who were in their fifties and sixties.

"You may wonder why I would put you through that exercise." The youth leader slumped into a chair as he rubbed a pink hand across the bridge of his forehead. She spied a name tag with "Timothy" scrawled in a hard-edge font. "We do like to play a game before the lesson each time we meet, but this one certainly was a little more interactive."

"Better than the time you made us eat random foods out of a paper bag. Couldn't go down the Vienna sausage aisle in Publix for a month after the Josh incident." Someone in blue tennis shoes piped up, sending a giggle all the way to the next-door seat neighbor to Priscilla. He pretended to hurl.

Timothy cut him a severe look, and the soft carpet in the room absorbed the silence.

Whoa, this felt different than her church back home. Sure, the people here wore sandals and tanks instead of dresses, but wow. No wonder that one kid with the curly orange hair wanted to skip tonight.

She wiped her sweaty fingertips on her shorts, then chewed on her lip.

Maybe she had given him a hard time, but she didn't *do* bad boys. Not after her mom had dated one, gotten pregnant, and he'd left a month later. Mom said it was for the best anyway. He liked to nurse a bottle more than she liked to nurse her baby child. Lucky for them, Grandpa Silas took them into their house for a few years.

Or so the dusty-scented photo books in his basement had told. By the time Priscilla had turned three, Mom had moved to Brooklyn, and that was that.

Priscilla swallowed, tasting the remnant of the snacks they'd left at the table during the meet and greet time. She didn't absorb many of the names but did get to meet and greet some delicious buffalo chip dip.

Timothy cleared his throat. "Does anyone have a guess as to why I had you play that game?"

All fingertips dangled toward the carpet. After the reaction to the paper bag remark, no one had any answers. So Timothy decided to venture one.

"We like to do a lot of teamwork exercises here. With the human knot game, it requires everyone to contribute a solution on how to straighten out the circle, the loud *and* the meek. If you want to untangle in time, you need to hear every voice."

He shot a glance at a girl in the denim skirt. She shrank, and her chair gave a metallic squeak. A flush shot up her neck and cheeks. Poor thing, why would he be mad at her for not speaking up?

Why's the leader trying to stare her down? It's not like the kid in the orange tank was going to let her offer a solution on how to un-knot the circle.

When Timothy released his stare, the girl breathed as though his gaze had been fingertips gripping her hand in the human knot. "Now, before we dive into today's lesson, I'd like to talk about our youth group's community service projects."

A girl in thick eyeliner gave an eye roll but stopped short when Timothy's eyebrows darted to the bridge on his forehead.

"Folks, as a youth group, we're called to serve the community. I was very disappointed to see how few people signed up for each of the service projects we listed on the Service Board by the snack table last week."

His beefy hand gestured toward a Corkboard stationed right above the buffalo chip dip.

"Lucky for us, we have a lot of needs in our community. There are three listed on there that can use a lot of love: mulching in the Palm Lake development, devoting a handful of hours to the soup kitchen two miles down the road every Saturday, and of course, weekly visiting the residents of the Country Acres Assisted Living Facility."

Priscilla perked up so high in her chair that her back ached from the metal behind her. *Assisted living equals older people. Hello, knitting club.*

Hand slightly-a-shake, she raised her arm.

Timothy squinted at her as though peering at the sun. The curly-haired boy had done the same earlier in his driveway. *Ugh, why does he have to live only a few doors down? He seems like the persistent type.*

"Yes'm?"

"Sorry, new kid." Her eyes darted to her flats. She dug the black tips deep into the carpet. "But can you tell me a little about that last one?"

His pink face brightened until it almost formed a shade of white.

"Certainly, lucky for us, this opportunity just opened up. They're usually not too keen on non-family visitors, but they just recently allowed volunteer groups to come spend time with the residents."

He leaned over his chair to grab a clipboard he'd stuck in between his feet.

"Let's see. Ah," he slapped a paper secured to the clipboard with the back of his hand, "starting tomorrow afternoon, we're having volunteers go in to play some rounds of bingo with the residents."

He squinted at the paper. Maybe he'd forgotten to wear contacts today. Instinct took over, and Priscilla shoved her glasses up the bridge of her nose.

"I also only have one volunteer signed up currently. Since his school chose the community service project for him, I'll have to remind him to come tomorrow. They officially open their doors tomorrow. We'll see if he shows."

Smirks and knowing glances passed around the circle. They all seemed to be searching for someone and no one at the same time.

"But if you're going to sign up for that one, do it tonight. We'll have a van pick up the volunteers in the church parking lot tomorrow afternoon at two."

Interesting.

Even though Mom made her go to youth group, she could recuperate some of her time spent with older people, besides with Grandpa, of course. Some of the residents probably didn't know how to knit, but she could teach them.

And they could teach her.

That's what she loved about those ladies in the knitting club. Everyone seemed to have a voice. And could actually un-knot something, even if they were just detangled yarn skeins.

Timothy cracked open the spine of his Bible that weighed down his huge hand. Swirls of dust spiraled from the pages in the orb of light stationed at the center of the circle of chairs.

"Let's turn to Hebrews 11."

After they finished the lesson, Priscilla folded her chair, handed it to an assistant boy who looked worried she had the gall to fold the thing in the first place, and marched to the sign-up sheet for Country Acres clear across the room.

Walls of chatter passed behind her as the youth group goers grabbed handfuls of chips and burst outside the doors. The girl in the jean skirt stayed behind and signed up for the soup kitchen with a purple pen attached to the bulletin board by a yarn string.

Priscilla placed her name in neat cursive. She'd worked on her calligraphy at home. The *r* went a little crooked, looking more like an *s*, but overall, not a bad job for a faulty ballpoint pen the youth group had provided.

She was the only one to sign up, besides the boy's name right above hers, already printed out on the sheet: Carter Irvin.

Chapter Four
PRISCILLA

THE WHITE CHURCH VAN about blinded her from the sun overhead.

She shielded her eyes and spotted a Timothy now sporting a puce face as he paced back and forth between a column supporting an awning by the front entrance and the van illustrated with a cross and "Prince of Peace" logo.

"A deal's a deal, Miranda. I don't care how tired he is. If he doesn't show up today, I have to call the principal. They can still revoke the diploma at this point."

Priscilla eyed the open door to the back of the van. Best hop in before anyone else arrived and snagged the best seats. *Probably shouldn't eavesdrop on the conversation anyway.*

Ducking inside, she gasped at the blast of AC that stunned her right in the temple. *Praise!* She got the whole back row to herself. The youth pastor probably hoped for a few more sign-ups before borrowing the church's twelve-passenger van.

A shudder jolted through the van when Timothy slammed the back door shut. He slid into the driver's seat and clicked the red button on his phone, shutting off the call. He craned his neck and offered what she could best describe as a crocodile smile—all fake, like someone trying to grin after being punched in the stomach. No one in New York gave that kind of look.

In NYC, when people make an expression they mean it with all their hearts.

"Ready to brighten some lives?"

Squinting, she nodded, unsure of what else to say.

They stewed in painful silence for a minute before Timothy clicked on the radio to a Christian station. Their van rode the right lane the whole way, behind slow elderly drivers as teens in jeeps and other topless vehicles blazed past on the left.

Timothy's neck swung back and forth. "Kids. I sure hope you don't drive like that at home. No offense, but your generation is full of reckless people. Probably texting on their phones."

Heat prickled in her cheeks. "Your generation" echoed in her ears. Along with "kids." *The boy with the orange hair called me that the other day. Kid.* She'd gotten used to women in her knitting club taking on a condescending tone with her when first introduced. But after an hour or two spent together, they'd drop the high-pitched voices and speak to her as an equal.

She tore off some skin on her lip. *Time for a subject change.*

"You may have noticed, Priscilla, that traffic's pretty weird here. Most places you go, everyone's going insanely fast or slow. No in-between." Not that she could comment. She didn't exactly drive in New York. Not many people there did.

He drummed his fingers on the wheel. "Florida's interesting. It's split between retirees and snowbirds, and teens. It's like two worlds down here."

"Snowbirds?"

"People who spend half the year here and half the year up North. They chase the good weather. Mostly fifty years and older."

With a swift swipe of the hand, he clicked on his blinker and rolled up the asphalt to a shiny gate. The female guard stationed inside slid open a drive-thru window. Priscilla glanced out the other side of the van and observed the one solitary building that stretched across a huge plot of land. Palm trees and well-trimmed hedges decorated the edges of the building. A winding, white sidewalk swirled every which way, and between two palm trees she spotted a fountain near the parking lot. Cool water sounded like heaven right now.

Strange. *I thought this would look more like a nursing home.*

In New York, her youth group had visited one nearby their church. The assisted living center there reminded her more of a hospital with the mobile beds, mashed-up cafeteria food, and nurses bustling from one room to the next, bags hanging low from their eyes.

"You'll wanna head to the South End. That's where you'll find the Jean Recreation Center." The guard jabbed a well-polished fingernail around the brick corner of the gate. "Any residents who wanted to meet your volunteers ..." She paused at the word as she peered into the van. "If you have more coming, make sure they say they're with you."

She thumbed her nose.

"The director doesn't want to let too many new faces in. Residents can get a little shy around newcomers, and we want to make sure to keep them happy and comfortable."

"I'll make sure to tell the others."

Others?

His voice ran through the lie so fast that he spat out the words together like the pureed food back at the New York nursing homes. Like Priscilla, he appeared helpless when it came to stretching the truth.

Great, I guess he and I have something in common now.

Up swung the bar blocking the entrance, so they cruised past the gate and to the left. A young man, perhaps eighteen or nineteen years old, strolled on the winding sidewalk and threw a wave at the van.

Hmm, weird. Why did he wear knee-high socks and long shorts in this weather? She hadn't seen clothes on men like that, except for some 50s movies set in the summer.

Then again, a girl in youth group had worn a denim skirt to her ankles. Sometimes homeschool kids had different fashion. She'd learned this back in New York when her mom made her do activities with other co-op kids like speech club and theater.

If they wanted him to head to the Jean Rec Center, he was ambling in the wrong direction, but maybe the path that disappeared behind a grove of trees would lead him there. A nurse in navy scrubs sidled next to the man, continuing what looked like an amicable discussion.

Priscilla cleared her throat. "Pastor Timothy—"

"Call me Tim."

No thanks, he didn't seem like a Tim or that he *could* belong to a nickname. "Pastor Timothy, are there other youth groups volunteering today?"

"What? Oh, er, perhaps. If so, they didn't let me know."

Maybe they'd passed the elusive Carter Irvin. That would explain why he sounded angry on the phone call earlier. Carter must've beaten them here and decided to walk to the center. But why wouldn't Pastor stop and give him a ride the rest of the way?

He must not have seen him. That nurse with him will show him to the rec center. Hopefully.

They rolled to a stop in front of a lodge-shaped building with "Jean Rec Center" beaming in gold letters in direct sunlight.

"I'll meet you inside." Timothy tapped the steering wheel. "Have to park."

She swallowed.

Oof, have to head in there, alone. Inhale, hold it there, exhale. *You got this, girl. It's not like youth group. You actually like people in this age demographic.* Electricity tingled in her fingertips. She swung open the door and her flats hit the hot pavement. Should've chosen a different shoe to wear everywhere in Florida. By July, these bad boys would be melted like a crayon.

Ducking under the shade of a sloped roof, she ambled toward a Latina woman stationed at the entrance who wore a vest. She squinted to spot a "Country Acres" stitched in white on the lapel.

The woman beamed at her. "You with the youth group?"

"The" as in just one? Would other youth groups show up today? "Yes, ma'am."

She reminded herself that perhaps people had come to visit grandparents. Maybe they *were* the only youth group making a stopover today.

"Wonderful, meet with Patty at the concierge desk." She spun around and punched some numbers into a keypad. The glass doors slid open with a click. Priscilla nodded to the woman as she walked past the doors into a blast of AC. She heard them slide to a close behind her.

Strange, this place smelled more like Bath and Body Works's ocean lotions than the stale soapy scent she recalled the nursing home back home wore.

In front of her, a squat, pale woman in a fading mom blonde haircut fiddled with an arrangement of pens in a mug stationed on top of the desk. She tilted up her chin to make eye contact. With a twitch of her lip and a churning hand, she waved Priscilla over.

"I'm Pat." She extended her hand. "You with the youth group?"

Again, with the "the." Weren't there more youth groups here than just hers? Priscilla squinched her eyelids. "That's right."

"Do me a favor and sanitize your hands before we head to the game tables." Pat gestured at an automatic dispenser by the doors. "Can never be too careful, you know."

Priscilla slid her palms underneath the machine which spat out a glob of foaming Purell.

Pat adjusted clear glasses that had slipped too far down the rim of her nose. "I suppose I should give you the rundown of the assisted living center before we begin. Sometimes younger people can be a little"—she eyed Priscilla up and down—"uncouth when it comes to interacting with the residents."

While rubbing the foam between her fingers, Priscilla paused, clenched her fingers, and unclenched.

It's fine. People assume. They don't know that you're practically a senior in a teenage body.

"Now as an assisted living facility, most of our residents are independent, with sometimes needing care assistants to help with changing, showering, or they may use a walker, cane, or wheelchair."

Yes, ma'am. Well aware of the meaning of assisted living. She chewed on her tongue, then forced a grin until her cheeks hurt.

"Our residents can vary on levels of independence, but we're not a twenty-four-hour care nursing home." Pat raised a pointer finger. "An important distinction."

Priscilla stared at a replica painting of *Starry Night* behind the welcome desk.

"As always, some important ground rules to cover. I must ask that you do not patronize the residents."

Focus on the yellow swirls. The residents would warm up to her just like the knitting club ladies.

"Or ask them their age. Last time we had someone from ... another youth group here ... let's just say one of the residents didn't come out of her room until the next day."

A girl in a red 50s style dress passed by in Priscilla's periphery. Same style as the dress Priscilla had decided to wear, except with a Peter Pan collar. She turned and watched the girl wave at Pat. At last, someone else who loved vintage clothing *and* had decided to volunteer here.

Maybe more than one youth group would show up today. Or she was simply visiting a grandparent.

"Hi, Dorothy. Good to see you." Pat nodded at the woman who disappeared around the corner.

Pat fiddled with the pens in the mug on the desk again. "Any questions?"

"No, ma'am." Her shoulders relaxed.

Doors slid open behind her, tanning her legs with a burst of warmth. Pastor Timothy must have parked.

She spun around and stopped. Eyes wide, she took in the boy from the neighborhood. Auburn curly hair a tangled mess, wrinkled white shirt with sunglasses attached, and leaning to the left whilst gripping his temple. She spotted him mid tearing off his sunglass. Bad choice, considering how his eyes looked.

No doubt, she'd seen plenty of characters like that when she and her mom would walk in Central Park. And the neighborhood boy decided to come to the nursing home hungover. *Yeesh, glad I didn't go with him on his late-night "adventure."* Her arms folded on her chest, as she quirked a brow at him.

A lip-gloss grimace formed on Pat's face. "Hello, young man, are you here with the youth group?"

Curling his fingers, he gave a combination of a wince and nod to Priscilla. Gosh darn, he recognized her.

"Yes. Name's Carter Irvin."

Chapter Five
CARTER

PRISCILLA GAVE PAT THE STINK EYE when the woman from the concierge desk made them put on name tags. Busted, now he finally found out the name of the mysterious girl from the neighborhood.

Huh, "Priscilla." So a pretty name *did* go with those pretty eyes.

He slapped the badge on his chest and glanced down at the wrinkles on his shirt.

In a rapid motion, he tried smoothing down some of the ripples, but to no avail. Should have set his alarm earlier. He rubbed the bridge of his nose.

Also he should have said no when the girl in the backseat suggested "getting margs" at her friend's house. He didn't catch her name last night. His toes scrunched in his socks. But he did manage to catch plenty of sand from the beach and bring it right along with him to Country Acres.

Welp, you're definitely hungover. You wouldn't have put socks on during SUMMER if your head hadn't pounded so much this morning.

Rubbing some foamy sanitizer on his fingers, he squinted at the bright lights hanging in the hallway on their way to the "game room." Clutching at his stomach he leaned a little too far to the left and nudged Priscilla toward the wall as they passed some watercolor paintings by the residents.

She glared while Pat faced straight ahead, talking about weekly activities.

He leaned again, this time on purpose.

"Do you mind?" She hissed this. Pat, oblivious, continued on about physical therapy schedules after mentioning one of their favorite residents, Scarlett, contributed eighty percent of the paintings in the hallway.

"The principal making you volunteer here too? Are we detention buddies now?"

Her eyebrows pinched, as if computing everything he said. "I volunteered because I wanted to."

Weird flex.

A boy, about his age, eighteen, or maybe a little older, in glasses passed by on the other side of the hallway with a nurse. Carter caught the tail end of the conversation, and maybe it was the hangover talking, but what he thought he heard was "back in the sixties, it would cost sixty-nine cents for a ticket. Boy, do I miss those days."

Ringing filled his ears. *Nah, definitely the hangover talking.*

And maybe the light stinging his eyes decided to play tricks, but did that guy wear knee-high socks? In this weather? Maybe the assisted living center had volunteers and visitors from other states, who hadn't grown used to Floridian temperatures yet.

They ambled under a wooden archway into a carpeted cafeteria full of square tables. The din of conversation from various teens in the echoing room pounded his headache.

"Welcome to the game room. It looks like we have more residents to go around than volunteers, so they may have to share you. We'll start bingo in five minutes."

Teens swarmed the tables, with only a few spare chairs with soft padding remaining vacant.

Above the tables, on the wall, scrawled in black paint read:

"'People who say such things show that they are looking for a country of their own.'"

What a weird thing to put on a wall. That didn't even make sense. Say what things? Did someone forget to paint the beginning of the quote?

He shook his head, then gripped his temple again. Ay, yi, yi, what a headache.

"Carter, I'll have you sit at this table with Ethel, and I'll grab some more residents." Pat slid back a chair at a table closest to the door. He slumped into the seat and faced a girl, a year or two younger than him, in a headband, hunching into herself, reminding him of his grandmother. "Priscilla, follow me. I'll have you sit at this table over here with Paul." Pat's voice trailed off behind him.

Wait, why would the nurse lady pair a guy with a girl? They felt really traditional here … then again, the nurse's hair flit in every which direction. She probably didn't think over decisions all that clearly this morning.

Like Carter and his choice to put on socks …

Facing Ethel, he watched her dollop red chips on her BINGO board. No one else had parked at their table.

Harsh light blinked overhead as he tried to get a glance around the room. What dressed these teens? The *I Love Lucy* reruns his mom loved to binge? They surrounded him in full skirt dresses, polos, ties, and suits. Maybe he needed to pay more attention to social media. Weird fashion trends might have happened when he was busy marg-ing it up last night.

By instinct, he palmed his pocket. Oh wait, Pat had taken their phones at the front desk.

Normally, that would've sent him into a panic. But hangovers tended to make his reactions slower.

"Another one of our rules here. We want you to stay present with the residents during your time with them." Her voice from a few minutes earlier bounced around his skull.

No wonder Ethel decided to form a picture of a heart with her bingo chips on her board. She had to occupy her thoughts somehow without something to scroll.

"So, Ethel, interesting name you got there."

Her neck snapped up and she gazed at him with watery eyes, brown curls obscuring her lips. "What?"

A girl in their youth group who wore a denim skirt had a strange name too. What was it? Birdie? Betty? Maybe these kids came from similar backgrounds where the parents taught them at home, and they sewed their own weird vintage clothing. That could explain the dress Priscilla decided to wear today.

He rubbed two chips together. "Anyway, what youth group do you come from?"

"Whoo, looks like someone had fun last night!"

Carter whipped around, too fast, head a-spin. When his vision adjusted, he watched a young Latina girl, maybe sixteen or seventeen, with deep red lipstick and a dress to match, scrunch her shoulders and wink. Pat followed behind her to guide her to the table.

She slipped into a seat next to him, twirled a red-polish fingernail in a large curl of hair, and waited until Pat disappeared to help another teen who had spilled their bingo chips all over the floor.

Then she leaned closer, flowery perfume strong. "So, young man, just how many did you have last night, eh?" She made a drinking gesture with her hands and then laughed.

Ethel shrank into her seat more and said nothing.

Blood disappeared from his face until he felt the heat drop into his neck. "Listen, you can't tell anyone, okay? They could revoke my diploma if they knew I showed up with a hangover. Already threatened to take it away since I showed up late."

The girl threw a dismissive wave and let her laughter ring again. It sounded like low music. She probably sang alto.

"Oh, *dios mio*," She swiped a tear from her eye. "And I was worried I would have to sit with someone *boring*, like Ethel. All those youth group kids need to de-starch their pants or something. Secret's safe with me. After all, I've had my share of excitement in life." Her long nails traced a ruffle in her dress.

She leaned back, and he noticed the dress had formed a deep neckline. His ex used to wear outfits like that around him.

He glanced away. "I see you don't have a name tag."

"Oh, I don't need one. Everyone here knows my name. Some more than others."

Mm, don't like the way that last sentence sounded. "I don't."

"Scarlett. Scarlett Riviera."

Feedback pierced his ears. Up front, the bingo caller tapped the mic, testing. No one else in the room appeared to flinch.

Scarlett tapped her nails on the table, one at a time, chin rested on her other hand. "I do hope he speaks up. This one can't e-nun-ci-ate. Can't tell a B from a G with him."

Squinting, Carter scanned the crowd again. "Where is everybody?"

Maybe the residents got the wrong time. Fine by him. Scarlett seemed like—as his grandma would say—a hoot, minus the weird fashion choice of the dress. He wondered what youth group she went to.

She scrunched her shoulders and played with a red rose clip in her dark hair. "It's a pretty full house. Bingo's the most excitement you'll experience around here. See, these people don't know what a good time looks like." She smirked. "Anyway, you didn't answer my question. I want to see if you beat my record. How many?"

He frowned. If this girl was sixteen, it was mildly concerning that she could hold liquor. Even at the party last night, he threw up after the fourth margarita, and at seventeen, he had at least a year's worth of practice. *She's gotta be older than that. Sometimes Latino people look a lot younger*. "How old are you anyway?"

Ethel shot back so far into her chair, the seat almost tilted. She flailed her arms and grabbed hold of the table. A nurse passing by in blue scrubs helped her steady her balance. He turned to Scarlett who left her mouth agape, mid-laugh, and clutched a fist to the center of her sweetheart chest.

"Ay, young man, didn't that starch-pants lady at the front walk you through the rules here?"

He scrunched his nose, trying to recall the instructions which had blended into a puree in his mind.

Scarlett sighed and cocked her head, expression amused. "That you aren't supposed to ask anyone their age?"

"Oh." He swirled a finger through his chips, as though testing the consistency of a drink. "I figured you wouldn't mind."

She simpered. "Ah, young man, I guess you're right. Age before beauty." She flicked a curl off her shoulder. "And I do have both."

"Yeah?"

She straightened herself in her seat, as though receiving a crown.

"My name is Scarlett Montez-Riviera, and I am eighty-four years old."

Chapter Six
CARTER

HE CHUCKLED. THIS TIME, SHE DIDN'T.

She cocked an eyebrow and folded her arms over her chest. "Something funny, young man?"

"Umm, no"—he jabbed a thumb at his name tag—"name's Carter and ... it's just, you don't exactly look eighty-four."

Was this some weird prank people were pulling now? Teens pretending that they're eighty-something?

Scarlett melted, arms to her side and face aglow again.

"Oh, how adorable. I bet the girls fall all over you, Carter."

He craned his neck over his shoulder to watch Priscilla help another teen in a gray suit place a chip on his FREE SPACE spot. Three-piece suit, in this heat? The guy wouldn't fit in any century. "Yeah, not all of them." He swung back, and Scarlett twirled her fingers around a necklace draped on her neck with a string of pearls gathered at the bottom.

"N 33. N 33." The bingo caller had begun reading balls that a circular cage spat out next to him.

Carter checked his sheet. Nope, no N 33. He glanced at Ethel. "And suppose you're eighty-six or what?"

She growled, shoved her chair back, and stomped away.

Scarlett clicked her tongue. "Lucky thing doesn't have to carry around a walker or cane. One of the few who isn't dependent on one of those around here." She giggled and placed a chip on the N 33 space. "Look at her fly. Like she has to train for the Olympics or something."

It was so hard to tell if she was joking. Maybe she had an odd sense of humor. Well, two could play at this quirky game. "Yeah, I left my walker at home."

"Now, Carter, I know you're funny and all, but I have to draw a line somewhere." It was hard to tell if she was joking or serious. A smile still played on her lips. "If you had a heart condition like mine, you wouldn't be so keen to carry around a cane with you everywhere."

"B 3. That's B as in boy. Three."

She lifted her eyes until the whites showed. "At least he said the 'boy' part. You can hardly hear back here."

They sat ten feet from the elevated platform on which the bingo caller stood.

Carter leaned closer toward her. "You can't hear him?"

With a growl, she pinched his earlobe. "I don't exactly have ears like I used to. Now, stop breaking Pat's rules and shut up so I can hear the caller."

This has to be a hangover dream. Need water or something to wake myself up.

When she released her grip, he shoved his chair back and stood up. Whoops, too fast, he gripped the table and steadied himself. He needed to get water or something. The alcohol must not have worn off from last night yet.

He spun around to find Priscilla's lips forming an O. Her eyebrows quirked with a question.

"Water break."

Glancing up, he spied Pastor Timothy at the door, arms strapped across his chest, buttons on his polo about to burst from the effort.

He made a jerking motion for Carter to sit.

Woozy and finding his feet had grown heavy, he slumped into a vacant chair in front of Priscilla and pretended to fiddle with the chips on an open board.

"O 66. O 66."

"What are you doing?" Priscilla hissed.

Throbs filled his skull with a faint chorus line of drumming. "I don't know if the alcohol has worn off. I might still be drunk."

Priscilla leaned in, eyed the Asian kid next to her, and muttered a quick apology to him. Apparently his name was 'Paul.' He had a weird haircut that didn't go past the ears, but a nice, sharp jawline. Ugh, why did his hangover make him notice weird things like people's jaws and the weird quote on the back of the wall. He twisted his neck to check and make sure that the writing hadn't disappeared. Nope, the cursive lettering still burned into his vision.

"People who say such things show that they are looking for a country of their own."

Priscilla's sharp voice pulled him back. "What do you mean, Carter? That's not how alcohol works."

He shrugged. "Scarlett was saying some weird stuff over there. I think my brain made up half of it." He gestured at the woman in the crimson dress.

A soft chuckle bounced in Paul's throat. He threw a quick eye-flick toward Scarlett's table and hunched over his BINGO board, as though frightened she caught him staring. Paul rubbed the bridge of his nose. "She can be a joker. Everyone here loves her."

Flush shot up Paul's necks and cheeks. He tugged at the color of his white oxford.

Yep, know that look. The same one he gave whenever he thought about Mia Patel. He smirked. "Paul, why don't you go talk to her?"

"I 18. I as in Iris. 18."

Priscilla slammed a chip onto her board. "Carter, that's not your business."

"No, but what if I made it mine?"

Eyes locked across the table. Her glare withered and she held a green chip at the ready for the next call.

Paul cleared his throat. "I don't think she would care if I sat with her or not."

"Why not? You're a strapping young lad. She'll fall all over you."

Priscilla's eyes widened at this, but she remained fixated on her board.

"G 46. G as in goose. 46."

With a shaky hand, Paul placed a chip on the G 46 space. Like Priscilla, he kept his neck hunched over the table. "I don't ... I don't think I'm ready today." This came out as a whisper.

"No problem, dude. You still have plenty of time."

He gave a sad smile. "Not much."

On the ride back in Pastor Timothy's borrowed church van, Carter took the whole middle row. Owing to the fact that when he reached the vehicle, Priscilla darted to the back and stretched her entire body over the length of the back section.

He scrolled on his phone, clicking through his social media apps while Priscilla and Timothy held a strained conversation over the soft strum of a guitar on the Christian radio station.

"Think you'll come back next week, Priscilla?" Pastor Timothy had to shout this. Probably to make sure sound carried all the way to the back of the van.

"What? Oh, yes."

"Some of them took that bingo game pretty seriously." He chuckled and swung the hammer down on his turn signal. "Hear most of the prizes are coupons to places. The week they offered a free meal at that 50s diner was cutthroat from what Pat told me."

Instagram: Three more likes.

TikTok: A couple hundred more views on his video.

Snapchat: Four new Snaps from friends.

"Um, Pastor Timothy?"

"Priscilla, what did I say about calling me that? I'm Tim."

"Mhmm." She didn't sound convinced. "How many teens come each week to Country Acres?"

"Well, aside from family visits, I reckon you two are the first two teens they've seen in a while. Besides some choir groups from local schools who stopped by during spring semester."

"Do you think there were any family visitors playing bingo?"

"Possibly. You never can guess at people's ages. Some people did look like they could pass for their upper middle ages."

"Any teens?"

Carter stopped scrolling. *Wait a minute. Did Priscilla just say "teens"?*

He glanced up as Timothy merged onto the right hand of the highway, approaching a stretch of blue sky and cumulonimbus clouds.

"Mmm"—Timothy swung off his blinker—"not from what I could tell, but it was a packed hall. Wheelchairs and walkers everywhere. For all we know, a teen or two could've been hiding in the mix."

Craning his neck, he spotted Priscilla chewing her lip, flicking a glance at him and then out the window.

She saw something. Maybe I'm not drunk.

"Now, Carter."

His head snapped back to the front where Timothy hoisted a finger directly under a brown splotch on the carpeted ceiling.

"I expect you to stay at your table next time. We only have so much of the youth group to go around, and those folks can use all the bright faces they can get. Much as I appreciate you hanging with friends your age"—he motioned to Priscilla who scrunched her nostrils—"for the two hours we're there, I need you to spend time with some of the residents."

"No worries." Priscilla's voice tickled his ear from behind. "It won't happen again."

Great, she didn't seem all that keen on speaking with him. So much for finding out what she knew.

Then again, maybe if he played the timing just right ...

Minutes later, they arrived at the church parking lot. Carter waited for Pastor Timothy to cut the ignition and exit the van. Once the door slammed, Carter sprawled out his legs, barricading Priscilla from the side door.

In time too, because she'd already lurched forward as soon as the van had rumbled to a stop.

"What the heck, Carter?"

"Under the church pavilion. We need to talk."

"Or what?"

He shrugged and pointed at his legs blocking the door.

She rolled her eyes. "I could always go out the trunk."

"In that dress? Be my guest." He smirked.

Priscilla glanced at her outfit and back at him. "Fine. Two minutes."

Two seconds after he swung away his legs, she raced out the door and skidded to a halt in the shade of the pavilion. Pastor Timothy gave a curt wave before jamming his keys into the front door of the church and slipping inside.

She bounced once, twice in her flats and hugged her stomach. "Well? Talk."

"I wasn't drunk. You saw that the whole place was filled with teenagers."

"I never said you were drunk." She threw up a hand, closed her fingers into a fist, and dropped her arm. "But I don't understand what I saw. Maybe we both had too much to drink. Grandpa does like his sangria. Even if I didn't have any last night." She sucked in part of her cheek, perhaps to chew on the skin, and then, suddenly, reached up to her shoulder and pinched herself, eyelids squeezed shut.

Her shoulders slumped when her eyelids flew open.

"Sorry, sweetheart, it's not a dream."

"Priscilla."

That voice could cut him in the throat if he stood any closer, yikes. Okay, so she didn't like "sweetheart."

He shuffled back two steps. "Yes, I know. Now that we've discovered you are, in fact, awake, let's try to find out what the heck just happened during the past two hours."

Scrunching her nose, she stared at a crack in the sidewalk.

"Maybe they were pulling a prank?" Her shoes kicked against a loose stone. "Does Florida have any reality shows that pretend to have teens act like elderly people?"

He hooked his thumbs on the crook of his elbows and gave his best impression of a Scarlett laugh.

"Maybe you *are* drunk, Priscilla."

Fire flashed in her pupils. Sparks died after two seconds, and she wedged her heel back into the flats. It had fallen out. "Whatever, your two minutes are up."

"Priscilla, I didn't mean—"

She marched past him and toward the neighborhood. "Don't follow me."

"Priscilla."

"See you next week."

"Why do you hate me?"

She skidded to a halt and whipped around, curls glimmering in the sunlight. A wince captured her for a moment in an expression of pity.

"Don't take it personally. I don't really like anyone our age."

With that, she spun around and disappeared down the sidewalk.

Chapter Seven
PRISCILLA

UGH, BOYS.

Drunk, the audacity. She slammed her back against the door as she closed it. *I am not like Dad.* She slid to the carpet by the front door and breathed in the scent of taco seasoning from the kitchen down the hall. *I am not and will never be drunk.*

She steepled her fingers and exhaled through them, allowing the bitter scent of the hand sanitizer to intoxicate her for a moment. *Inhale, hold it, release.*

Moments later, a rock punctured her stomach and fell all the way into her gut.

He was just joking, Priscilla. You overreacted.

But that's how she dealt with people in the city who tottered too close in Central Park or hanging near Subway stations, clutching the neck of a bottle stuffed into a brown lunch bag. She couldn't let him get too close. Bad boys like him got nice girls like her mom pregnant.

She'd rather be good than nice.

Even if he did see the same phenomenon she had at the rec center. The quote on the back wall—what did it say again? Something about a country?—the residents in vintage clothing, all appearing sixteen or seventeen years old.

Releasing a sigh, she heaved herself forward, stood, and peered out the window next to the front door to observe Carter trudging up his driveway two doors down. His neck sloped like the body of a shrimp, all curved, dejected.

Maybe we should've talked longer. Bet we could've figured out some reason for what we saw.

He paused at the center of his driveway, whipped out his phone, and started scrolling.

Nope, never mind. I can figure it out myself. Too many ladies at her knitting club liked to go on and on about how her generation couldn't stay off their phones. Couldn't be associated with that.

She peeled off her flats at the front door with her toe and made a mental note to grab sandals next time she left the house. Everyone seemed to wear those in Florida anyway. Advancing toward the family room, she halted between the hallway and kitchen when she spotted a bright yellow bowl of guac resting on the counter.

Stomach afire, she grabbed a chip, dipped the edge, and let the salt and lime fill her mouth before sliding her fingers into the bowl again.

"Like it? I think Maria put a little too much cilantro in the mixture."

She spun on her heel and found Grandpa Silas on a white leather family room chair with a book cracked open on his knee. A grin split her cheeks. "It tastes great."

He rubbed the whiskers on his chin. "I can see you're not a true Floridian yet. Not a guac snob. Give it time." He winked and returned to the book in his lap, licking a finger like a postage stamp before flipping a page.

The book.

That was it. She could find answers about Country Acres that way. Like she did for all her other research projects for school.

Her sophomore year, her history teacher had them do a ten-page report on another time period, and they had to show up to homeschool co-op—a classroom for homeschoolers that met a few times a week—in full costume. No surprise, she chose the 50s and focused on popular movies from that era. She spent weeks at the library borrowing movies and perusing books about the Golden Age of Capitalism.

Ever since that project, she'd bedecked herself in all vintage clothes. Wouldn't her teacher be so proud?

"Grandpa, do you have any libraries nearby?"

Chin turned downward until the sagging jowl hit his neck, he glanced at her over a pair of reading glasses. "We sure do. If you head down the road and hang a right, it's about half a mile away."

Like New York, here she could reach most buildings in walking distance. And *unlike* NYC, half a mile wouldn't take her a million minutes to traverse a short distance.

"Here, let me give you my library card." He dug into his capri pockets and pulled out a leather wallet.

"Won't they get concerned that you and I don't share the same last name?"

"You can say you're getting some books for your poor elderly and frail grandpa." A twinkle from the dangling glass light fixture glinted off his pupils. "After all, I *am* an old man."

He returned to his book. As she turned to go, she read the title: *The Fault in Our Stars.*

She reached the brick and glass building, cursing the sore that had developed between her big toe and the one beside it. Sandals, what a rotten idea. How did the Floridians ever get used to this?

Hobbling past a fountain, everything inside her yearned to dip her feet in the bubbling clear water, but she forced herself forward, under the jutting pavilion, and into the row of glass doors.

Everything smelled of wood from the dimly lit bookshelves and winding staircases a ways down the hall. At the end sat a squat coffee shop with dangling Edison bulb light fixtures and plush green chairs. Man, Grandpa had been holding out on her. Probably because if she knew about this place, she wouldn't want to leave.

On her right, a girl about her age, stationed at the front desk, clacked on a blast-from-the-past computer. No doubt, the monitor had time-traveled from the early 2000s based on size alone. Weird that they had a teenager working here. Back in New York, they required anyone employed in libraries to have a fancy-schmancy library degree, but maybe in Small-Town Florida, they would hire teens as assistants.

The girl up front swabbed a finger through a dark pixie cut and turned to the shelf behind her to grab a book. Her blouse matched the color of her hair, and a healthy dab of eyeliner completed the outfit. Now all she needed was an eyebrow piercing to match the getup. Maybe she did have one, and the librarians made her take it off for the shift. Priscilla thought back to the ladies from knitting club.

What would they say? Considering they tsked about grandkids getting cartilage piercings.

Chest expanding, retracting, she practiced how she would word what sort of books she needed. Not many opportunities had presented themselves for her to talk to someone her age, apart from co-op.

Hi, do you have any books on people who've bathed in the blood of the innocent so they can live forever as a teenager?

No, too morbid and a terrible introduction. Even though librarians dealt with a lot of crazies, that one might warrant a 9-1-1 call.

Would you happen to know if I could read a book on group hallucinations? Yeah, just two people vibing together and seeing the same mirages?

How long had she been standing in the Florida sun?

By now she'd reached the counter and the girl behind the computer leered at her, pale face awash in the bright light of the computer.

"Can I help you?"

"Do you have books on ... reverse aging?"

The girl behind the counter scrunched her eyebrows, confused. *Well, better reaction than her dialing the ambulance or police.* "Or maybe a book on people staying young and never aging?"

"Fiction?" Her fingers already ran across the keyboard before Priscilla could answer.

Not exactly.

"Yeah, fiction." *Nonfiction would sound crazy, right?*

Bright words danced along the assistant's dark irises as she scrolled. She paused, slid open a drawer, and slapped a bright yellow sticky notes pad onto the counter. "And no specific genre? Just fiction?"

"Fiction's good." The words came out through a tight throat, scratchy and squeaky. She wished she knew the finesse of small talk. Even when going to her favorite pizza shop in downtown New York she had to rehearse the order five times in her head before approaching the counter.

Even though she got the same thing every time.

"We do have quite a few titles. *The Mysterious Case of Benjamin Button, Picture of Dorian Gray, The Fall of Hyperion* ... " Click, click, she tapped on the mouse and then scribbled some numbers on the sticky note pad. "We do have a local author who just sent us a book." Her voice sounded as if someone had turned it into a black and white movie, missing all color. She glanced out the glass windows of the door, longingly at the sun. "I can read the description if you like."

Priscilla bobbled up and down until the sore between her toes burned.

"Umm, sure."

"*Of Adonis and Ambrosia*: A middle-aged archeologist finds the source of the fountain of youth at the ruins of an Ancient Greek temple, turning him into a younger version of himself. But a jealous scientist by the name of Heinrich Zelos wants to uncover the secret of the temple site." The lights in her eyes extinguished, perhaps from clicking off the search engine. "Think *Age of Adaline* meets *Seventeen Again*, I guess. At least, that's what the description says."

She hadn't seen those movies, but she bobbled her chin. "That book sounds perfect."

Sure, the architecture from Country Acres read more like Abe Lincoln's log cabin than an Ancient Greek site of mystery, but besides that...*The book seems to match what we're looking for.*

The girl finished scrawling book numbers on the notepad and clacked the red pen on the counter.

"I assume you know how to navigate Dewey Decimal?" She curled a pencil-thin eyebrow and glanced Priscilla up and down. "You look like you live in a library."

Rude ... I think? "Yeah, I should have no problem finding the books, thanks ..." She squinted to read the name on the silver name tag on the girl's lapel in the dim lighting.

"Mia Patel." The girl waved her off like a strong, pungent whiff of men's cologne. "Don't mention it."

Chapter Eight
CARTER

AS SOON AS CARTER SWUNG OPEN THE FRONT DOOR of his house to the front stoop, a frantic voice greeted him.

"Carter, I'm helpless."

There he found Mrs. Elena Patel, Mia's mom, in a pencil skirt and a bulbous yellow flower clipped in her hair, right next to her ear.

He stepped backward, and she shuffled in and kicked off a pair of tall, black heels. Without them, the top of her head met at the halfway mark of his chest. She hobbled toward the kitchen, tights probably pulled too far down and causing her to waddle and peered her head into the living room on the right.

"Mom's not home?"

"She took Grandma out to shop. Anything I can do to help?"

Mrs. Patel planted herself in the middle of the turquoise family room carpet and bent over, hands pressed against her thighs. Like she was catching a breather or something. She did live a couple streets down. He stole a glance at the window and spotted no cars in the driveway.

"Can I get you something to drink?"

"No, too dangerous. I have a date. Tonight."

It took him a moment to register what she said. "I meant something like water or sweet tea."

She unbent herself and twisted around toward the kitchen after a great deal of effort. He felt his face redden when he spotted the outfit and how it bunched on the lower half. *Should I tell her to stop in the bathroom to fix it?*

"That's sweet of you, but I don't think I could keep anything down." She clutched at her stomach, waddled to a brown couch stationed by the windows, and slumped into the cushions. "I was hoping your mom was home to give me some advice. Haven't done one of these dates in a while."

How Mrs. Patel and his mom managed to maintain a friendship after the whole purpling incident, Carter couldn't say.

Something about their children engaging in frivolity could bring two women together under the bonds of kindred spirithood. After all, who better could they talk smack about their children to than the parents of the other actual said kids?

Carter wrinkled and smoothed out his face in one fluid motion.

"No offense, Mrs. Patel, but Mom isn't exactly the poster child for a good relationship." Divorces apparently took a long time to hammer out details.

She fanned herself with a round pillow. "Oh, yes, dear, terrible shame you've had to go through all of this. Can't blame you entirely for what happened in that parking lot at the school with all this happening at home."

Heat filled his cheeks and he distracted himself with a brown lizard that had crawled into the house again. The reptile stared back at him from the ceiling.

"But your mother is my best friend, and well, best friends give great advice that they never intend to follow themselves."

His lips curved and he marched into the kitchen. He swung open a cabinet and clinked two medium-sized glasses on the countertop after he clinked ice into them. Turning to the fridge, he heaved a huge jug of sweet tea and poured.

Much as he couldn't stand adults ... Mia's mom had always been an exception. Sent him several messages as soon as he found out about his parent's divorce, brought him more casseroles than his mom had ever baked him in his life.

She helped him then. Surely, now ...

"Well, maybe you don't need my mom's advice. Don't you work in a government office? Isn't there a marriage department or something? Maybe some people there have some tips."

"Lewis will be no help, trust me." She put the round pillow back on the couch and proceeded to fan herself with her hand. "He just gets people their licenses."

Carter's lips twitched, lifting a brow. "Well, maybe he can give you one of those for your date tonight. In case it goes well."

She snickered. "That's not how it works. You can't just get a license. There's premarital courses and a waiting period of a few days. Although I do know he makes exceptions. Waved the waiting period for a bride who had terminal cancer this past spring. They held the ceremony a day before she passed." She rubbed her chin. "And he does owe me a favor."

An ice cube clicked against his teeth. He swallowed. Mrs. Patel buried herself further into the couch.

Welp, she's not going anywhere anytime soon.

"Tell me about your date, Mrs. Patel." Patel, the name was reminiscent of Mia's father. He had no idea why Elena kept her married name after the messiness of that divorce.

"Well"—she pressed her palms to her knees—"I don't know much. It's a blind date. From what I can tell from my friend at the salon who set me up, he's from up north. But instead of snow birding, he permanently moved here this past spring. She said he's tall, dark, and handsome, so of course, that narrows down nothing."

They did have a lot of those in Florida. Mia's new boyfriend fit every part of that description. Well, except for the tall part.

"Do you have a name for the guy?" He reached for his pocket.

"What's in one? No, dear, you can put away the phone. I doubt you'll be able to find someone on Facebook by just typing in 'tall, dark, and handsome.'"

He shoved his device back into his pocket and forced his lips into a straight line, though they wanted to twitch into a smirk. *No one my age is on Facebook.* Carter scooped up both glasses and stepped into the family room. He handed Mrs. Patel her glass, and she set it down on a coaster that featured a conch shell.

"It's not like I haven't done a blind date before." She placed a finger on the cup to stop a water droplet from sweating onto the table. "But us Patels ... we're hopeless romantics. Emphasis on the hopeless."

For real? Maybe she'd adopted Mia.

Glass in hand, Carter parked on the floor and crisscrossed his legs. No sooner had he set his cup on the coffee table between himself and the house guest than did Mrs. Patel lean forward and place a coaster underneath his glass. Mothers . . .

"Eh, maybe I should cancel. I have an hour beforehand to do so."

His skin prickled. The words "hopeless romantic" bounced around his skull. Gosh darn, he'd have to intervene, didn't he? Like all of his friend's romantic endeavors.

"No, don't do that. Maybe I can help."

"You?"

"Sure, I might be young, but I have"—he paused before the word *experience*. Not the best choice in front of the mother of his ex-girlfriend—"I have some ideas on how you can put your best foot forward tonight."

She cocked her head, calculating, then leaned forward.

"Do tell." One would think that Mia had no relation to this woman at all. How Elena and Carter could carry on conversations like this, after everything that happened. But then again, Mia never really seemed to fit in with her family. She'd spent countless dates swearing she was adopted.

And Elena was the type of person to make friends with everyone, whether they wanted that or not.

Carter gestured at Elena's hairline. "First things first, ditch that flower. It looks like it's eating half your head, and you have beautiful hair that it's hiding."

Hesitation seized her hands for a moment before she reached up and unclipped the flower. She placed the accessory on the couch and smoothed some flyaways that had gone astray.

"Better?"

"Better. He'll be blown away. Now, on first dates, guys do like it when women make a move. Lightly touch his elbow or hand. That way he can know you're a little more comfortable around him."

She grazed her elbow with her middle finger, testing out the idea.

"Another thing"—he uncrossed his legs and bumped his toe against the curled foot of the coffee table—"make eye contact." Shoot, there were Mia's eyes again. "And laugh at his jokes, no matter how painful they are. Try to talk like you're not on a date."

"How do you mean?"

"Just be natural and be you. He'll love you. I promise."

Mrs. Patel spun her thumbs round and round before leaning back into the couch and reaching for her glass of sweet tea. She swigged from the rim and let out a satisfied "ah."

"My dear, that helps a lot. You're wise beyond your years in a number of ways." She set the cup down and pressed against her knees to rise. They crackled. "Best be heading out. Want to finish getting ready."

They ambled down the front hallway, Carter an inch ahead because the width couldn't hold two bodies side by side. He held open the door as she slipped her heels back on and waddled to the front step.

"Young man, I have no doubt you'll make some girl very happy someday."

She took two steps, paused at the bottom of the stoop, and twisted around. A shriek of delight from neighborhood kids nearby filled the silence of the moment. Then a splash followed. A dip in the backyard pool sounded nice.

Mrs. Patel hmm'd. "It's just too bad it wasn't Mia."

After a sad glance, she clenched the yellow flower clip in her hand and clip clopped down the driveway and to the right. Carter exhaled long and slow before slipping back inside to let the AC cool his cheeks and neck.

"It's too bad it wasn't Mia."

He sighed.

Maybe I should be Mrs. Patel's best friend. I'm apparently good at giving advice, but bad at talking to women.

Through the square window, he watched as Priscilla hobbled down the street with something clutched to her chest, books. He fought the itch to swing open the door. He didn't move until she'd paraded up her driveway and disappeared inside the house.

At least you'll have more chances to talk with her at Country Acres.

Unless she quarantined herself to the other end of the rec center to avoid speaking to him. What was it about their conversation in the church parking lot that set her off? He didn't mean to say she was drunk—even in jest—but no one would've expected her to storm off after that.

Ugh, women.

He clung to the curved end of the banister and pulled himself up. Might as well watch some videos to take his mind off today. His fingers inched toward his pocket. He curled his fist. No, not social media. Every time he scrolled, Mia had posted something new. Maybe that job at the library kept her bored out of her mind, so she had to upload a picture or video every hour to keep from suffocating.

She liked the sunshine. He remembered how much she did.

He trudged into the family room and slumped onto the couch. With a limp arm, he reached for the remote and switched on the television. His mom had left it paused on one of her favorite movies, *Back to the Future.*

Stealing a quick glance at the remote, he shrugged. "Beats having to choose something to watch." He clicked the play button and buried his neck into the cushion while the character Marty McFly goggled at a high school-aged version of his dad. They must've passed the part of the movie where he traveled back thirty years to 1955 ...

I wonder what it would be like to see Dad and Mom as teenagers. Wait a second.

Tapping the pause button, he leaned forward to analyze the younger version of Marty McFly's dad. Something about the way he gelled his dark hair and those sharp cheekbones reminded him of that kid, Paul, at Country Acres.

No, not kid. He's apparently eighty or ninety-something years old. Like Scarlett.

Maybe he had a solution ... or maybe it was back to the drawing board.

Chapter Nine
CARTER

CARTER APPROACHED PRISCILLA in the church's playground. "Didn't you get Pastor Timothy's text?"

Priscilla glanced at him sideways as her swing on the playground by the church glided backwards. "I never have my phone on me."

"He said they needed to postpone the visit by an hour. I guess the activities coordinator had a family emergency. They had to call in backup, but I guess she couldn't show until an hour afterwards."

For some reason, Country Acres couldn't simply ask another worker there to read off the bingo numbers. According to Pastor, the skill to do so took a certain amount of finesse. But with how much Scarlett criticized the guy they had last time, maybe the real reason was because no one else had the gall.

Priscilla stopped the swing by shoving her flats into the dirt.

Mud smeared her ankles. Florida saw a lot of rain this time of year. Besides a brief sprinkling yesterday, they hadn't seen much precipitation, though.

Carter moseyed down the line of swings before he dove backwards onto an empty seat, two spots down. Enough space between them that she wouldn't scamper off again. She busied herself with picking at the dirt with her nails. Then she sighed, leaned back, and began swaying again. He followed suit, trying his best to match her pendulum.

"Maybe we should get some paper towels for your ankles?"

"I would go inside, but they locked it up." She pushed and pulled on the swings' chains. "Why are you here early, anyway?"

The fence bordering the church playground and parking lot fell in and out of focus.

"My mom's out of the house and it was just me and Grandma. We don't really know how to have a conversation, so I figured I'd get here early."

Priscilla fell silent. She went forward while he lagged behind.

When he neared the center, he gave an extra sturdy kick to catch up with her.

"Listen, Priscilla, I think we started off on the wrong foot. I didn't mean the drunk comment ..."

Past the red bar at the top of the swings, he approached a beautiful blue sky.

"What I'm trying to say is, I'd love to start over."

Her swing faltered and she didn't kick this time. Her toes dragged on the ground until they almost reached the short grass behind the swing set. He skidded to a halt to peer at her through the triangle in the chains, but she wouldn't meet his eyes.

"What exactly does 'start over' mean?"

"You know, have a chance to be"—he winced—"friends."

The word tasted like bitter coffee grounds. A number of girls had given him similar talks back in school when he'd attempted to ask them out on dates.

She swayed back and forth for a moment before kicking off again.

"I don't know, lover boy, I don't really make friends with anyone under the age of forty."

"Lover boy?"

"You called me 'sweetheart' the other day, so you get a nickname."

"What you want a different one? How's princess?" Those flats, sans the dirt, did look like queenly type shoes.

"Eww, no." She was fighting a lip twitch, he could tell. Her mouth curved back into a frown. Maybe she did like the nicknames after all. Why did all girls play so hard to get? Priscilla's face slackened. "I didn't exactly like how you were trying to get Paul to talk to Scarlett."

"Why not?"

An ibis obscured the sun for a moment while they swung back and forth, each missing the other's pendulum.

"If you'd been at the table when they started calling numbers, Paul explained how his wife died about a year ago, right after their sixtieth anniversary. People don't just rush into a relationship after something like that happens."

"You didn't see the way he looked at her."

"I saw. It's not going to happen."

"What, does love have an expiration date or something?"

Crickets and frogs behind them hummed in a grove of trees. Her jaw loosed, shut, and then she chewed on her lip. Five back and forth sways later she spoke.

"Even if you were fifty, we couldn't be friends. Men like you get eaten alive where I come from." She made a gargling noise like she'd choked on the words. "Besides, I'm practical. You're an idealist. At least from what I can tell. We'd never work in tandem."

"Well, you know what they say about opposites."

"Actually"—she jabbed a pointed finger to the sky before clinging back to the chain-link— "psychologists have proven the contrary. Donn Byrne back in the 1960s conducted tests to see if similarities in relationships were the glue that held them together. Opposites don't attract. At all."

Nerd alert.

She flung herself off the swing and staggered a landing in the grass ahead. Rubbing her ankles on the brown grass, she gave a heavy sigh when the dirt still clung to her skin.

"Our grass down here is dry." He skidded to a stop. She probably didn't want him to land next to her.

Why do you want to pursue this girl so badly, dude? She's clearly given you all the signs that she isn't even interested in the friend zone. You can't get any farther apart from her than now.

Maybe because he kept hanging out with chicks who, like him, checked Instagram feeds every five minutes, and could do with an old-fashioned girl for a change.

And no matter what that psychologist dude said, opposites had to attract in some way, because man, oh, man was this girl attractive.

"I noticed, about the grass." Priscilla pinched her nose and sighed. "It's fine. Since I can't go inside to wash up, at least I still have plenty of time to develop my theory about the residents of Country Acres before Pastor Timothy gets here."

He perked up at this and detangled his arms from the swing to set his hands on his lap.

"That so? Well, I've developed a theory too, and it's better than yours, princess."

Creases formed on Priscilla's forehead when she halted on the way to the fence. Then she straightened her spine and proceeded to grab a tan bag slumped against the fence. She swung it over her shoulder and cocked one eyebrow.

"That so, lover boy?"

The direct sunlight could've played tricks on his eyes, but underneath the shadows her fluffy hair produced, he thought he caught a smile—not a smirk—one that actually went all the way to her eyes. *Was all that nerdy talk about the psychologist her way of flirting?*

"Sure is. Now why don't you tell me about your pitiful theory first, so I can show you up afterwards?"

Her eyes bulged for a moment, and she belted her chest with her arms. "Well, okay then." She paced forward, planting herself right between the fence and the swings, her hair blocking out the sun, cowboy at high noon style.

Good Lord, this girl likes a challenge.

Lucky for him, so did he.

"My theory is that the residents have received a taste of the *fuente de la juventud*, a fountain of youth concoction, if you will ..."

"Yes, most Floridians understand some Spanish."

"... whether via direct exposure in a food or water source or in medication, they have both medically and scientifically experienced a DNA change that has returned them to the age when they were most active and vibrant, their teenage years, but they have to stay on site to receive supplements to replenish their youthful complexions and bodies."

Yeesh, did this girl memorize a dictionary on occasion? Mrs. Patel had a work friend from the library who liked to use what she called "erudite" vocabulary to "intimate the plebs." Mrs. Patel called it a defense tactic to try and keep those she deemed dangerous away.

Is Priscilla trying to scare me?

He rubbed the back of his neck and curled his fingers when he felt the growing sunburn across his skin. Why did they choose to lock the church on non-Sundays? "You know, for the fact that you speak Spanish and English, you're not coming across easy in either language, princess."

She pressed her glasses up the bridge of her nose. "The fountain of youth is at Country Acres. That's why they're teens again. Simple enough for you?"

Behind him a chipmunk skittered across the grass and disappeared into the trees.

"And how did you come up with this theory?"

She dug into her bag and flashed a book with a Greek statue on the front.

"A book? Seriously? Google could've given you better answers."

"Okay, then let's hear your *wonderful* theory, since you obviously put in so much research."

Carter's shoulders bounced up and down. "Easy. Country Acres is a time capsule."

Her head tilted, her look making him think of someone trying to unscrew a pickle lid using telepathic powers.

Finally, "A what?"

"You know, those things where you put in stuff you want future generations to remember? Like old diaries, newspapers, baseball cards, smallpox."

"Yes, I know what a time capsule is."

He lifted his chin, triumphant, and battled the rim of water forming in his eyes from gazing directly at the sun that glowed like a halo atop her head. His chin buckled down on the sunglasses attached to his shirt. About dang time he put those on.

"Whenever a resident steps into Country Acres, they step back into 1950 or 1960 something. They become the time capsule. It's like time traveling, but cooler."

Now was her turn to stiffen her neck. "That doesn't make any sense. Why wouldn't Pat look like a teenager?"

"She's not a resident."

"Oooh"—she raised her hands and voice in a mocking fashion—"so the time capsule is omniscient now and can pick and choose who to give youth too, ooooh, scary. Seriously, what TV show did you get your 'inspiration' from?" She threw up air quotes.

"Not a TV show, a movie. *Back to the Future*. And your theory doesn't exactly explain why they're all wearing outfits from the past. Did they have to dip their clothes in the fountain of youth too?"

Priscilla spun around, pressed her hands together like a prayer, and breathed into them. Then she twisted back, red skirt forming a bubble from the spin.

"Well, we can both agree that they are teenagers. The fountain of youth and time capsule theories mean that somehow the residents went from being eighty to being eighteen." She fiddled with the strap of her bag hoisted on her shoulder. When she placed the book inside, the bag bulged. "Maybe we'll find out today who's right."

"What does the winner get?"

"Who said anything about winners?"

"What? You scared your theory isn't good enough, and that you're going to lose to moi?"

She balled her fingers into fists.

"Fine, dude, when I win, you don't talk to me for the rest of summer. Deal?"

He flung himself from the swing and advanced two steps forward. A foot separated them.

"Fine, and when I win, I'm taking you to get ice cream. Sound good?"

A thrill rushed through him as the words spilled out. He hadn't meant for them to.

Her jaw slackened and she tucked a stray hair behind her ear in a nervous fashion. The curls forced the strand to bounce back to its original place. She inhaled, held the breath for a second, and then released.

"Okay, lover boy, deal."

Carter watched Scarlett lean back in her chair in the Bingo Hall and throw a laugh up toward the ceiling.

"Ah, my bingo partner came back. I thought you'd ditched me for some other fair lady at Country Acres." Scarlett plumped her lips with so much lipstick today, it looked like red bees had stung them. "That's usually how it goes. Eh, what can you do?"

A woman with creases around her eyes and gray hair devouring the blonde on her scalp tapped the mic. No doubt, a worker the omniscient time capsule hadn't granted the gift of youth to. "I apologize for the delay. We'll begin in two minutes."

The volunteer woman heaved a sigh and rolled the cage of balls at the front before disappearing. Maybe she needed a last-minute thrill before back to business as usual.

Scarlett rubbed two chips between her fingers. "I'm feeling lucky, *muchacho*. Think the bingo gods will be kind to me today?"

The woman tapped the mic again. "Sorry, one more announcement. Unfortunately, our activities coordinator just informed me that her mother passed at the hospital. She will not be able to drive the group to the fair being held at the pier tonight. We're hoping to get a group together to go next Tuesday. Thank you."

"Ack." Scarlett threw down her chips and slumped her cheek against the heel of her fist like a sad chipmunk. "Of course someone had to go and die during our one night out of the Country. Typical."

He recalled how when he went out with the neighborhood kids, someone at the ice cream veranda had spoken about setting up for a fair in a week or so. Maybe if he proved his theory today, he could double up on the date: ice cream and a fair.

"You can leave the site, Scarlett?"

For some reason, he'd been under the impression that these worked a lot like the psychiatric hospital his brother stayed at during high school for OCD. Because he'd been involuntarily committed, he couldn't leave until the doctors deemed him well enough to reintegrate into society.

Scarlett pursed her lips, the blue straps on her dress making a stretching noise as she shrugged. "Yeah, sometimes you might have a group go to Wal-Mart or get the senior special at Bill's Barbecue, but we don't get a whole lot of adventure outside these walls. That's why bingo gets so competitive. Those coupons are practically gold."

Because that would wear off the time-capsule effect. Once they leave, they become old again. He held onto the back of his seat as he twisted around and shot Priscilla a smirk. *Guess whose theory is winning, baby?*

Priscilla had chosen to face the other wall this time, leaving Carter to only stare at the back of her hair. Next to her, crimson flooded Paul's forehead and cheeks as he snapped his neck down.

Caught him staring at Scarlett again.

He twisted back to face his bingo partner who evidently hadn't finished the woes of missing the fair.

"Sure, we can't ride the rides, but they have a man there with a chainsaw who likes to carve animals out of wood stumps. Talk about a thrill. Sure beats painting picture after picture in our art group." She flicked a curl off her neck and darted a glance over Carter's shoulder. "Ack, do me a favor and switch seats with me."

"What? Why?"

"Didn't your parents ever tell you not to question your elders? Now, up. Let's look lively. Before I turn eighty-five, *muchacho.*"

Carter shoved his chair back. He lurched forward to help Scarlett right as she white-knuckled the rim of the table, to steady herself. She waved him off.

"I got it. I got it."

A woman in navy scrubs and a tight ponytail behind her offered assistance, but she made a pushing motion with her arm. Any closer, and she might've landed a bullseye directly on the nurse's chest.

They switched seats and Scarlett threw all her hair back until it formed a cape around her exposed shoulders and back. "That oughta do it."

"Do what, Scarlett?"

"One of the residents keeps staring at me. We don't want to encourage him."

Paul, in Carter's periphery, had hunched his neck so far, he looked as though he wanted to bury it inside his chest.

Carter grimaced before smoothing out a loose wrinkle in the white fabric tablecloth. "Oh, come on, Scarlett. There's no harm in him staring. You are beautiful after all."

"Lies are not beautiful things, young man. They age you faster." If she had a fan, she would've poked it at him. She settled for two fingers jabbing against his shoulder instead. "And besides, he wants a marrying woman. You can't make me put on a wedding dress again."

"Again?"

Her ring finger didn't even have a dent left behind. How long ago did she have a husband?

"Questions age you faster as well, now hush. I think the caller's about to begin. Let's hope the bingo gods look down favorably on me."

She slid a green chip onto the FREE SPACE. Carter mirrored her as he glanced at the empty chair on his right side.

"Mind if I ask another question, Scarlett?"

"Jeez, I'm stealing your friend next time for bingo. No wonder I lost last time. You bring bad luck with you."

"Friend?"

"Yeah, the one who keeps stealing glances at you from over her shoulder when you aren't looking. Why do you think I moved seats? So she could get a better look at you."

Priscilla? Yeah, right. Maybe to try and kill me with her glare.

"Anyway, you had a question. Out with it, *muchacho*. You speak too slowly."

"What happened to Ethel?"

He twisted in his seat to scan the crowd. Maybe his age comment last time had scared her off to another part of the rec center. Pat had mentioned during their orientation that teens frightened the residents easily.

Lots of big curls in the hair and large sun hats, but no Ethel.

"Oh, she had a heart attack on Thursday. Died before they could even rush her to the hospital. Only reason they found her was she hadn't come to dinner, and they checked in on her in her room. Must not have been able to hit the call button to alert the nurses."

He blinked. "What?"

"She died, Carter. That's what happens to people here. You get used to it. Doesn't prevent us from wanting to get barbecue or go to fairs."

That made no sense. *If this was a time capsule, she shouldn't have gotten a heart attack.* Teens rarely got those. Only athletic ones or ones with cardiac issues.

So much for the time capsule theory. Or the fountain of youth. If the residents had eaten ambrosia or whatever he had spied over Priscilla's shoulder in the car as she read that library book, that should've kept them young and healthy.

"How old was she?"

Scarlett held up a chip to her eye like a monocle. "Ninety-three years old."

Chapter Ten
PRISCILLA

HIS HAIR LOOKS NICE FROM BEHIND.

She chewed on her lip. *Why did you have to talk nerdy to him about that psychologist though? We know that nerdy = flirty. Girl, you're slipping.*

A mixture of fried food and ocean sea salt swelled in the air as she, Grandpa, and Maria stopped by a ticket booth at the entrance of the pier. Grandpa had mentioned wanting to stop by the fair when she returned from Country Acres. Something about enjoying a man who made sculptures out of tree trunks using a chainsaw.

Why did she even flirt with him anyway? He positively revolted her when they first met.

Those pretty eyes didn't help ... and that hair. And the fact that he and Scarlett seemed to get along, and no one else her age would give someone in a nursing home the time of day. Ugh. *Stupid heart, stop fluttering.*

No-See-Ums bit at her legs, causing her to dig into her bag to spray bug repellant on her calves. Yikes, that stung.

When the man at the ticket booth whipped around again, her chest deflated. Too bad the front of him didn't look like Carter's face. Had the same red hair though.

I didn't notice until he was on the swings today that his freckles on his face form constellations. Right by the nose she even spotted a close resemblance to the Big Dipper, her favorite pattern in the night sky.

Heat surged into her cheeks as she held out her wrist to receive a stamp in the shape of a starfish from the auburn guy at the entrance to the fair. In the distance, a looming Ferris wheel with flashing bulbs highlighted the booths and rides planted on the beach and near the pier in shadows, under the glow of a tangerine sunset.

"Good thing we got here on time." Grandpa waved his stamped wrist at Maria and Priscilla. "We'll be able to catch the chainsaw man's last show before everything goes dark."

They melted into a hefty crowd who all seemed to surge toward a row of bleachers stationed around a clean stump of wood and man beside it snapping on a pair of clear safety goggles. Bordering both sides of the boardwalk, vendors called out about throwing darts at balloons and rings around the lids of goldfish bowls, with the lure of stuffed animals and new pet prizes.

Priscilla stole a glance at one of the vendors when he had his back turned and flush crawled up her neck when she caught the back of his head in the fiery glow of the sunset.

No, that's way too orange to be him, Priscilla. Looks like he washed his hair in orange juice. His looks more like the color of copper. Stop looking for Carter anyway, you weirdo.

She forced herself to glue her attention to a whirling ride parked next to a row of portable restrooms. Shrieks and squeals of laughter disappeared in the suction of the swirl on the ride, and her eyes traced the circles of the ride until she had to wrench her gaze away because her stomach had turned sour.

"You doing all right, Prisca?"

Her lips curved into a smile that didn't quite meet her eyes. "Yeah, Grandpa, doing great."

"You look deep in thought."

Those watery eyes could see through anything. He must've passed down that trait to her. "Just thinking about a boy." She flushed when he started to chuckle. "Not like that."

Grandpa Silas's legs skittered to a halt as a teen dropped a corndog that sputtered mustard on the sand. Wrapping his arms like wings around Maria and Priscilla, they dodged to the side. They'd reach the stands for the chainsaw show in about fifty feet.

"You know, Prisca, your grandma gave me the hardest time before our first date. She worked at a diner, and I would stop in every day to ask her to give me extra butter for my eggs and go see a movie with me when her shift ended. She refused to give me either. Skimped on butter, even."

Maria and Priscilla shared an amused glance in the fading light of day. Grandpa had told this story many times.

He continued after they passed the slope of a slippery slide that had so many people giggling and screaming that he couldn't get two words out.

"Eventually, I wore her down. Her coworkers and everyone else teased her so mercilessly that she decided to go on a date with me just to prove a point. Five months later, we got married." He paused and chuckled when he spotted a stand selling fried butter, amongst other items that could give even the youngest person the best chance of a heart attack. "So Prisca, tell me, how much butter have you been skimping on that boy?"

She groaned, wrapping her arms around her stomach. Even though the weather warmed her skin at a balmy eighty-five degrees, she wished she had brought along a sweater to tuck herself into like a turtle shell.

"It's not butter that's the problem, Grandpa." She sighed and watched the dark ocean waves in the distance lap over each other. "He reminds me a lot of Lucas." Her dad's name, only spoken by her mother like a curse word. Her mom still kept a picture of him hidden in her nightstand. Priscilla never got more than a glance across the room at the photo, not a close enough view to catch any distinguished features except the huge sleeves on her mom's wedding dress. Mom henceforth marked her room off limits when she caught Priscilla spying through the doorway.

Lucas.

A seagull squawked overhead.

"And my *other* grandpa."

Her grandpa on her dad's side had cheated on Grandma (who went by Mimi) and gone out with another woman on the side. Even "married" her, as Mimi had found out later in pictures of the woman in a quarter-sleeve gown. Those were the only details about the photo she gave to the family when asked. No one could argue or suggested any differently as she had ripped all the images to shreds.

"How so, Prisca?"

They'd reached the stands and Maria helped ease Grandpa up the step to the second row. They dodged around the sun-kissed ankles of a group of teen boys before squeezing into the only open spots left in the row. *Dang, we got a good spot. Especially in this crowd.*

"Well, I never met either one, but he seems like the kind of guy who switches loyalties based on how he feels."

Even if this wasn't true, he wouldn't be able to handle her erudite vocabulary that her mom claimed Priscilla used as a defense mechanism to scare boys away. The sheltered lifestyle and obsession with vintage movies didn't help, for sure.

Grandpa frowned at the thin makeshift chain-link fence that surrounded the tree stump.

"Let me ask you this, Prisca, do you like this boy?"

Her nostrils flared. "What? Of course not."

"Oh, sweet girl, your shoulders just went all the way to your ears. Don't lie to your grandpa, now."

She scooped her knees into a tight hug against her chest. "I don't care that he's cute. Mom thought Dad was cute, and he disappeared from the picture entirely."

The man began to rev his chainsaw. Soon they wouldn't be able to hear any conversation.

"True, I don't know this boy, Prisca." He chuckled and then coughed. Grandpa out-laughed his lungs sometimes. "But I do know myself when I was his age. And I know I didn't deserve that extra butter ... and I didn't deserve that date with your grandma. But she gave me a chance."

"Seems like bad advice, Grandpa, based on what Mom went through. She took a chance on someone too."

He hmm'd. "True, Prisca. I guess love is risky business. It's up to you to determine if something is worth the risk."

Teeth crashed down so hard on Priscilla's upper lip that she tore away a layer of skin.

She hunched more into herself. *He did ask to be* just *friends. I suppose there's no harm in that. Not like he wants me to give him extra butter and a movie.*

He did ask her out to ice cream, though, if she lost the bet ...

Revs from the chainsaw drowned out her thoughts as the man in a flannel jacket tied across his waist began chipping away at the base of the stump. She watched through a crack between a woman nuzzling her head on a man's shoulder in front of them while wood chips flew in every direction. Thank goodness for the fence.

Legs aching, she unbound them, but they kicked out faster than she could contain them, nicking the man in front of her in the back. He twisted around.

"Oh, I'm so sorry, sir—"

She froze. Why did he look so familiar? Those dimples that showed, even when frowning, those broad shoulders. A mixture of longing and regret boiled in her stomach. *Don't be ridiculous, Priscilla. You're in Florida. You don't know anyone here but Grandpa and Maria.*

He also appeared petrified, eyes bulging and jaw unhinged by the slightest degree. Perhaps he'd recognized her too, but from where?

The woman beside him, a woman with a yellow flower clipped near her ear tapped his shoulder.

During a pause in the chainsaw revving, she asked, "Everything all right, Luke?"

Tension sent thousands of electrodes up and down Priscilla's arms. Lucas and Luke. She never did get a close look at that picture on her mom's nightstand, but those dimples ... oh, those dimples.

Luke twisted around and mumbled something, but the chainsaw blocked out the words. Inhaling, exhaling, Priscilla pressed two fingers to each of her temples and leaned forward, eyes squeezed shut. As if blocking out all the senses which had decided to blare red lights to match the sunset.

He had the same dimples Priscilla did.

But no, surely the dying light played tricks on her eyes. Yes, he had a much lighter shade of skin in the photograph than the man did now. Sure, Mom didn't talk about Dad much, but what on earth would he be doing in Florida anyway? Same as Mom, before she moved to New York. They'd both lived in Wisconsin, worlds apart from this place. And he wasn't old enough to retire and snowbird. She knew his graduation date from college, at least. She had found clues on LinkedIn when curiosity had struck her one day when she finished her classes early.

Two fingers tapped against her shoulder and her eyelids flung open. The couple in front of her had disappeared. Had they gotten up? Did she imagine them?

She found the source of the touch as Grandpa Silas retracted his arm. "You all right, Prisca?"

Shivers ran up and down her body, caused not solely by all the humidity evaporating from her skin. "Yeah." She tried a weak smile and hoped the dim lighting could prevent him from seeing through the lie. "Might be a little hungry."

That much was true. She hadn't eaten much since she returned from Country Acres. Maria had a steaming crock pot full of white chili when she'd arrived, but her stomach churned at the scent of the chicken mixed with corn and spicy peppers. At least, she couldn't eat anything after what Paul had told her in between bingo calls.

"Paul, why do you look so down today?"

"Oh it's"—he jabbed a finger over at Carter's bingo table—"my good friend passed away this past week. She would often go on walks with me outside. Knew more about Scarlett than any other resident here. I think they had a healthy competition in art class." He blushed and flicked his glance away from Carter's table.

"I'm so sorry to hear that. Was she eating plenty? Taking her meds? Drinking water?"

He shrugged and traced a flower pattern on the tablecloth with his finger. "She did all the right things. I guess it was her time. It's what happens when you get to our age."

So much for the Fountain of Youth theory. If Carter's checked out, hello, ice cream date.

She smirked. Then again, if Grandpa Silas stood a chance with Grandma, *may she rest in peace*, maybe ice cream wouldn't taste so bad, even if she'd lost the bet.

Besides, neither of our theories seem all that strong. Best we can hope for is a tie—that neither of us got it right.

"Prisca, do you want me to get you some food?" Grandpa Silas pulled her away from her thoughts as the chainsaw man paused to suckle on a bottle of water.

"That's all right, Grandpa. I can grab something for myself. Do you two want anything?"

Maria and Grandpa jerked their chins to indicate no and faced the tree stump again. By now, the chainsaw man had begun working on the grooves of a tortoise's shell. At least, so stated a bright white sign on the fence, in large black letters, read, "Subject of This Show: A Tortoise."

Priscilla smoothed out her skirt when she rose, then ducked unsuccessfully to let the back row continue watching.

After playing a game of hurdles over the legs of those in the second row, she bounced off the step toward a white food stall that advertised in green bubble letters all sorts of fried goodies, hot dogs, and hamburgers. A small, snaking line stretched all the way to three stalls over that featured two specials of the day: fried shrimp and pierogies.

A weird assortment. Hot dogs it was.

In front of her a short guy with tan skin and a baseball cap tapped his shoes against the sand. His pocket buzzed loud enough to outdo the carnival-style music from a nearby carousel, and the glow from his pocket stung her eyes. She glanced away to watch the strings of colorful lights on the Ferris wheel chase each other in a slow circle.

"Yeesh." The boy's gravelly voice pulled her away from watching the wheel. After he shut his phone off, he waved the dead device at her. "Shoulda left this thing at home, eh?"

Doesn't want to be on his phone, eh? I believe I just made a new friend. She had, after all, mentioned that opposites don't attract.

This boy, with carnival lights dancing in his eyes, had a good start at being *similar*.

Guess she didn't have to worry about giving Carter any butter now.

"I always forget mine." She shoved her hands into the pockets of her skirt, rubbing her fingers on the wallet contained inside. "I mean, when you look at all this"—she gestured to the booths and rides—"how can you afford to be distracted by something else?"

He eased his weight on his hip, mirroring her by placing his hands in the pockets of his jeans. Lips curved upward. Maybe he liked the idea of a friendship too.

"Marcus."

"Priscilla."

"You're not from around here, huh?"

"Is it because of the accent?" One of the youth group kids had mocked her nasal the other day when they exited the building.

"No." He jerked his chin down at her shoes. "Your socks are showing. We don't do that here."

Sure enough, she tilted her chin down and only spotted his ankles peeping out of the curves of his white and black no-show Adidas.

"Although, that skirt is beautiful. Green's a great color on you."

Was he ... flirting? So hard to tell with the men down here. Up in New York men didn't hold doors for strangers and talk so friendly. Still, she gave the skirt a twirl, and the fabric flounced out until she formed a summer Christmas tree. Any excuse to show this baby off.

"There's a nice vintage shop near our apartment back home. Found this one on clearance."

He switched his weight onto his other hip. "Do vintage dresses have pockets?"

"Oh, pockets can go as far back as the 1700s. Women used to keep coins and other important items in their petticoats' pockets, and—" She stopped herself. *Oh no*, when she flirted she talked way too nerdy. Sure, he was cute, but she just met him, and men seemed to scare easily when a girl knew her pocket facts. She would know. She used it as a defense mechanism to frighten them off. "Sorry, my mom is an editor at an imprint that specializes in history books. I can get a little carried away."

She hadn't flirted with someone in a while. Not after everything Mom and Mimi spilled about their past lives with males. She'd sworn off men. So why did this one warm her stomach and feet?

Marcus's lips twitched and the line moved forward two feet.

"No, it's good to be passionate about something. Now tell me, Priscilla, has anyone been able to give you a tour of the area?"

Was ... was he offering to give one?

Prisca, no, the whole point of your mom sending you to Florida was to prevent you from sidling into the car with some stranger. Even if he doesn't use his phone nonstop, what else do you have in common with this guy?

Despite herself, the words, "Oh, no, not yet," slipped out. She needed to eat something fast. The world tilted a little, and she steadied her balance on the sand. Stupid blood sugar levels dipping, always made it so hard to think straight.

"Would you want someone to—"

"Marcus! Where is your phone? I've been trying to text you for the past fifteen minutes. Couldn't find you after the Ferris wheel."

Priscilla's stomach soured as she watched a girl with a boyish haircut and lacy black dress march up to Marcus. She cradled her arm around his hip, hanging on for dear life like a sloth. She then planted a kiss on his lips before flicking a horrifying scowl at Priscilla and twisting both herself and her boyfriend to face the front.

Even with the faint glimmer of red remaining in the sky, she recognized the girl from the library: Mia Patel. That girl had already made a rude remark about her living in libraries but now probably thought Priscilla was making moves with her boyfriend. No, she had it all wrong. She didn't do that, like whoever Mimi's husband married on the side. She vowed never to be the *other* woman.

I guess he was just being friendly. Typical Florida.

They'd almost reached the front of the line, but her abdomen burned. Not hungry anymore. Why was she so upset about this boy anyway? She'd just met him. Maybe it had something to do with the injustice of his match. That girls like Mia could get guys like him.

And girls like Mia thought that people like Priscilla would try to snatch him away ...

Just like what happened to Priscilla's Mimi all those years before.

Blinking away a glaze that stung her eyes, she slipped away from the queue and tried to catch her breath, but the swarming crowd made it so hard to breathe. Scanning the area in a circle, she spotted a tunnel that had something painted in a bubbly font on top, but she couldn't tell through the haze in her eyes blurring her glasses.

Craving the darkness, she slipped inside, glanced around for any other bodies, sighed when she found none, and slid to the floor in a ball.

Air through the nose, out through the mouth. Still her heartbeat thundered so loud, as if she had just dodged a bullet.

Chapter Eleven
CARTER

"STAY WITH GRANDMA, I'm going to see if the 4-H stalls are extra or if we can get in for free."

Carter's shoulders slumped as he and his grandma stood alone as the crowd rushed past them like a river swirling around rocks. Grandma pushed her glasses up her long nose and squinted at the lights. He sighed. Grandma's legs wobbled. He scanned the area for a bench and found one nestled between two food stalls, one with a strong whiff of sauerkraut.

"Come on, Grandma, rest your feet." He motioned for her to sit, standing beside her as a nearby child licked cotton candy from sticky fingers.

Silence somehow managed to find its way between them despite the shrieks, old-timey piano music, and somewhere in the distance a man calling out raffle numbers through a microphone. Lights from the carousel danced in his grandmother's eyes. They reminded him of Ethel's.

A hole bore into his stomach at the thought of the woman at Country Acres. How could someone so young could die of something so old?

How many more years until Grandma became an Ethel?

"So, Grandma—"

She peered up at him, face aglow at a long-missed interaction.

He cleared his throat, question lost on his tongue. How to start a conversation with someone four times his age ... "Did you ever have fairs like this, growing up?"

The beams from the bulbs on the carousel illuminated her features. Something about the wash of light blurred her wrinkles, making her look ten years younger. Warmth spread in his stomach, and he felt his shoulders relax as she began to speak.

"Let's see if I can remember. Lots of livestock." A pungent swirl of manure ventured from the 4-H stalls nearby. How did that manage to outdo the sauerkraut? "Rides like these"—she gestured at one that brought a train around a circular track—"but far more dangerous. I suppose not much changes about these events." A girl in jean shorts cut high up her thigh scurried up to the sauerkraut booth to grab a handful of napkins. "Except for the clothing."

Huh. Maybe both the fair and Country Acres served as a time capsule of sorts. He wondered what would happen if he checked Grandma into Country Acres. Would her clothing suddenly turn into a vintage swing dress? *Was she ever a teen once? I mean, yes, she was obviously once a teen, but it's hard to picture it. What did that look like?*

Memories bounced around his skull for any photos Grandma used to hang in her old house of herself and Grandpa. But the images blurred in his mind in a sheath of black and white.

"Grandma, if you could be a teen again, would you take that chance?"

She flashed a smile, a bottom tooth so crooked it shielded one of others in the row. "Isn't that the question?"

They wavered in silence until the merry-go-round made a full circle. "Does it have an answer?"

"Well—"

"4-H stalls are free." His mother's statement had cut his grandma's short. The other, who had left her mouth slightly agape, sealed her lips and groaned as she made an effort to stand. Mom helped her rise, then they both sped off toward a barn with a yellow glow on the inside and a lantern hanging on the outside.

Strings of flags decorated the interior when they stepped inside, greeted by a punch in the nose from scents of hay and manure.

Carter paused to gawk at a white bunny so large it took up half of the cage. A blue ribbon adorned the outside. In a stall right across the way, a brown cow curved its neck backwards so it could lick a fly off its back. Ahead Grandma and Mom stopped to poke their fingers into a cage full of baby chicks. He started to angle in their direction but dead-stopped again when a burn-your-eyes-out yellow flower captured his attention on the left.

Elena Patel turned from admiring a black chicken with a bright red comb atop its head. She squeezed the arm of a man in a straw fedora before she turned to Carter.

"You, young man, should go into matchmaking."

Carter fought an amused quirk of his mouth. "Umm, I think there are dating apps for that. Plus, I didn't set you up with him. Didn't you say a friend from the salon did?"

"Well, yes, but—oh, you should do something with this whole dating business. Have people pay you for advice. A Dear Abby, but for lonely people."

She lost him on the Dear Abby part.

"What do you mean, Mrs. Patel?"

Elena jabbed a thumb behind her where her date had stood a second ago. Now he'd ventured a foot to the right to check out a rooster whose tail feathers poked out of the silver bars on the cage.

"I kept the yellow flower in, since you said to be myself, but I followed all the rest of your advice. We've gone out more than once.

Which I think is a win. And he seems to want to move fast. Most people do when you get to my age." She clasped his shoulder. "I appreciate your advice. I may have to pull in a favor from Lewis—the guy who does marriage licenses—after all." She winked. "Because if we play our cards right, you might be attending a wedding at the end of this summer."

He glanced up at her date and something about the curl of his hair sent his mind reeling. Where had he seen spirals like that before? And those dimples.

"Well, I'm glad to hear it."

She gave his shoulder a squeeze before rejoining her date. Arm in arm, they meandered down the stall, dodging around a cow pie left on the center of the strip.

Carter met with his mother and grandma near the "gift" from the cow, and tried to maintain their slow, leisurely pace. But he grew bored after the fifth fat bunny in a row. The whole point of him wanting to come to the fair was to have some artsy pics snapped of him in front of the Ferris wheel for Insta. No luck with getting that Instagram photo with the sun about to set. And this barn reeked of un-inspiration for any videos to post later.

Mom eyed him over her shoulder as he trudged through the hay-littered floor.

"Sweetheart, I'm getting thirsty. Why don't you run out and grab us some lemonade, and we can meet you somewhere?" She flashed her phone. "I know you have yours on you."

As if on cue, his device buzzed from his pocket. He fought the urge to check the notification until he'd left the barn. Eh, just a spam email.

Eyes adjusting to the darkness that had fallen over the fair, he chased down a stand with a yellow lemon logo in the burnt glow of the sunset. By now, a mere strip of scarlet burned in the horizon. In minutes, it would fade to purple. He dodged around a couple heaving a sand-friendly stroller and swerved into a line three-people deep. No doubt with the night air cooling, he had the best chance to grab a cold drink now, when no one wanted one.

"Ugh, why isn't he answering?"

Familiarity stung his ears. Despite himself, he swerved on his heel, sand biting his skin, and watched Mia Patel click a red hang-up button on her phone, exit out of the app, and click the Snapchat logo at the top of her screen. No doubt to message whoever wouldn't answer the call.

Back when they dated, she did text a lot. Despite acting aloof most of the time.

Her neck snapped up, perhaps feeling the burn of his gaze. She froze, faltered, and then returned to her white screen. "Didn't think I'd see you here."

"We don't exactly live on Daytona Beach. This fair's one of the only fun things our town does, you know." Especially with all the snowbirds gone, half of their city's population had disappeared up north.

She scrunched her shoulders, strap slipping down from her dress. "Yeah, but it's not like tonight's the only night they're running it." She growled at her screen and muttered, "Come on, I Snapped you. DM'd you on Instagram. Pick. Up. Your. Phone."

Mia slid her phone into her jean shorts, which, like the girl back at the sauerkraut station, she'd trimmed them short until only strings hung down from the fabric, like a clothing waterfall.

She folded her arms to cut a look at Carter. "At least you got back to me whenever I messaged, except for that weird month you went AWOL. He almost never has his phone."

He meaning her new boyfriend.

Carter approached a mustached man behind a register who drummed his fingers on the counter. "Two medium lemonades, please." He handed him a ten and received four one-dollar bills back. Wow, some expensive juice right there.

"Ugh, is she *flirting* with him?"

He spun around to the tune of the man in the counter digging a scoop into the ice and pouring it into a cup. Mia planted her hands on her hips, and he followed her line of vision to a girl with large hair talking to Marcus at a food stand nearby. He could recognize those dimples anywhere, especially with the electric lights that hummed all around them.

"No, Mia, she did the same smile for me earlier today, and she hates me with a burning passion. Trust me, I don't think anyone our age is her type."

Mia snapped her chin to him, lifting one perfectly plucked eyebrow in an oh-really fashion.

No way she was flirting with me earlier. She said she didn't want to even talk with me if she won that bet. Good thing they both lost. Maybe he could convince her about ice cream some other time.

"Two medium lemonades. Have a nice day!"

He turned to retrieve them from hands so large they looked like they could wrap completely around one of the cups. Cartoon lemons decorated the cup and green lid. Twisting on his heel he found Mia had disappeared from the vicinity and had begun marching toward Marcus and Priscilla.

A crowd barricaded Carter from following, not that he wanted Marcus to see him tailing his ex-girlfriend anyway.

Mia made a large gesture with her arms (like she always did when angry), planted a kiss, and moments later, Priscilla swabbed a finger under her eye as she pulled herself away from the line. She glanced around, found the entrance to the red Fun House tunnel, and disappeared inside.

Lord Almighty, what did Mia say to that poor girl?

Playing dodgem with a crowd, including a man whose ice cream cone looked ready to decapitate itself, he found a break in the stream of people and stepped into the Fun House. Priscilla uncurled herself to glance up at him.

"Sorry, don't want to bother you, but you ran into my ex, so just wanted to check to see you're okay."

She cleared her throat and knuckled her eyes. No tears, but she'd crinkled her face like she wanted to block them if they came. "Mia's your ex?"

"No, the guy with the ridiculously long jeans for summer. Yes, of course, Mia."

He planted himself on the opposite end of the wall, then slid to the floor, sure that she didn't want him sidled next to her. He set the lemonades beside him and threw a glance down the tunnel as an array of mirrors glimmered reflections of the line of bulbs that decorated each wall.

"I'm fine, lover boy. I'm just not used to people being friendly down here." She exhaled as she pressed her legs down. Maybe worried he could see something up that long skirt of hers. "Speaking of friends, I was too hard on you earlier on the playground. Don't worry about that deal we had earlier. No one should ever prevent someone from speaking to them for the rest of their life." The whites of her eyes showed. "Even if they say stupid things from time to time."

"Stupid friends are great to have around anyway. They make you feel smart." He grinned, brushing off some sand that coated the toe of his shoe. "Besides, the bet is off anyway. One of the residents died of a heart attack. Not that you can't die from that at a younger age—but it is less likely. And they mentioned canes and walkers ... which means that they *are* the age they're claiming to be. Eighties and nineties. For some reason we can see them as their teen selves."

"I know."

They met eyes before splitting apart, each gazing at the walkway of mirrors. In a nervous fashion, he reached for the sunglasses strapped to his shirt.

"Wanna take a look at these mirrors while we wait for my ex to leave, princess?" He swung his neck in the opposite direction. Through the sheet of darkness, he watched Mia park at a table with an umbrella with Marcus. "Looks like they won't be leaving for a while."

Her gaze appeared to follow in his periphery.

"Well, I guess we don't have anything better to do."

He rose and offered a hand. She frowned at his palm. He made a little *Pac-Man* out of it, talking in a high voice. "I'm not Carter. I'm Carter's hand. We both don't like Carter. Now take me, and we'll get faaaar away from him."

She squeezed her eyelids together until wrinkles formed on her forehead. "You're ridiculous."

Still, she gripped his hand until she steadied herself on both heels. Then she let go, and they ventured down the hall of Fun House mirrors. He glimpsed at his reflections on the left, each growing taller, fatter, or head-bulging, like special effects on a camera filter.

He paused at one that made his torso short and elongated his legs, giraffe-style. "You know, I've heard of these places before. Mind snapping a pic of me for Insta?" He already had wrenched his cell phone out of his pocket.

"Again, you are"—she grabbed the phone from him—"ridiculous."

Posing with his hands on his hips, in Superman fashion, he watched the camera flash once. She handed him back the phone. Strange, this chick didn't take five to ten pictures with different angles. He glanced at the photo. A little blurry, but something told him Priscilla didn't do photoshoots with a lot of people. So much for Insta. At least he'd have something for his story.

"This is hilarious, princess. Look at the difference between my actual self and my reflection."

The phone glinted in her dark irises for a moment before her entire self brightened. "Wait a second. I think I understand Country Acres now."

"You do?"

Priscilla palmed one of the mirrors, one that somehow made her already slimmer than before. She wasn't exactly stick-thin, but that allowed the Good Lord to bless her in a few areas. "When you and I look at the residents, it's like looking at them in a mirror. But everyone else sees them as they are." She appeared to read the confusion on his face and pointed at the picture on his phone. "We perceive them to have 'long legs.' Everyone else sees them as they normally appear, with normal-sized legs."

A few seconds later, the spark set off in his brain. And like her, he could feel every one of his features illuminate. *We're looking at the residents through a fun house mirror.*

"So it's like you and I are looking at them with a filter?"

"Exactly. That explains why Pastor Timothy and even the residents can't see it themselves. Only us."

He had wondered why Pastor Timothy didn't seem to observe an entire Bingo Hall full of teenagers. "But why us?"

The question buzzed between them as a light overhead flicked on and off. Someone needed to change out a bulb on the right wall.

Whatever sentient something, whether God or some medical phenomenon that caused them both to hallucinate the same thing— chose them, He or it picked two complete opposites for the task at hand.

"Isn't that the question?" Priscilla said at last.

"Does it have an answer?"

She thumbed her chin. "I wish I knew. But I can tell you that meeting once a week for bingo isn't going to help us solve it. I can barely get Paul to say two sentences before the caller starts going. Once that happens, complete silence."

And Scarlett wasn't exactly a conversationalist when her board could determine if she got the Gift Certificate to Bill's Barbecue that night.

No doubt, bingo was a poor use of the "gift" apparently bestowed on both of them.

"We need to find more time with the residents and fast." With the corner of her dress, she wiped off her handprint left behind on the mirror. "They might look like teens, but you and I both know they aren't getting any younger."

Chapter Twelve
PRISCILLA

"YOU MEAN TO TELL ME, Mr. Carter, that you—who has missed youth group consistently and begrudgingly are required to volunteer your hours at Country Acres to secure your diploma—want to spend *more* time each week at the assisted living center?"

"Actually"—Priscilla raised her hand but then dropped her arm, fighting claustrophobia with the two walls of bookcases in Pastor Timothy's small office—"we both do."

The pastor palmed a pink face with his sleeve and clicked the window fan on a higher setting. It appeared the church didn't like to run the AC during weekdays. Strange considering how much the buildings baked in the summers here.

Conversations she'd heard from the one girl over the Cheetos back at youth group proved her no-AC-during-the-week theory correct. At least Grandpa liked to blast the AC in his house.

Oh, Grandpa ... she couldn't think about him now. Not after his medical scare this morning.

Sweltering in a silky dress, she lifted the fabric above the calves. *Oh, the scandal in a Baptist church down South.*

"Much as I appreciate the heart to serve the elderly, Country Acres doesn't like to open its doors to non-family visitors. There are protocols and such. I don't know how they would react to you two stopping by whenever you feel like doing so."

He leaned back in his rolling leather chair, the fabric squeaking from the effort on both sides. Priscilla and Carter each adjusted in their seats, her sincerely praying that she didn't leave any sweat marks behind on the faux leather upholstery for when she had to stand up. Why hadn't he gone for a softer, cooler fabric in this heat?

"I suppose I could give Pat a call to see if they would be open to seeing you more often than on bingo days, but I doubt Country Acres would let anyone waltz in unless they're family. Even then, you would probably have to schedule visitation hours. It could be easier to cut through that red tape if you do it through the church—because it's an organization they trust—but I don't know how much easier."

Priscilla curled her fingers around the armrest and released.

Well, so much for the gift. I guess we'll just have to learn what we can during bingo. Now, time to leave this uncomfy office.

"Thanks anyway, Pastor Timothy." She rolled her chair back, pushed herself up, and checked the fabric. A miracle, no sweat marks left behind.

The two of them burst outside of the office door and into the hallway to catch some fresh air away from the towering bookcases. She waited until Carter had shut the door before she took a breath through her steepled fingers.

"You know, for someone who lives in the city, you don't do well with tight spaces, princess."

She dropped her arms and glanced at pieces of paper dangling from a bulletin board, what looked like sheets torn out of Bible-themed coloring books. The paper closest to her featured the art style of a child too obsessed with squiggles, the color maroon, and drawing outside of the lines in crayon.

"At least we have AC in the city. Can we step outside? Somehow it's colder out there."

They ambled down the hallway, to the left, and out the doors into bright, blinding sunlight.

"Gonna head back home, Priscilla?"

She shrugged. "Grandpa had a coughing fit earlier, sounded like bronchitis, so Maria had to take him to the doctor. House is empty now."

"But I thought introverts liked being alone."

"We do." She popped her heel back into her shoe which had gone wayward. "But not all the time. Mom works all the time, so sometimes when I'm left home alone too long I can get cabin fever. I might go stop by the playground to—" she finished the sentence in her head, *stop thinking about Grandpa.*

She'd managed to avoid that topic so far in her head while in Pastor Timothy's office—well, mostly. No doubt, her focused attempts on staying conscious in the heat had occupied her thoughts. But now, in direct sunlight, with no sunglasses to shield her eyes ...

Grandpa Silas.

He'd gotten winded from the fair the other night. Barely making it up the steps without having to gasp and grasp at his sides. How much longer could he live like this before he needed to head to a place like Country Acres? Although Maria helped with meal prep and daily activities, she couldn't always be around when he became breathless.

And even though having Maria around wasn't all that different from assisted living, Grandpa Silas seemed to think so. There was just something stubborn about him wanting to stay in his own house.

Give him one bad night alone in his room, and, like Ethel, he could disappear.

Just like that.

She scrunched her toes, kicked off her shoes, and winced at her instantly singed skin courtesy of the blacktop parking lot. "Do you ever get used to the sand in your shoes?"

"Well, you're not exactly wearing proper footwear for beachside Florida." He angled his shoulder down to seemingly catch her flailing arm. She let him balance her, but for a moment only. "I also wouldn't suggest going down the slide." The dark green snaking playground equipment gleamed in the sunlight. "Unless you want to get second-degree burns."

"Swings it is, I guess."

The sun's rays tanned their skins as they strolled toward the playground. She winced at the thought of how the chain strings attached to the swing would brand her palms because they sat in direct sunlight all day. Maybe she could gather folds of her fabric skirt and cling to the links that way.

She squinted at the wisps of clouds remaining in a picturesque sky. Although New York had days like these, they came fewer and far between, mostly in summer.

"Also, how in the world do you get used to the sun here? You'd have to have the visors down all the time in your car when you drove."

"Here, borrow these." He unclipped his sunglasses from his shirt.

Priscilla hesitated before she grabbed them and shoved them on her nose over her glasses. The world faded from a bright blur to a sepia brown. She glanced at the sun without a stinging sensation that filled her eyes with moisture.

"Can you see better now?"

"Yeah." She slid the glasses down her nose with a wince at the return of the burning light. "It's crazy what a pair of sunglasses can do." She pursed her lips as she kicked a loose rock on the pavement with the toe of her shoe. "It's like looking at the world through a filter."

Bugs buzzed in the trees ahead, the tune of a perfect summer rhythm. She prayed for no more No-See-Ums and mosquitoes. A fair share of bites ran up and down her legs.

Memories flooded her vision of the night before in the Fun House.

Realization struck her.

"Carter?"

"Yeah?"

"Do you think Country Acres is like a pair of sunglasses?" She unsheathed the glasses from her face, then handed them back to him. He nuzzled them on the nape on his shirt. "Maybe we're given the chance to see the residents in a different light for a purpose."

"What do you mean?"

"Pastor Timothy can't see them through sunglasses. I've been thinking about it since we talked in the Fun House, and I can't fight the feeling that somehow us being able to see the residents as teens can help us to help them."

He frowned as he scooped up a brown leaf that he prodigaled onto the parking lot. Twirling the stem in his fingertips, the oval shape whirled round and round until it blurred from the speed.

She was losing him. Plenty of kids from homeschool co-op had short attention spans too.

"Think about it this way, I can't look at the sun until I put on those glasses. Maybe we can't fulfill our mysterious purpose at Country Acres until we put on ours."

"I think I'm tracking. So if we saw them without the glasses, they would burn our eyes out. You know, because they're old. If an elderly lady wore what Scarlett had on in the Bingo Hall, I think I'd want my retinas hosed down with Clorox."

Hopeless, hopeless, hopeless, she smeared a palm from her forehead down to her chin.

"Priscilla." Pastor Timothy burst out the double doors of the church, panting. "Carter." He halted in the parking lot, hands on knees, to catch a breath.

He gulped.

"I just got off the phone with Pat. Apparently two residents had overheard her conversation, and specifically requested you visit them whenever you have free time to do so. I would say that's awfully convenient of them to overhear it, but those residents do like to hang around that front desk a lot. You don't even have to schedule visitations. Just call an hour ahead of time to let them know you're coming. You start Monday."

Carter threw up two hands, sidling up next to Pastor Timothy in the shade of the church entrance. Sunburn threatening to crawl up her arm, Priscilla followed. She gasped as the cool touch of the shadows chilled her skin.

"One thing at a time, Pastor Timothy. Who requested that we come?"

"Oh, gracious, Carter, I'm terrible with names." He unbent himself to stroke the scraggly whiskers on his chin. "Paul, remembered that one. Good church name."

Priscilla scrunched her lips and cheeks. No way would Paul have eavesdropped on the conversation. He didn't seem like the type. Must've been nearby another person who overheard it. Images from the bingo game flashed through her mind.

And then the movie reel stopped at a woman with large red lips and a sweetheart neckline dress to match. Like a perfect Ann Miller or Hedy Lamarr. Maybe even an Elizabeth Taylor. Names from her favorite older movies flickered through her head.

Carter cleared his throat. "Pastor Timothy, did the other person happen to be a resident named Scarlett?"

He snapped his fingers, then twirled his index once like a baton. "That's the one."

Scarlett must've asked for Carter, and Paul his ol' bingo buddy Priscilla.

"But you two will have to spend time with that specific person who requested you." Pastor Timothy greased his shirt with his forehead sweat when he went to wipe off the moisture. "That means no scampering off to talk to another resident if yours doesn't appear to entertain you enough." He cocked his head as he flicked a brow at Carter who was hastily shoving a cell phone back into his pocket.

Priscilla rubbed a thumb up and down the cleft in her chin.

Hmm, this might confirm my theory. We're given this gift for a purpose, and we've been assigned to a specific person to use that gift. Me to Paul, and Carter to Scarlett. At least that narrows down our focus, so we don't have to talk to every single person there to figure out why we see what we see.

Good thing too, the personalities of the residents appeared to match their requested visitors.

"Pat said to start visitations on Monday, since they do most of their outings during the weekends, and you can start fresh." Pastor Timothy was spinning a key ring on his index finger. "I'm afraid that other groups in the church will need the van. Other than bingo nights, you'll have to find rides there."

Oh, whoops, the gift had hit a snag. No way could she let her grandpa drive.

Her last time on the road with him was three years back. In his attempt to merge into four lanes of heavy traffic, he simply shut his eyelids, as if in prayer, and slammed his foot against the gas. Apparently, Florida residents had great reflexes when it came to hitting the brakes.

"Shouldn't be a problem." Carter's voice, which shot up an octave, indicated the opposite. "I could ask my mom to borrow her car. She might go for it, knowing that I'm only planning on driving to

Country Acres." He flicked a glance at Priscilla. "And that I have an eyewitness who can confirm we just went to that place, and nowhere else."

"Sounds like a plan. If you two excuse me, I have a call at two." He jerked his wrist around to read the time, which caused his eyes and mouth to bulge in panic. "Which I'm running late for."

With a curt wave, he rushed inside, leaving Priscilla and Carter behind in the gust of his odor: a combination of too much cologne and sweat.

"I guess that answers that question."

Carter frowned as he threw up a passive, nonchalant wave in a poor attempt to diffuse the scent left behind from the youth pastor. "What question?"

"*The* question."

"Oh no, sister, we're nowhere near answering that." He unclipped his sunglasses and slid them up his nose, covering the Orion's belt constellation of freckles with the bridge of the glasses frame. "But at least we're closer to figuring it out."

"Oh dear, no, there's been a misunderstanding."

Pat clasped her hands in front of her vest as she spoke. Priscilla tried her best not to keep staring at the second to last golden button the woman had failed to put in a buttonhole.

So much for Carter haggling with his mom over the car. If there's been a misunderstanding, we drove all this way for nothing.

But according to him, when his mother found out about Priscilla riding with him, she relented and handed him the keys. And so Carter arrived to pick Priscilla up that morning to the tune of some indie pop Spotify playlist.

"She says that your grandpa's been a great neighbor. Trimming grass and cooking meals for us, especially when my brother... was checked into a hospital a while back." He'd turned up the volume on the speaker. Maybe to drown out the sound of his voice. "Says goodness probably runs in your family."

"But Pastor Timothy told us that Scarlett had called for me and Paul for Priscilla." Carter pulled his finger out of a bowl of potpourri on a cabinet near the front desk. He'd been stirring the mixture like some weird, fragrant soup. "Do they not want us to visit anymore?"

"Oh, they want you to visit. They've been asking me nonstop every time they pass this desk."

With a huff, Pat grabbed the potpourri bowl and shoved it into a drawer full of sliding folders. Cinnamon and orange had disappeared from the room.

"Then what's the misunderstanding?"

"The misunderstanding, young man, is Paul did not ask to be visited by Priscilla, and Scarlett didn't want you to accompany her when you stopped by Country Acres."

That made no sense. That would mean ...

"Scarlett asked specifically for Priscilla. And Paul for Carter."

Why hadn't Pat mentioned this before? She did often seem flustered, so maybe she forgot to.

Priscilla focused her attention on a fake stone fireplace (Grandpa said no one had a real fireplace in Florida) stationed by the door, surrounded by couches with vintage swirled fabric, like the comforter Grandpa had put on her bed. Concentrate. Why on earth would those patients request this? From what she heard about Scarlett, the woman made Carter seem reserved and calm. And she doubted Carter could yank any conversation out of Paul by showing him TikTok compilations.

"And as a reminder"—Pat slid open a drawer, withdrawing blank name tags that she slapped on the countertop—"I'd told Tim over the phone that you are to accompany the resident, and only the resident, to any scheduled activities and unscheduled. Since you haven't scheduled a set amount of time, we highly suggest you take at least two to three hours to dedicate to each visit."

Priscilla plugged her nose without touching it, a trick she'd learned as a child, to prevent a groan from sliding out. Much as she'd loved to spend time with the residents, Scarlett acted like how she looked ... sixteen years old.

Based on Carter's nose wrinkling, she guessed he'd taught himself the same maneuver.

After the two of them scrawled their names under the "Hello, I'm:" to display on their chests, Pat motioned for Priscilla to follow her with a jerking wave.

"Scarlett is currently in the salon getting her hair done. Carter, stay put. I'll come back in a moment with Paul. He likes to go walking during this hour."

Priscilla shot Carter a help-me sort of glance before slackening her features. *Stop it, Prisca. Just because he sang like Frank Sinatra on the way over here doesn't make him any cuter. You live in New York. You can help yourself.*

Bracing herself for the longest two hours of her life, she distracted herself with the objects on the right side of the narrow, carpeted hallway, on the way to the salon. Paintings of fruit baskets and sailboats lined the beige wallpaper.

Sconces served as guides down the hallway, until they reached the last door on the right.

She coughed as the pungent punch of hair spray caught her right in the lungs. With an impatient motion, Pat flicked her arm toward the door. Priscilla praised the good Lord for the invention of glasses. She didn't want to know what would have happened if that hair spray had landed right in her eye. Priscilla stepped into the brightly lit room, almost bumping into a side table with a vase full of fake pink flowers.

"It's about time."

Craning her neck to the right, she found Scarlett beaming at her. The stylist, wand in hand, twirled out a beautiful black curl which fell to frame Scarlett's face.

"Hi, Scarlett." Priscilla's voice squeaked. She coughed to bring it down. "You're looking good."

Indeed she did. In her turquoise sheath dress, belted in the middle, lacy gloves, and false eyelashes, she looked like they'd torn her out of a 1950s fashion magazine.

The stylist behind her, who either had all gray hair by choice or by age, Priscilla could never keep up with the trends, cracked a smile so wide she could split an apple in half with a bite. "Doesn't she look just precious?" She slapped her long-taloned nails together with a squeal. "Oh, the residents here are the cutest."

Heat prickled in Priscilla's cheeks. Even though Scarlett had powdered on a decent amount of rosy blush today, from in the bright lighting of the squat room it appeared her face and neck had also darkened in color.

Cute. All the ladies at the knitting club *hated* that word. Especially when younger people wielded it against them like a weapon. *"Aren't old people just the cutest?"*

Scarlett paled but unclenched her grappled fists from the swivel chair that sat in front of a large, rectangular mirror.

"Heather." She said this through gritted teeth.

The stylist swung with a wide lean to the side of the chair to face Scarlett. "Yes, dear?"

"I think I left my rose hair accessory in my room. Do you mind grabbing it for me? I'd get up but—" Scarlett's arms trembled. Or at least, she purposely made them do that.

"Not a problem, sweetie. I'll go grab that for you."

She disappeared out the door. Scarlett glanced from her right to the empty chair on her left, which would be occupied by some other resident soon, before she looked back at Priscilla. "No offense, dear, but I cannot stand young people." She pinched her nose to mimic Heather's voice. "So cute. So precious. Ack."

Definitely on purpose, the shaking arms. *I guess the stylist also chose to dye her hair gray. Should've guessed. No wrinkles.*

Scarlett swiveled her chair around and played with the stem of a fake flower in an ocean blue vase. "I sent her to the other end of the building and scheduled a hair appointment during knitting club"—her lips sagged—"to avoid any other residents coming here during this time, because I wanted to address the question I can see firmly planted behind your lips."

Priscilla grazed her mouth with her fingertips. Was she that bad at holding secrets back?

"You certainly didn't expect me to request you. After all, we haven't met."

Priscilla side-saddled a plush chair stationed by a painting of three girls putting on ballerina slippers.

"Although I convinced Pat I needed the company, I *am* company myself."

Priscilla chewed on her tongue to hold back the word "true." Instead, "So why did you request me?"

Scarlett fluffed out a curl that had gone flat in the mirror. She had ungloved her fingers to do the trick before putting the lacy skin back on.

"I want to ask you a favor and give you one in return."

Her breath hitched. Maybe Scarlett would reveal the reason she was given the gift to see the residents differently. She could complete a favor and give a purpose behind her gift.

"Which would you like to hear first, Priscilla?"

She kicked out her feet, knocking over a bottle of nail polish remover that landed on the floor. Lucky for her, the stylist had screwed on the black cap. Priscilla lurched forward to set the bottle back on a porcelain side table.

"I'd love to hear what I can do for you."

Every part of Scarlett beamed as she swiveled back around. "Wonderful answer." She brushed off a loose hair on her skirt. "I'd love for you to help me prevent Paul from trying to get fresh with me."

"Trying to what?"

"The man is head over heels. Won't stop staring. Even eavesdropped on the conversation I had eavesdropped on when Pat got a phone call. Talk about rude."

"But you said you also eavesdrop—"

"Don't interrupt, dear. I didn't take you for being that type." Her gloves made a silky sound as she crumpled her fists on her lap. "Now, do you promise to help me prevent any of his attempts to make me fall in love with him, or do I need to hold back my end of the deal?"

Priscilla gripped both arms of the chair to steady herself. The world, for a moment, had tilted sideways.

"I'm sorry, I'm just having a hard time following all of this and feel like you're rushing me into a contract to sign over my firstborn. I don't even have kids." She un-hunched herself when the room stopped spinning. Too many hair spray fumes. "I don't even know what the other part of the deal is."

"Oh, darling, it comes from me. That guarantees it simply must be wonderful."

"Granted, but much as I'm all for stopping men from trying to stick their ... noses where they aren't wanted, from what I've heard about Paul ... well, he *is* a nice man."

"Yes ..."

Scarlett rested her chin on her fist, like posing for a perfect painting. Two seconds passed before she lifted her head again.

"My dear, although I haven't learned much in my many years of life, I do know one thing. *Nice* boys are very different from *good* boys. You can find more nice boys than lying politicians. As for good men? I have yet to find one."

Priscilla's jaw unhinged and then shut again.

After all, what could she say to change Scarlett's mind? *Your grandpa on your father's side—not the lovable one from Florida— cheated on his wife and married another woman on the side. And Dad?* Images from the fair spun in her mind like the tilt-a-whirl ride. *Lucas abandoned Mom not even a year after he'd gotten her pregnant.* Had he come to small-town Florida at the same time as her, after hiding from her life all these years before? Did she *really* see him at the fair the other day, or had her imagination played tricks?

She had to grip the sides of the chair again with slammed shut eyelids.

"So you want me to help you do what exactly?"

"Find out precisely what he has planned to woo and entice me and help me to thwart those ploys. And oh, he has a plan. I know those quiet types."

Like pranks? She didn't enjoy doing those. Back in middle school, the eighth graders had saran wrapped toilet seats, causing one student to have to call her mother to bring an extra pair of underpants to school. For the rest of the school year, they'd referred to the girl only by the nickname "UnderWraps" because of the undergarment and saran wrap. Hence why she convinced her mom to let her do homeschool for high school.

"Will anyone get hurt?"

"Excluding hearts, no. Do we have a deal?"

Scarlett had outstretched an arm. Leaning forward, her shadow covered a blotch of purple nail polish that had smeared on the white tile. Priscilla chewed on her lip. *Pat did say we had to do what they wanted. And maybe if I agree, I can figure out why I got this gift in the first place.*

She rose and clapped her hand in Scarlett's.

Weird, she felt no wrinkles either. Just smooth, lotioned skin. The gift must have an effect on the other senses. That would explain why Scarlett's voice didn't shake but came out musical and yet firm, like a sad poem. And why Country Acres smelled like flowers instead of age.

The plump lips on Scarlett's face retreated into a thin line as she released her grip. "Those dimples."

Drooping into her chair, those once vibrant eyes clouded over.

In an automatic motion, Priscilla reached for her cheeks. "Yeah, everyone likes to talk about them. I guess they show up whether I'm frowning or smiling. Now"—she stepped backwards and fell into her seat—"what did I just agree to?"

Right then a squeal sounded from the door as the stylist snapped a pretend photo of Scarlett from a "camera" made with her fingers.

"Don't you just look precious? I couldn't find the rose, but will this do?"

She unfurled an object in her grasp, a blue gingham print headband tied in a bow Rosie Riveter–style.

"I suppose that will have to do."

The stylist clapped and handed her the headband as Scarlett pressed her fingers against her dimple-less cheeks.

Chapter Thirteen
CARTER

Paul walked fast for a young old man.

The two of them circled a round garden with an assortment of long, pointy plants and colorful flowers. Paul hadn't spoken a word yet. Carter reached for his pocket before he remembered Pat had collected their devices again at the welcome desk when he arrived. He licked his lip and found the taste salty. It was hotter outside than he'd expected today. Should've gone for the tank instead of the red t-shirt. At least he wore sandals, unlike Paul who decided to keep on long pants. He hoped the sunglasses effect just made it look that way. Maybe the resident had worn more weather-appropriate clothing in reality.

Well, might as well try some conversation.

"So, umm, Paul, I hear you have a crush on one of the residents."

Based on how the other dead-stopped on the path, hunched into the collar of his letterman jacket, and shoved his thumbs into his pockets, he *might've* chosen the wrong way to start off that conversation. A man passed next to them on the winding sidewalk in a green-brown army uniform. He tipped a cap as he ventured on.

"Sorry, what I meant to say was"—he also shoved his hands into his pockets and let the sprinkle of a fountain glaze his heated skin—"she seems like a great woman. No wonder you've fallen head over heels."

One side of Paul's mouth momentarily quirked up to his cheek. He spun around, sat on one of the stone benches that rimmed the fountain, and patted the spot next to him.

Carter took it, then squinted at a blue jay flitting across a blue sky in the sunlight. A stone fountain swan spurted a stream of water nearby.

Finally, in a soft tone that could barely out-burble the sounds of the fountain, "I was hoping you could help me."

"Me, help you?" They hadn't so much as exchanged a hello yet.

Then again, Priscilla had talked about wanting to know our purpose here. Paul could've chosen me for a reason. I can see him through sunglasses to help him finish XYZ task.

Speaking of sunglasses, that bright bulb in the sky had started to incinerate the corners of his eyes. He unplugged the pair from his t-shirt and shoved them up his nose. The world dissolved into a sepia. Two women, accompanied with nurses in tow, giggled as they adjusted the rims of their hats, each black headwear featuring a different colored bow on the center. One of them called the other "Derinda." Down the path, a man in a striped tie and oily hair paused to watch two squirrels chase each other up a tree in spirals. In the distance, a row of red roof buildings glimmered in the sunlight. They led all the way to a tennis court and fenced pool beyond.

"Yes." Paul's chin bobbed up and down, pulling Carter from the distractions around the Country. "Some sources have told me that you are quite the matchmaker."

Sources? What sources?

Visions flashed from the Bingo Hall where Scarlett rubbed two green chips together. She had mentioned something about how all the ladies fell over him. And he did help Elena prepare for that date, yellow flower chewing up half her head and all.

A woman with deep dimples halted at the fountain, two white heels clicking in delight as she outspread her arms like a bird to take in the cool sprits of water. "Isn't this place just divine, boys? Like a piece of heaven."

Those dimples. They reminded him of a certain girl with hair so large and beautiful, especially when the sun glowed right behind her.

The woman by the fountain disappeared with a swish of her skirt. Carter hunched over his knees until he hung inches away from the concrete. "I don't know how reliable those sources are. If I've learned anything, it's that I *can't* talk to women."

Paul's hands came into view in his periphery. He spotted a red indent where a ring once had adorned the skin.

"I mean, *you* know more than me, Paul. Priscilla said you'd been married for sixty years. That beats my longest relationship ... it didn't even last more than one year."

Two bees buzzed over a patch of dry, brown grass, which seemed to be the only interruption of "heaven" in this place that smelled so fragrant and warm. He thought back to Ethel. Yes, even in paradise, she too had to leave heaven's clutches.

A faint chuckle tickled his ear.

Carter lifted his chin as he massaged out the ache forming in his neck from hunching over too long.

"You know, Carter, I've been to many weddings. They always have a dance for the married couples. They keep sending couples off the dance floor based on how long they'd been married." He tallied the numbers on his fingers. "One year married, five years, ten, all gone from the dance floor. My wife and I were always dancing the longest."

He exhaled and rubbed his knees, shielded by gray pants. The man must've been burning up in this weather.

"At the end of the dance, when no other couples remained but us, a man with a microphone would always ask us what the secret to a long marriage was." The corners of his eyes crinkled. Even as a teen, he looked old. The soul peeking through the cracks of young, supple skin. "We never had a good answer."

"Why was that?"

Water from the fountain nicked him on the knuckles when he leaned back. He didn't care. This felt amazing.

"Although my wife and I learned to love each other, even had a beautiful daughter together, our families pressured us together. They were ... different times. I liked a girl who wasn't Korean. She liked me back. Neither one of our families approved, so they presented an alternative."

He pinched the skin of his ring finger.

"You mean, like, an arranged marriage?"

"We learned to love each other over time, but I didn't have to woo her, prove myself worthy of her. She had me and I had her, and that was that."

Paul's Adam's apple bobbed with his pause. The two wavered in the silence of bugs and frogs buzzing somewhere far off and the rumble of cars whirring on a distant road beyond the gates to Country Acres.

"So, you want me to help give you tips on how to flirt with Scarlett?"

"She's not reserved like me, and I don't know how to be"—he paused, swinging his chin back and forth to decide upon the word—"bold."

Carter leaned back so far, the trickles from the fountain spouted on the hairs toward the back of his head. Maybe he was given the gift for such a time as this. But would he lead Paul astray, since he'd failed with both Mia and Priscilla?

"Tell you what. I'll help you if you can help me."

"Help you?"

"The girl who played bingo with you. I'm head over heels for those dimples, but she wants someone a little *less* bold. I don't know how to do that. Maybe we can coach each other?"

Paul pressed against his knees, rising from his spot with a groan. He outstretched a hand. At first, Carter thought he was trying to help him up, but as he gripped, Paul yanked once in a shake.

Paul swallowed, grimaced. "Let's knock 'em dead."

"Grandma, where'd Mom go?"

He kicked off his shoes and dumped the car keys in a wicker basket. A lanyard with the name of a Quilting Outreach Group that Grandma participated in weekly "Stitches of Love" hung off the wooden side table at the front door. He stepped into the family room. The flashes of light from the television reflected in his grandmother's eyes. Twisting on his heel, he saw the weather forecast displayed on the television. Grandma did like to watch the news.

"Grandma?"

She perked up, clicking the mute button on the remote. "Sorry, dear, hearing aid needs new batteries." She gestured at a tan-colored device nestled above her earlobe, then flicked an itch on her long nose.

"Did Mom head out for something?"

"Yes, she and your father are"—she glanced away, preoccupied with fluffing a smooshed green pillow on the family room couch—"there was a lot of shouting. I'm happy you missed it while you visited Country Acres."

Pity tore at his stomach until a trace of nausea crept up his throat. He'd been home plenty of times to hear their screaming matches, nuzzled in a corner between his door and the wall in his bedroom. Air pods and videos couldn't drown out the door slams and muffled sobs right below his room.

Poor Grandma. Having to listen to that while quarantined in this house. Mobility, or lack thereof, had hindered her from snatching those keys from the basket, jumping into the front seat of her daughter's car, and slamming the gas.

She rubbed at a glaze in her eyes before plastering on a grin.

"Why don't you tell me about your visit today?"

She patted the cushion next to her. He parked in the designated spot, but closer to the armrest which had a dent from his brother sitting on it too many times.

"There was a weird mix-up. We thought wrong on which resident wanted us, but I got to spend time with one. Doesn't say much." He rubbed his toes in the carpet. *Like another elderly woman I know.* "We talked about his marriage for a while."

He glanced at the jellyfish glass paperweight his late grandpa had given to them during his beach trip to the Outer Banks a few years back. In the dimming glow of the light outside, a phosphorescent green glimmered on the sides of the glass tentacles. According to Grandpa, in a note he scrawled to the family, North Carolina had great waves but too many families playing bocce ball and boogie boarding. They blocked his view of the ocean waves over the covers of a book he was reading.

Grandpa had never visited. Carter only saw him during Christmas gatherings up North. Paul spoke more words to him today than Grandpa ever had in his life.

Tangerine light spilled through the slits in the blinds onto Grandma's ring finger. Like Paul's, she had a red indent from where a band used to reside.

"Grandma, I never heard many stories about your marriage. You stuck with Grandpa for a long time, so you have to have plenty."

Maybe this'll get her talking. After Paul's shoulders had dropped, they walked away from the fountain, then he spoke more freely. Maybe the "gift" was already working. If he could talk to Paul, why not this woman?

Black and white photo book images flashed across his mind of Grandma in a white ball gown stationed at the front of an altar with two somber bridesmaids flanking her side. No one smiled with their teeth. Mom made him look at those dusty books during the annual Christmas gathering. They would peruse them together in a basement that smelled like a mixture of cold and dust, while his Aunt Cheryl played a hymn on an out-of-tune piano.

His grandmother frowned at the ring. A gloss, like the covering sheets in the photo books, filled her eyes.

She jerked her chin. "Lots of shouting. Not many great memories."

"Are you saying it was an arranged marriage?" Paul had later spoken about some other people in the Korean community who ended up in unhappy marriages but couldn't break free so easily from one another.

"No, but it was a little more difficult to un-arrange anything in those days."

Spirals of dust swirled from the windowsill, like snowflakes falling in a fiery glow. He'd never ventured up North during the winter, but plenty of snowbirds had advised against going. "It's beautiful for five seconds and lasts until April." Or so said their balding neighbor John who disappeared between the months of

May through September. Maybe Grandma had a marriage like snow. Beautiful at first, but then long and miserable.

"Did you ever love someone, Grandma?"

She beamed as she leaned forward to cradle the jellyfish paperweight. "Oh, yes."

"Did you love Grandpa?"

The light dimmed. She knocked the coffee table with her palm to steady herself. She clacked the paperweight back onto the surface before retreating into the cushions.

At last, she spoke. "Dear child, you ask too many questions."

Chapter Fourteen
PRISCILLA

BECAUSE SCARLETT AND PRISCILLA spent the rest of their day together flitting from activity to activity, Priscilla had forgotten all about *the question*.

The one about the other half of the deal.

Scarlett had fumed leaving the salon after the stylist snapped ten pics for "the Gram" as she uttered a sling of words like "cute," "adorable," "just precious," and other insults. The two of them retreated to her room in a building known as "Gravesmill Grange," which boasted a painting of a tractor roaming down a brown hill, sprouts of corn lining each side.

Aside from that, the walls wore a robin's egg blue color and convex light fixtures hung from the ceiling. The narrow halls reminded her of some hotels she'd stayed in when her mom brought her along for writing conferences. But industry cuts along with lower pay at those events made it difficult to drag her daughter in tow. How she missed perusing the conference book-store and hearing pitches from authors across makeshift plastic tables.

She wondered how they could fit more than one wheelchair in the tight space, and if two residents ever collided on their way to their complex.

According to the incensed Scarlett, who was busy fumbling with keys in one hand and tearing out the Rosie Riveter headband with the other, each resident had an apartment of sorts, without a large kitchen, since they had most meals in the Trumbull Dining Hall. Depending on the attention they needed, they might have a care assistant with them for most hours of the day, like with Grandpa Silas and Maria.

Scarlett claimed to be "built like a stomach that ate food from the Depression." When she jabbed the keys into the hole, she mentioned how her mother had eaten peanut stuffed baked onions for some meals. So she didn't need a nurse to accompany her for most tasks.

Inside, Priscilla tried to soak in every aspect of the room, while Scarlett rummaged through her drawers to find the hair clip the "asinine stylist" could not manage to locate.

A walk-in bathroom hummed, light on, next to a queen-size bed, furnished by a red quilt comforter. On the other corner of the room, she spotted a TV and a sink with a microwave situated right above it. Scarlett, or some worker, had decorated the room with seashell lamps, assorted succulents, and a diffuser by the window, spurting out clouds of a lavender scent.

"Aha."

Scarlett had found the turquoise rose, a few frills surrounding it like rays of blue sunshine. She spent a few moments attaching it to her head. She paused when she spied a picture frame on her desk, flicked a glance at Priscilla, and then shoved the photograph inside a drawer of her nightstand. The drawer wouldn't close all the way and jutted out an inch.

That feels familiar. Mom had, after all, a photo hidden in her nightstand too.

With a sweeping motion, she gestured for Priscilla to scuttle out of the room to their next activity: Pinochle. An hour or so later, Scarlett sent Priscilla home.

It wasn't until Priscilla arrived at the small-town coffee shop "Bean Juice" (*horrible name for a place with such a classy atmosphere*) armed with a book that she remembered she'd forgotten to find out how her new friend from Country Acres would "help" her.

She exhaled through her mouth as she approached the counter to order an iced chai. A barista scribbled her name on a clear cup, then she found a padded scarlet chair wedged between a bookshelf and hanging shelves from a wall carrying assorted goods from coffee beans from Ethiopia to decorated mugs with pun-filled sayings like "Bean There, Done That" and "I Love You a Latte."

A grind of coffee beans interrupted an overhead speaker where a guitarist with a raspy voice crooned about disappearing with her lover into a second heaven.

In her element, people-watching but not having to interact with any of them, she gandered at the customers in the shop. A man with a bald spot on his deep tan forehead spoke with a woman in a pantsuit who had straightened her spine so much, if you punched her, she might snap in half. During a pause in a ukulele solo from the speakers, she thought she caught the question, "So why do you think you're a good fit for this position?" from the balding man.

Across from their circular table sat three girls, perhaps middle schoolers or freshmen, giggling over a video. They huddled around a phone on the table, with blended drinks swirled with a dome full of whipped cream.

The barista called her name. Moments later she sipped on cinnamon and nutmeg, only to find when she spun around, someone with Adidas had slid into her seat. Her scrunched eyebrows popped apart when she recognized their owner.

"Marcus?"

Recognition donned his face when he glanced up at her. She doubted he remembered her from the fair. She'd tried to forget about her failed attempt at flirting with someone who, she later learned, already had a girlfriend.

Who just happened to be Carter's ex.

Didn't want to repeat Mom or Mimi's mistakes.

Marcus un-slouched from the chair, rising to engulf her in a hug. "Priscilla, so good to see you."

She reached for his hand on her left side and gave it a firm shake. "Yeah, haha, likewise." Her arms retreated to coil around her chest. "So, what are you doing here?"

Waiting for your girlfriend Mia, no doubt.

A low-hanging light brushed the top of her hair. She ducked, then slid onto a lime green couch, a decent distance away from him. He chose the cushion right next to her. Seeing him in this bright light harshened some of his features. Some acne lined the bottom of his chin where black whiskers sprouted and yellow glinted in his teeth when he smiled. Decisions were best made not in the darkness, she decided.

He stretched out his arm on the back of the couch, so she scooted toward the armrest to avoid his reach. "I like hanging out here, you know. You come here often?"

Not after today. "Nope, first time."

His eyes glinted. "Want a tour?"

Ugh, what was with this guy and giving tours? Starting to think we aren't that much alike at all. "Oh, haha, no thanks. It's a pretty small shop." Four square walls of this place could maybe fill the space of her grandpa's family room. Three of these shops could recreate the Jean Rec Center where she played bingo.

"I meant of the city."

"Oh, I'm not sure how your girlfriend would feel about that."

She scanned the walls until she found a green exit sign next to a bulletin board stuffed full of business cards and posters of local events and missing dogs.

"My ex won't mind."

She spun back around before sucking a nervous sip through the plastic lid on the drink. The storefront sign had boasted they'd done away with straws a year back. She swallowed. "You broke up with Mia?"

"Other way around."

"Really?"

Crocodile smile again. Why did she ever find him attractive that night? "She doesn't like nice guys apparently."

Scarlett had mentioned something about nice guys earlier today.

Nice boys are very different from good boys. You can find more nice boys than lying politicians. As for good men? I have yet to find one.

Marcus liked to talk with his hands to the near detriment of an empty mug on a coaster on the table behind him. "You know, the ones who get you flowers, treat you well. Apparently, her last boyfriend was too old-fashioned. Wanted to save himself for marriage and propose when both of them graduated." He stretched out his legs underneath a glass coffee table. "Guess what two things didn't happen for that poor guy? Surprised they even went a whole year. He probably had tried to make it last as long as possible."

Was her last ex Carter? He hadn't mentioned how long ago they dated. And from the sound of it, Mia went through a man a minute. Old-fashioned didn't really seem to fit the bill for him anyway.

"Anyway, I guess I weirded her out too much by opening doors and paying for dates. Girl has daddy issues, since he disappeared from the picture when she was a kid, I guess. So how about that tour?"

By now he'd scooted so close, he was leaning inches away from her neck. Thousands of worms, or so it felt, wriggled in her abdomen.

"Thanks, Marcus. You seem like a *nice* guy. But I'll pass."

He held his position for three exhales but then retracted his arm and stood.

"Catch you around."

Warm relief untightened her stomach as the worms stopped wriggling.

Marcus shoved his hands into the pockets of a letterman jacket, far too warm for this weather, and bumped shoulders with a tall figure in the door. They stood frozen for a moment; Carter's fiery curls came into view.

Great, not him.

Appearing to notice her sagging side-lip, he ordered some sort of frozen drink that had caramel in the name and selected a bean-bag chair in the farthest corner away from her. Seriously, they chose the weirdest arrangement of furniture. Maybe the name Bean Juice did fit the atmosphere after all, in spite of the classy lighting and music.

Why did he choose the farthest seat away? And why didn't relief fill her gut like it had when Marcus exited the shop?

She rolled her eyes, groaned as she heaved herself from the couch, and scooped her cup and book. "Call me old-fashioned"—she marched over to another beanbag beside him and slumped into it—"but you usually say 'Hi' to people you know when you see them at public venues."

He made a move, perhaps to get up, but the beanbag absorbed him further. She giggled, then stole another sip of the cold drink. By now, some of the ice had melted and watered down the mixture.

"No offense, princess, but most of the time you look unhappy to see me, so I figured you wanted to be left alone."

"Well, I coulda used you a few seconds ago. Mia's ex was very eager to give me a tour of the town." She shivered.

"I never said anything about giving a tour."

"No, I meant Marcus."

His jaw unhinged, but the shriek of the coffee bean grinding machine drowned out his question. She could hazard an easy hypothesis, even if she couldn't read lips.

At last, the machine silenced with a doo-woo. "I guess she's skittish when it comes to guys who are a little more old-fashioned. He told me about her last ex, and—"

Carter bolted from the beanbag to rush to the counter, even though the barista hadn't called for his name yet. His leg bounced back and forth as the man behind the counter, a short bald man with a tattoo sleeve, applied whipped cream to his beverage.

Wait a second, was Carter her last ex? That meant he wanted to wait for marriage and to propose, old-fashioned style. That also meant some part of him did belong in another time period. Like her.

Maybe they weren't complete opposites after all.

But still, he *had* changed. At least, had changed for Mia. She still had to be careful around a guy like that.

The barista handed Carter his drink. He returned, licking a trail of whipped cream that had begun to snake down the dome on the cup. He slumped into his beanbag and busied his gaze on a ladybug crawling on the windowsill beside them.

"How was your time with Scarlett today?"

"Oh, fine." She stirred around the cinnamon in her cup with a flick of the wrist. "She had me agree to do something for her today."

"Really? So did Paul."

He had? Since when did innocent Paul ever want anything out of anyone? And how the heck did loud-Carter-my-voice-can-be-heard-across-any-room ever let the poor man get in two words edgewise?

"What favor did Paul ask you?"

"He wants me to help win over Scarlett. Doesn't have a whole lot of experience in talking to women."

And Carter did?

She scrunched her brows at her cup, rubbing her thumb over the embossed title of her book. Carter had already made a bad first impression with her and a terrible last one with Mia, it appeared. Paul had turned to the wrong man for advice, especially with Scarlett wanting to pull pranks to disrupt wooing attempts. "That so?"

"Yeah, we want to try with my first step on Wednesday. They have an outing planned at a local diner, decor's all retro. He wants to pay for her ice cream and sit by her on a swivel stool, just like old times. I've even taught him a few of my pick-up lines."

It was a struggle to hold back an eye roll on the pick-up comment. "I thought we could only meet with our residents inside Country Acres."

"Paul and I checked with Pat after our walk. You're welcome to join us if you want. Scarlett's already signed up to go."

She nibbled on some loose skin on her bottom lip. There was no doubt what that woman would do when Paul tried to pay for her ice cream at the diner. But just like Priscilla had agreed to go to youth group, she couldn't go back on any promises. And those vows included going with Scarlett and doing whatever Scarlett wanted. Even, shudder, pranks.

Besides, you're already feeling wary about him trying to set up Paul and Scarlett. Scarlett kept getting silent over Pinochle whenever one of the residents talked about their former husbands. From what you've heard from Carter, her marriage didn't end all that well.

Priscilla smiled around the plastic lid on her cup. "You know, that sounds like a wonderful idea."

"So you'll go?"

"Yes, but I'm paying for myself."

He lifted his drink to his lips. "We'll see."

Chapter Fifteen
CARTER

WOW, PAUL'S PLAY-IT-COY TIP ACTUALLY WORKED.

On their walk through a patch of sunflowers at Country Acres, Paul had suggested Carter had come on about as strong as black coffee so he needed to show a calmer side of himself. Although he didn't expect to find Priscilla in Bean Juice, he figured he best leave her be, on Paul's advice.

Somehow, that worked.

Should listen to my elders more often.

Paul the elderly seventeen-year-old held open the door to "Sandman Sweets" for Scarlett, Priscilla, and a number of other women in large skirts, belted tops, and small hats adorning about every head. For some reason, the teenager effect hadn't dissolved when their white bus chugged out of Country Acres. When they'd passed the gates, he half-expected walkers and canes to materialize, held by their wrinkled owners.

So the fun house mirror effect follows them everywhere.

The sunglasses must've wanted them to see the Country Acres residents in the same sepia no matter where they went. Although, as they rode the right lane all the way to the corner shop painted in pastel pink, he wondered why he didn't see his own grandma or anyone else as their younger selves. Maybe part of his theory was correct. That only the *residents* appeared younger, no one else.

Waved in by Paul, who refused to let him hold the door for anyone, Carter stepped inside onto a checkerboard floor.

Too bad Pat confiscated their phones before they left with the tour group, because what he wouldn't give to snap some photos in this place. The red padded bar top stools, the jukebox bubbling an Elvis tune in the corner, records mounted to a wall, and teens in period appropriate clothing to match everything.

"Blue Christmas" oooOOOoooOOhed in the background, as a woman in roller skates glided to a milkshake machine to spin the contents in a silver cup. Paul eyed him before approaching Scarlett during one of her hair twirls. Scarlett, who had been laughing whilst in conversation with Priscilla, tightened her lips and turned to him.

Carter inhaled and exhaled along with Paul, running through the steps he'd given his friend on the bus ride over.

Step one: Compliment something about her.

Paul shuffled a shiny black shoe on a white tile as he palmed his neck. "You look beautiful in that dress, Scarlett."

She played with an invisible necklace strung around her neck. With a spin of her dress, the red skirt fanned out and she angled her foot like a pageant model. Something told Carter that she had done some sort of performing in the past.

Priscilla nudged him in the ribs. She leaned over to whisper, "She told me she was a majorette during high school."

"A what?"

"A baton twirler. Look at how she's fidgeting with her hands, like she's used to holding something there. She knows how to twist."

Step two: Try out a pick-up line.

He'd given Paul a number of them on the bus, all ice cream themed. But the way the man bobbed his head side to side with his hands shoved into the pockets of his gray pants made Carter wonder if there would be follow-through on this step in particular.

Paul picked at the collar of his white oxford as his Adam's apple bounced.

"Scarlett, I can't help but notice that you're a sweet woman."

Carter sucked in a breath through his teeth. His friend decided to go for it after all.

Before he could finish the line, Scarlett spidered her hands on her hips. A blue stripe crossed her cheek from an overhead neon light. "You tryna say you have a sweet tooth?"

Paul's lips twitched and he played with the cuff links on his shirt. He turned to the jukebox in the corner, as if plotting an escape plan, then squared his shoulders. "Would you like to sit with me at the bar? I'd love to pay for your tab." Carter could tell he was uncomfortable asking, especially since Scarlett seemed to show little interest. But maybe Paul trusted in Carter's plan ... enough to skip some steps.

Wow, advanced right to step three: Just ask the girl out already.

Priscilla's eyelids squinched when the two lovebirds grabbed barstools by a napkin dispenser, right under a poster from *I Love Lucy*. He couldn't tell if she wore a grimace or genuine grin, the dimples would never reveal their secrets. Back when they'd first visited Country Acres, she disapproved of the two trying to get together, but maybe she'd warmed up to the idea.

Speaking of temperatures ...

"Priscilla, I see two bar stools over there calling our names." Carter gestured to two seats down from the lovebirds where a girl in a pink poodle skirt taped orders to a small metal window that led into a kitchen. The tinkle of pots and pans disrupted the rhythm of Elvis's croons.

She folded her arms to where her thumbs fiddled with the pockets on her chest. "Fine, but I pick up my own tab, got it?"

Hey, at least they still got ice cream together.

They straddled a seat beside an array of yellow and red ketchup and mustard bottles. Next to him, Scarlett was going on and on about how Paul should order a strawberry malt for himself. Poodle skirt girl slid open a door and rolled toward some of the residents who were laughing loudly in the booths that lined the other wall. Other non-resident customers dotted the various tables of the off-site restaurant.

Carter plucked a menu from a holder on the side, and the two of them glanced at the items together.

"I bet you think you're pretty hot stuff." Priscilla jabbed her finger at a cold item on the menu, a lime phosphate. "Having Paul go along with whatever plans you told him on the bus to win her over. By the way, you can't whisper. You're incapable." Her lips twitched, fighting a smirk.

"Well, it seems to be working out pretty well for him. If he ever gets stuck, I told him to meet me in the men's room and I'll go help him recover."

"Speaking of restrooms, be right back."

Priscilla slipped off the stool. Her golden skirt swished as she marched down the corner, disappearing into a room on the right. Poodle skirt lady swung by and took his order: a chocolate malt. He asked for a lime phosphate for Priscilla since she'd turned away from the menu after she knocked her knuckle on that listing.

She did give me a significant look after that. Maybe she wanted me to pick up her tab but pretended the opposite.

Mia would sometimes do that on dates. Say she wanted to pay and then disappear into the restroom when the bill arrived. Not that he minded. Southern manners always dictated that the man take care of the meal.

Next to him, Scarlett ordered a vanilla malt, and Paul, a strawberry one (on her orders). The woman behind the counter started to work on the drinks after giving a tight tug to her ponytail that was situated underneath a white sailor's cap.

Priscilla emerged from the restroom, shaking off wet hands covered in soap suds. She leaned over the counter to the waitress who had a canister of whipped cream in hand to swirl on the strawberry malt.

"I'm so sorry to bother you, but someone scattered all the paper towels all over the restroom floor. Looks like they sprinkled water all over them too."

Whites of the waitress's eyes showed. "Not a problem, ma'am. We had some kids in here earlier. Family of six. One of them probably decided to have too much fun." She set down the canister of whipped cream to tighten the bow on her apron, then she glided to the bathrooms.

Palms drying, Priscilla slapped them together. "I think I want to test out that jukebox but have absolutely no musical taste. Paul and Carter, wanna help me pick out a song?"

Carter knew nothing about 50s music, but how could he pass up an opportunity to spend more time with her? *Should try the being coy trick more often.*

Paul passed a wary glance to Scarlett, almost as though if he took his eyes off her, she might melt away, but she pushed her fingers against him in a playful shove. "I'm not going anywhere. Now help the poor girl pick a song."

He beamed when she gave his shoulder a squeeze and strutted to the jukebox with Priscilla followed by Carter.

Bubbles chased each other in the amber liquid of the machine as Priscilla ran her finger down a list of songs placed on the front of the juke on a yellow plate. She flicked a glance over her shoulder before snapping her neck back to the machine.

Priscilla thumbed her chin. "I don't know, Paul. 'Jailhouse Rock' and 'Splish, Splash' sound like great hits. And oh, '16 Candles,' how can anyone choose?"

Paul hunched over the names while wind rushed from Priscilla's hair as she glimpsed over her shoulder again. Carter waited until she turned to the jukebox again to check behind himself. Scarlett, behind the counter, placed a ketchup bottle back in its holder as she stirred the straw in the strawberry malt. She tapped the straw against the lid of the cup and returned to her seat.

What is she doing?

Once she stationed herself back at the stool, she cleared her throat, then coughed into her sleeve. Priscilla's eyebrows lifted.

"Got it, I think 'Jailhouse Rock' sounds perfect."

"You sure—"

"'Jailhouse Rock' it is, Carter." She slid two quarters into the machine and pressed the button next to the name. "Now, let's get back to our seats and chow down."

Poodle skirt girl emerged from the bathroom with a whir to back behind the counter. She jostled the whipped cream canister, swirled a mountain of cream onto the cups, then handed the four of them their drinks.

Everyone sipped except for Priscilla who clutched at her abdomen with one hand, stirring the green liquid with the other.

Moments later, Paul sputtered, strawberry malt landing on his pants and the bottom of Scarlett's dress. His blush pinker than the ketchup bottles behind the counter. Wait a minute, ketchup bottles, Priscilla leaving for the bathroom, and Priscilla making him and Paul help her choose a song so they couldn't watch Scarlett from behind.

Everything clicked.

He slammed down his drink, whipped cream spurting onto the counter, and leaned toward Priscilla. "What did you do?"

"You're awful at whispering."

"Did you tell Scarlett to put that ketchup in his drink? What is with you wanting to tear those two apart?"

Paul hurriedly dabbed at Scarlett's dress with napkins from a silver dispenser. She threw a wave and said something about "not to worry."

"For your information"—Priscilla jabbed a finger inches away from his nose—"*she* set me up to it. If you recall correctly, she made you change seats in the Bingo Hall so he would stop staring."

Muttering something about a restroom, Paul rushed to the back, blotting the stain on his pants with the leftover napkins.

"Now I have to undo damage."

She pinched her nose with a groan. "Just tell him to give it a rest. The less he tries, the fewer pranks she'll pull."

Heat rushed to his cheeks. "And you can't just tell her you won't do it?"

"I'm under oath. Nothing can make me go back on a deal, okay?"

Carter clenched his fists, nails digging into the skin, and he glanced at the various clocks hung above the barstools, each displaying a different time around the world.

"Well, I made a deal with him, too. And as you can recall from what Marcus told you, I don't give up on commitments easy either. Back down."

Priscilla unhinged her jaw before crumpling a napkin in her fist.

"Fine, lover boy, I was hesitant about pulling pranks, but after seeing that you need to be knocked down a peg or two, I might be all for helping Scarlett out now. May the best resident win."

Eyes from all around the restaurant burned into his neck, but he didn't care. Surely some of the Country Acres folks saw Scarlett stirring the ketchup in the drink. If they didn't know now, they would eventually.

"Whatever, all's fair in love and war." He marched off toward the restroom, but Priscilla's firm tone managed to sting his ears one more time.

"Correction, neither are ever fair."

"Don't worry, Paul. We'll hit her with all we've got. She won't see you coming and can't help but fall in love with you."

The whoosh of the hand dryer echoed off the tile walls of the bathroom. Paul rubbed his pants with a fury until flakes of paper towels scattered onto the yellow tile floor. Carter thought back to Priscilla telling the waitress about the girl's bathroom. Did she really have the gall to steal all the paper towels, get them wet, and scatter them all over the restroom so Scarlett could mess with the strawberry malt?

With a groan, the machine halted, and Paul tossed the crumpled towels into a bin.

"It's a shame she put the ketchup in the drink." He licked his lips. "Before I went to the jukebox, we were having a wonderful conversation. We told each other about our former marriages."

"Uh huh?" Carter checked his hair in the mirror and fixed a wayward curl.

"Although they held a service at a church, it turned out not to be a proper wedding. Scarlett's wedding, I mean. A fake pastor officiating, no papers signed. He always said he'd take care of the legal stuff and for her 'not to worry.' The man had another wife and family back home. She didn't question anything until he'd disappeared one month, and she found the picture of the family."

"Her late husband sounds like a"—Carter paused, focusing on an old time Coca Cola ad on the wall—"a word I probably shouldn't say in front of an elderly man."

Paul grimaced as he smoothed out his collar in the mirror. It had upturned during the whole strawberry-ketchup debacle. His pocket buzzed, so he pulled out his phone to squint at the screen. At the sight, Carter thought of when Grandma bought a smartphone last year and had to have him walk her through some of the apps and functions whenever he stopped by for holidays.

"That a friend texting you?"

White light reflected off his eyes and the mirror. "My daughter. You know, she was the one who told me you were quite the matchmaker."

Wait a second, he hadn't overheard that from Scarlett? Or Priscilla? Then who told him?

"Your daughter?"

"Yes, I have a picture of the family somewhere." He hovered an index finger around, then tapped the screen when he found the photos app. "There, that's my family."

A hole tore into his stomach when he stared at the image. Next to Paul stood a woman with a yellow flower devouring her dark hair: Elena. In front of the two, Mia had her arms belted across her chest.

Chapter Sixteen
PRISCILLA

"OY, WHY DOES MY STOMACH HURT SO MUCH?" Scarlett clutched at her abdomen. Her head hitting against the window of the bus with a thunk. Priscilla drew up her knees with a cringe as her friend groaned. "I didn't even put ketchup in my own drink."

Adjacent she caught the profile of Carter, lips drawn to a thin line, patting the passenger next to him on the back. Poor Paul.

Fire seared her stomach too, but that happened whenever she did something wrong. Hence why she always went to youth group when her mom told her to and followed Mom's instructions to come home before darkness had fallen over the city. One curfew or youth gathering missed, and she'd have to pop Tums like candy.

Her mother called it her "conscience caller."

"Some people get headaches, others get a tightness in their chests. It's like our bodies set off warning bells to stop what we're doing and do the right thing instead."

She wished Lucas, her father, had a conscience caller. Maybe he fought constant stomachaches, deserved as much.

It didn't help she also chugged the sour, sweet lime phosphate when Carter had disappeared into the bathroom. She paid for her tab before he got a chance. Feeling guilty, she also grabbed the bills for Paul and Scarlett. After he had to chug ketchup, she figured he didn't deserve to have to pay for that concoction.

"You just drink too much of that malt, Scarlett? My grandpa sometimes has a problem with dairy."

Scarlett jerked her chin to gaze out the window in time for an ibis to soar past. "Had two sips, and then everything tasted like sand."

Hmm, maybe she has a similar conscience caller like me.

She nibbled on her bottom lip as she pressed her arm against her abdomen as if cinching herself in for a roller coaster. The pain didn't subside. "Scar, do you think we should hold off on the pranks?"

She'd heard some of the residents call her "Scar." About time she gave her friend a nickname.

Soon as Carter ran off to the bathroom, her abdomen had begun to burn. She didn't know if she could watch someone sip something so nasty through a straw again.

Her friend didn't respond at first as the shadows of palm trees strobed the lights in the bus. Bright yellow poles decorated the sides of the aisles and an escape hatch on the roof bounced whenever the vehicle hit a bump in the road, not that any of the residents inside could use it with their invisible walkers and canes and whatnot.

"We can't let him try to woo me," Scarlett said finally. She clutched at her stomach again with a moan. "I cannot be hurt by a marrying man, you hear?"

Then why agree to the date? Scarlett had mentioned some flings with other guys at Country. Maybe she'd hoped for one of those?

Priscilla winced but managed to overhear a conversation in the seat behind her about an upcoming dance event at Country Acres. One of the ladies had a squeaky voice that contrasted the gravel sound of the other.

Minnie Mouse voice: "Do you think Matilda can get her granddaughter to hang streamers?"

Low reptile voice: "I'm more worried about Linda remembering to ask her daughter for the other decorations. She runs a drama club downtown. Lots of beautiful props and set pieces."

Ahead, Carter leaned his head back against the seat to catch a brief nap before they arrived back at the assisted living center.

"I dunno, Scar, Paul has Carter on his side. And they're awfully stubborn. Maybe you could tell him 'no, thanks' and end it there."

"Ha, men understanding the word no? With my late husband, he saw me as a majorette at a football game. Asked me to a pizza parlor when I reached the sidelines. I was a good Catholic girl and said no. So he showed up at my house the next day to pick me up." She hunched over, resting her forehead against the black padded seat in front of her. "Asked me after three dates if we wanted to go steady. 'No.' After five more dates, 'Oh you want to marry me?' 'No.' Then I ask him, 'Should I be worried about the legal papers for marriage?' 'No, dear, I can handle those. Things work differently in America. You fix me supper, all right?'"

Her voice crackled like ice on the last word.

"I didn't know he wasn't a high schooler. That he was a twenty-five-year-old married man. Looked like a teenager."

She swiped at her eye as she twisted her neck toward the window again.

"He just happened to be at the football game where we performed—the majorettes and I. Said he had to cover it for his school newspaper." Even turned away, her jaw visibly trembled. "Found out later he'd graduated from his high school seven years back. He could've tricked everyone. Everyone said he looked ten years younger than his true age."

She drew in a breath, swabbed her waterline again with a sharp nail, and straightened herself against the seat.

"No's meant nothing to him. They mean nothing to the men at Country Acres." She chewed on her cheek. Carter had mentioned, on one of their car rides, that he thought she dated around with the men there. "So you just learn to say yes. And that's why I can't say yes to a marrying man. All the nice boys have broken me too much to deserve a good one."

And with Carter on Paul's side, they wouldn't reach that anytime soon. Onward with the pranks ...

"A shame." Scarlett sighed with a tap of her nails against a sticker for the exit door on the window. "He does have the most beautiful eyes. Like dark pools, filled with light."

"Stop flapping your arms like a skinny chicken."

Priscilla's arms went slack after she bumped into the nightstand in Scarlett's room. Why on earth Scarlett wanted her to learn the moves to the Jitterbug before a dance that was a few weeks out was beyond her.

"Ay, yi, yi, need to get that thing fixed. The drawer doesn't like to shut." Scarlett leaned in front of Priscilla to shove the drawer back in. Moments later, the wood slid out again.

"Scarlett, why don't we spend our last hour together doing something else? Pat will probably have me helping out that night anyway. So no dancing." She hoped.

Her friend's heels clicked together, ruby red, just like the *Wizard of Oz*.

"I won't have it, now let's try it again."

"But I don't even like dancing."

"O ho, no, no visitor of mine will proceed to a dance-themed event without knowing how to dance. I won't have it. My late dance instructor, Mr. Burgemeyer, wouldn't have it. And the sacred ground which you dance upon known as Country Acres will not have it. Now let's try that step again. Bend your knees this time."

She did so, stepping back inches away from Scarlett's mattress. The woman insisted on dancing near the bed since Priscilla kept tripping when they tried the bouncing steps in the kitchen. At least she'd land on the bed if she fell one way.

"Feet flat on the ground. You don't want to be taller than your dance partner."

Focusing on planting her feet, she tried to "pulse" her feet up and down.

"Shift your weight back and forth. No, no, not like that. You look like you need to use the restroom."

"Well, if you do recall, I didn't actually get to use it back at the diner. I was just throwing wet paper towels all over the place."

"Eh, you have a young bladder. You'll survive. Shift your weight again."

Leaning too far to the right, she bumped into the nightstand again, causing the drawer to slide out further. She slumped onto the mattress with a groan. "Scarlett, I really don't think people will care. They're using walkers and wheelchairs. I doubt anyone can even remember how to swing dance."

Cocking a brow, Scarlett stepped out onto the tile to face Priscilla. Forming triangles with her knees, she swayed back and forth, twirled, and shuffled her feet so fast that Priscilla had a hard time keeping track of the left foot from the right.

Although they'd never hammered down the exact details of the "gift," she had noticed that the residents walked slower than herself and Carter. They took longer to rise from their chairs and chew food. Even with sunglasses on, she could only see so much.

But that didn't stop this woman from dancing. In that moment, no one in the world could tell that she'd long passed her eightieth birthday. She danced like it was 1950-something again and tapped her heels against the tile to a tune of a bouncing piano rhythm that didn't exist except somewhere in the past.

Scarlett whirled around, arms outstretched at her conclusion. "You were saying?"

Priscilla hadn't realized her mouth had fallen open. She closed her jaw.

The other waved a finger like a classroom pointer. "You're only old if you let yourself be." She winced as she clutched at her chest, slumping next to Priscilla on the mattress. "Just wish I could tell that to my heart. It doesn't appear to understand the protocol."

"Well, you danced beautifully. What Paul wouldn't give to see you twirl like that."

Scarlett's eyes smiled as she winced again.

"Do you need me to get you anything, Scar? Water perhaps?"

Priscilla leapt to her feet, knees knocking the drawer. It slid from its holder and almost crushed the red heels of a certain dancer. The younger stooped down to put the drawer back in place, but a golden glint from a picture frame arrested her attention. Memories from her last visit in Scarlett's room whirred through her mind. She didn't want her to see the photo.

She slid the frame out of the drawer to find an older Scarlett in front of an altar in a wedding dress with lace so high up her neck, it could choke her. A tea-length skirt showed off two skinny legs attached to white shoes. Next to her stood a man with dark hair, a white vest, no smile, and ...

Dimples.

Like hers.

"Scarlett, why didn't you want me to see this?"

With tremendous effort, Scarlett opened her eyes. They bobbed back and forth from looking at the photograph to looking, well, anywhere else. She blinked and glanced at her palms.

Priscilla cleared her throat. "My Mimi had mentioned there was another woman who her husband would run off to every week or so to visit. Kept both women at bay by claiming to go on business trips. Were you—did you marry my grandpa?"

Tears sparkled in Scarlett's eyes. Priscilla knew that any no from her now would mean the opposite.

Priscilla's mouth curved upwards as she wrapped her arm around Scarlett to give her shoulder a squeeze. "Why on earth would you keep this photo? I mean, you're beautiful, but you always look that way, wedding dress or not."

She sniffed as she blinked away a glaze in her eyes. "I keep it as a reminder."

"Mind if I take it?" The words slipped off her lips unexpectedly, but her stomach didn't ache. No conscience call this time.

"Why would you do that?"

Priscilla rose from the bed, then slipped the frame into a satchel she'd brought into the room. Whenever Scarlett wanted to be left alone, Priscilla carried along some books to the home to distract herself.

"Because, Scar, some memories are worth letting go." She swung the strap over her shoulder, amazed at how much weight the picture frame added. "So you can hold onto newer ones."

Chapter Seventeen
PRISCILLA

"SLOW DOWN, PRISCA. Your old grandpa can only walk so fast." Grandpa Silas panted behind her while a woman parked underneath a striped umbrella slathered coconut-scented sunscreen onto her nose. "You'd think you'd learn to go slower with all those visits to that assisted living home."

Oh, Grandpa, you have no idea.

White sand burned her toes as she inched toward the darker sand that the water had glazed earlier. Although soggy, the grains cooled her skin.

"You'd be surprised at the residents. One of them can give some of those reality dance shows a run for their money."

By now, he'd reached her side.

They continued on foot, Priscilla placing her feet in someone else's large footprints left behind earlier. She dodged around shells and scouted the area for any conch or sand dollar collectibles. Maria didn't accompany them today. Grandpa decided to give her the day off after she worked overtime when he had climbed the stairs too fast, so she had to walk him through breathing exercises. Thus she arrived home late to celebrate her daughter's birthday.

Two teen boys passed a frisbee back and forth, one of them had turtle-printed board shorts that sagged too much so he kept having to yank them back up. She glanced back at the ocean with the hope this wouldn't be like that time Grandpa, Mom, and she traveled to Mexico. They had accidentally stumbled upon a clothing-optional resort on their way to a nearby village.

Fire burned in her cheeks at the memory.

She thought back to how she disposed of the picture from Scarlett's nightstand in Grandpa's green trash bin after she ripped her other grandpa out of the photo.

It killed her to destroy something vintage, but like she'd told Scarlett, some memories were not worth preserving. She did keep the other half of the photo. Scar looked beautiful in that wedding dress after all. With the way the bouquet of flowers curved over her arm with its twisted leaves and the veil trailed to the edge of the tea-length skirt: timeless.

Too bad it wasn't for a real wedding, a wedding Scar truly deserved.

"Grandpa, do you ever have any regrets?"

"I regret not putting on more sunscreen. Talk about vengeful rays this morning."

"No, I mean, about your past. About love."

"You've been asking a lot of questions ever since you started visiting that place, child. Why don't you tell me what you're thinking about?"

Foam from a wayward wave lapped her bare feet, then receded back into the ocean.

How would she explain this to him? "It's just, there's a woman at this home who has a chance at falling in love again, but she doesn't think she deserves a good man, so she's trying to do anything but get together with him."

Near the dunes wrapped in sand and spurting green grasses, a man and young child, probably father and son, laughed as they held up a string to a magenta box kite that added a dash of bold color to the already brilliant sapphire sky. She had to slow her pace again. Grandpa trailed behind by at least ten feet.

"I mean, Mom felt the same way about Dad. She's tried dating apps, even letting her friends set her up on blind dates, but hasn't settled on anyone yet. Maybe it runs in that side of the family. First my other grandpa, and now Dad, each preventing someone from future happiness."

They passed by a woman sprawled on a blue beach chair with a Kindle in hand. Her large, brimmed sun hat rustled in a cool breeze from the waters. Priscilla wondered how the woman could read in direct sunlight with sunglasses on. But then again, maybe she was blessed with perfect vision.

She nudged her glasses up the bridge of her nose.

"So I feel torn. No one should ever be forced into a relationship. But she did mention he had beautiful eyes. And, maybe I imagined it, but when I was choosing songs at the jukebox in the diner, I saw her hesitate"—*with the ketchup,* she finished in her head. She had to remind herself that she didn't tell Grandpa about the prank incident. If she had, maybe he wouldn't have minded. He did enjoy April Fools'. "I saw her hesitate before turning the man down."

Grandpa panted as he greased the back of his hand with his forehead.

Neither spoke for what felt like several minutes. They passed by two lifeguard stations and a pier with an ice cream shop just off the boardwalk before Grandpa spoke again.

"Sometimes the hardest person to forgive is ourselves, Prisca. People go entire lifetimes believing they only have one chance at redemption, when, in fact"—he stooped, grabbed a handful of sand, and let the grains run through his sifted fingers—"they have that many."

"So how do you convince them to love again?"

Grandpa halted as two pairs of legs darted in front of them when a wave threatened to slosh their feet. Priscilla squinted in the beams of light from the sun to spot one, a woman, in a pink frilly skirt, like a scarf tied over a bathing suit.

Bracing her eyes for moisture and pain, she glimpsed the couple before having to turn away in fear of going blind.

All parties had stopped, and now she understood why.

The man in a straw fedora had deep dimples. Just like the man in the photograph from Scarlett's room, he was grasping the hand of a woman in a bikini with a scarf covering the lower half of the bright yellow bathing suit. She'd seen the man before, but in a light far darker than this. At the fair. A man who looked like her dad, even though she'd never seen a photo of him up close.

Sunglasses off. That stare. Plus the dropped jaw from Grandpa Silas. It seemed the Floridian sun that burned her neck and forehead hadn't decided to start playing tricks on her mind with mirages or hallucinations.

She glanced at the man who hadn't budged yet.

Please say something, sir.

"Oh, sorry, just noticed we had similar facial features. You're not my daughter, after all."

Anything.

Nothing.

The woman beside him tugged at his arm to draw him toward the waves. "Luke, you coming?"

His stare, the pause, Grandpa's gape.

The dimples.

And now the name, the same name she'd heard back at the fair. It was all true. Alarm bells whirred in her ears until the ocean waves could no longer drown out the roar. She knew this, deep inside.

Electricity shot off in her chest, like her heart sped off so fast that she couldn't even count the beats. Even though she could try to run through every logical conclusion in her head that men with similar dimples could share her father's name and not her blood. The longer she stared, the more her mind reeled back to when she'd glimpsed at her reflection in the fun house mirror.

After seventeen years, she had found her dad. She couldn't fight the internal instinct of knowing, of seeing without sunglasses. She'd always played out this scenario a thousand times before in her head, and now it had arrived.

"Prisca."

Grandpa tugged at her arm, mirroring the woman. His voice sounded weak, like glass. She'd only heard it like that once before. On a phone call, with her mom and her, when he brought up Dad.

A curse word stopped short of her lips. She'd never sworn in her life. *It's really him, isn't it?*

But her feet seemed to have forgotten about movement as well. So much for the Jitterbug with Scarlett. Now a man who had abandoned her pregnant teen mother cradled a new woman, her shoulder squeezed against his large bicep.

At last, Priscilla remembered how to move.

She spun around and sprinted toward home. She kicked up sand with her heels, screwing a hand to her eyes when Grandpa behind her called, "Prisca! Slow down!" Hot streams of water surged down her cheeks as she fled past two lifeguard stations with a slight pause to dodge around a crab scuttling toward the ocean. Fire filled her lungs. She spotted the pier with the ice cream stand they'd passed on the way.

Longing filled her abdomen for those shady thatched roof shops where she could hide and cry in peace.

She curved up the dune slope onto the wooden boardwalk which singed her toes. Praying that she could avoid splinters, she rushed toward a t-shirt shack, stooped under the silver counter when the shop owner had turned his back, and muffled sobs into her palms.

She heard nearby footsteps halt, then scurry away, followed by a child asking a parent, "Why's that girl over there sad?"

She sniffed and found her nose had run onto her hands. Rubbing them on her shorts, she noticed her glasses had filled with a fog so she pulled them off her face, using a corner of her bathing suit to wipe them off.

"Priscilla?"

Even though the boardwalk had reduced to a blur, she could recognize that voice a mile away. One incapable of whispering.

"Go away, Carter. Not in the mood."

"Sorry." He had something cradled in his palm.

She placed the glasses back on to spot the red checkerboard pattern of a paper dish holding something fried. All of Carter sagged as he parked at a red table nearby with an umbrella hoisted over it. That looked shady ... in a good way. And the foot traffic on the boardwalk had given her a wide bubble of space. Maybe she should get out of the way to stop preventing business for the t-shirt shack.

Sniffing and knuckling away the moisture from her eyes and nostrils, she rose, then padded over to the table. She flipped up the umbrella before parking herself on the opposite side of the table. This time, tears wouldn't come.

"I won't ask if you don't want me to."

He swabbed away grease spilling down his chin with a napkin. Were those alligator bites? Maria had once brought some home from one of Grandpa's favorite restaurants for dinner.

She sighed as she thumbed the pockets of her plaid vintage bathing suit. Mimi had actually sewed this one, worried that a real bathing suit from the 1950s could carry all sorts of blast-from-the-past diseases.

Once again, she'd forgotten to bring her phone.

Not that she could text anyone. Half her friends back home, from the knitting club, weren't exactly tech-savvy, and what on earth would she tell her mom?

No, perhaps the only two people in the world she could mention anything to were Scarlett and Carter.

Had she truly become friends with teens? Albeit one actually far older than seventeen.

"I think I just ran into my dad on the beach." She explained the encounter.

Carter plunked his alligator bite back into the paper boat. His fingers frozen, outstretched as though ready to cast a magic spell. He dropped them with a whistle. "No wonder you want to be left alone. My parents aren't perfect, but I can't imagine how I'd react if I saw my parent for the first time, after he abandoned me."

Fresh tears surged so she turned away to distract herself with two seagulls pecking at some hush puppies that had fallen from an abandoned table next to theirs.

Inhale, hold it, exhale. "I'd always thought I'd react a lot calmer than what I just did, running away and all. Keep an even tone. Say something like, 'Nice to finally meet you.' But I can't stop thinking about his arm wrapped around that woman. How that could've been Mom. How Mom won't let that be her now with any man because of him."

She broke off, biting down on her trembling bottom lip.

Carter outstretched an arm but then pulled it back, like she'd burned him. He settled on grabbing another alligator fritter. "So your mom won't trust anyone else?"

Priscilla frowned, then cringed at how her abdomen seared. "Mind if I try—?"

"Be my guest. I probably shouldn't eat this whole boat anyway."

Plucking a greasy fritter in the shape of popcorn chicken, she dipped it into an orange sauce on the side before she popped it into her mouth. A tangy taste filled her mouth as she chewed. Not too bad.

"I think"—she swallowed, two loud teens carrying surfboards passed by their table, smelling of seawater and watered down sunscreen—"my mom is keeping a photograph of him by her bedside."

"I thought you said she didn't keep any photos of him."

"Metaphorically." Well, also literally. But no time to get into that.

She explained how Scarlett had an image of herself marrying Priscilla's grandfather, even though she discovered she hadn't really married him. Even though he'd tricked her, she convinced herself that she didn't deserve any good man because she'd stumbled into a relationship with a very bad one.

Carter craned his neck to watch an elderly couple giggle at each other as they tried on shirts that said, "I'm with a beach bum," with arrows on the shirts pointing at the other person. A woman in a navy bathing suit, perhaps their daughter, told them to pose for a picture.

Priscilla watched his fingers twitch toward his phone on the table. Instead, he shoved it into his pocket.

"I think everyone has a picture by their bedside, Priscilla."

Leaning back, she smirked while she folded her arms. "Yeah, lover boy? You seem to be fine from jumping from one relationship to the next no problem."

If he had been in a relationship with Mia recently, and let her go beyond a boundary he set, shouldn't he be hesitant to jump into something else?

He sighed, pulled out his phone, and clicked on the TikTok app. Shielding his phone with his hand like a sun visor, he tapped the screen before shoving the device back into his pocket.

"Again, I had a picture by my bedside, too. But I just destroyed it, like how you tore up that photo from Scarlett's wedding."

The photograph had given a good, clean rip when she did that. Imagine what relief her mom would feel if she tore apart her own photo of Dad and let herself trust a man long enough to go on a second date.

Imagine what relief you would feel, Priscilla, if you did the same.

Chapter Eighteen
CARTER

HE'D UNFOLLOWED MIA ON TIKTOK. What a good photo to get rid of from his bedside.

No, beyond that. He deleted her from all social media channels, even removed her contact from his phone. His hands shook when he placed the device into Pat's plastic bin she liked to call "the phone spa."

"Those devices work so hard for you. They deserve a little break too."

Name tagged, even though Paul and Scarlett hadn't given any indication they needed a reminder of their monikers, the two friends parted ways at the front desk. He headed to the left toward Paul's lodging to complete phase two of their plan to woo Scarlett.

Today Paul planned to serenade her with one of her favorite songs: 'Singing in the Rain.'

Carter nodded to a resident in blue shorts, waistline hiked up to his belly button as he reached the second door on the left in the men's corridor. Knocking once, he heard the faint "come in" before twisting the knob. He halted when something bright yellow, like Paul's daughter's favorite flower to wear on dates, arrested his attention.

"Umm, Paul, why are you wearing a raincoat?"

Paul slicked a U-shaped hat onto his head, stumbling a bit in his bright yellow slickers. The man looked like something out of a cartoon or old raincoat convention. Fumbling with the pockets, he pulled out a receipt that he shoved into a desk drawer stationed by his bed.

"Playing the part." Paul chuckled and la-dee-la-dee-la'd as he smoothed a wrinkle in the plain brown comforter.

"You do realize that my weather app says we won't get rain for at least another couple of days." A rarity in Florida in early summer. The weather seemed bent against raining this year for some reason. It drizzled on a few days when he and Priscilla weren't at Country Acres—almost like the weather stayed sunny during their time with the residents.

Paul held up three fingers, like Carter used to when he did Boy Scouts for a hot second back before other commitments at school overtook his life. "Always prepared." He flicked his wrist to check his watch, which had slipped down a yellow sleeve. "Speaking of, we want to get to the ladies before they leave for Scarlett's painting class." Once every two weeks, Scarlett and several other women would create reflections of a painting the instructor gave them at the head of the class: fruit bowls, birds, and mountainous terrains. Those who created the most beautiful portraits had their work hung up in the hallways.

He recalled someone mentioning that Scarlett and Ethel had quite the rivalry until Ethel, well, yeah.

Paul triangled his elbow with a nod at Carter to take it. Arm in arm, they strolled out of the room and down the hallway.

"We'll have to reach her from the outside. Men are prohibited from going down the women's corridor, unless accompanied by a nurse, family member, or the woman themselves."

Good luck getting Scarlett to agree to that.

They ventured into a lobby area for the men's corridor that featured dimly lit plaid couches and various spiky plants in pots adorning the corners and side tables in the room. Paul exchanged hellos with two gentlemen enraptured in a baseball game. They tossed an aloof wave at Paul before hollering at a pitcher to stop trying fancy throws and actually get the ball close to the plate.

Apples and oranges, wrapped in plastic, adorned glass bowls on their way to the outside. Carter clutched at his rumbling abdomen, wondering if anyone would mind if he snagged one of those. Not the oranges, though. He hated how the sour white pulp felt and tasted in his teeth if he forgot to unpeel it.

Eyes burned into Paul's raincoat from all around the lobby as they approached the door that slid open thanks to the motion sensors. *Wonder what some of the clothes they wear look like to other people.* After all, their own youth group director saw them as elderly people instead of teens. The "sunglasses effect" had to have worked on clothing as well.

But something told him that no eye could miss the raincoat, sunglasses or not.

"Paul, where did you even get that getup?"

Beams of sunshine illuminated his sheepish grin as they stepped onto a winding sidewalk on an angle toward the women's dormitories. Paul slid half of his fingers into the pockets. The shoe squeaks from his slickers mixed with the song of some bird nearby.

"A few times a week, Country Acres sends a bus to the Wal-Mart up the road. I decided to get this after you told me about the plan for singing outside her window."

Lavender punctured his nostrils when they passed bushes full of purple and red-yellow plants. Two women in plaid shirts and pants clamored about what they would wear to an upcoming dance. Paul and his friend had set a goal that by the dance, Scarlett would accompany him—or at least, let him have one dance with her.

A car rumbled past on the blacktop. Illuminated through the slight tint of the windows were the phone screens of two teens in the back. Most of the time, he could tell the visitors here apart from the residents by clothing alone.

Wonder how often Mia checks in on her Grandpa.

She hadn't mentioned him much on dates, but who knew when she would decide to get sentimental and show up here? But family was, well, family. She *must* have wanted to swing by every once in a while.

When they angled left toward a collection of windows that faced the gate that led to the pool they had for the residents, Paul halted a moment before he stepped onto the grass. He dug into his pocket to pull out smooth stones, similar to the ones Carter had put in a tank for his goldfish back in middle school: all purple and shiny.

Must've bought those at Wal-Mart too.

Paul gestured to a window with its dark red blinds drawn. "I'm going to need your help with this part. I need you to throw the stones against the apron."

"The apron?" No strings attached to a cooking garment anywhere in sight.

"That bottom ledge of the window. I'm afraid if we get too close to the glass, we could break something. Would you mind throwing these?"

Smooth rocks slid into his palms. He rubbed his thumb over the polished surface. *Forgot that Paul has a shaky arm now. With that letterman jacket he always wears, you'd think he could do it no matter what the age.*

Scarlett danced, what could stop him from throwing a curveball?

Better safe than sorry, though. Who knew how much vengeance Scarlett would wreak if they broke her window?

He wound back his arm, but Paul snagged his wrist. "One more thing, you might want to duck out of the way when she opens the window. Nothing can ruin a mood more than a wingman standing in the middle of the action."

With a firm jerk of the chin, Carter paced two steps to the side, then aimed the first stone at the apron. It thunked and hit a flower a bee had fallen asleep inside. Now abuzz, the insect flew in a circle before disappearing over the sloped roof on the building.

The second stone knocked louder this time, finally the blinds split open. He crumpled to his knees, away from Scarlett's line of sight, as she had Priscilla slide open the window with a squeak.

Paul spread out his arms, like a peace offering, as he started the lyrics to the song. Lips curving, Scarlett leaned out the window with her palms on the apron, soaking in the sunshine and the serenade. Then, she turned to Priscilla inside to whisper something he couldn't quite catch. They, too, ducked down, then both emerged at the window with something pink and bright green in their hands: water balloons.

Oh no.

"I'm singing in the—oof."

Priscilla launched the first balloon which landed on the dry path of grass in front of his feet and exploded water upon impact. Scarlett's balloons missed him by feet but still managed to spurt some "rainwater" onto the coat. Cheeks igniting, Carter lurched forward to shield his friend, but Paul made a jerking motion with his hands for him to stay put and continued to sing. Water balloons exploded like fireworks all around him. A perfect Fourth of July.

Minutes later, the two ladies had run out of ammo. Scarlett leaned out of the window, her arms dripping onto the pink flowers below.

"My, what a performance. Don't know if Gene Kelly coulda handled that line of fire."

"Not all of us look like movie stars, Scar, so I guess we have to muster on in other ways." The shadow of his hood failed to cover the smile hidden underneath.

"Indeed." She tapped her nails on the apron, one at a time, to the rhythm of the song as her lips twitched, like she was fighting to mirror him. "Well, thank you for the music, but I must be off to do a painting."

"They doing watercolor today?" He flicked off the drizzle on the suit as it dripped in a puddle around him. By now, the dirt had reduced to mud underneath his shoes.

She gestured at all the broken balloon pieces on the lawn. "How could they? We cleaned them out of water."

With a curve of the chin and lip, she slipped back inside, shut the window, and slammed the curtains shut. Carter uncrumpled himself from his spot, massaging a sore that had formed in his knees from holding the position too long.

Maybe I'm out of touch with older people, but did that sound like flirting?

Scarlett had scrunched her shoulders and chewed on her lip when she talked with Paul. Did phase two work a lot better than he'd thought?

Drips formed abstract patterns on the sidewalk as they trudged back to the men's half of the building complex. There were a few minutes of silence, filled with Paul's panting. They received some dirty looks from the workers as water dripped on the carpet near the couch where the men shouted at a player who swung at a terrible pitch.

Down the hall, Paul reached into his pocket for his jangling keys. He swung open the door, then disappeared into the restroom.

Carter spotted folded clothes on the toilet seat before Paul shut the door.

It's almost like he was prepared for Scarlett's attack.

He had wondered how Scarlett managed to figure out a plan ahead of Paul asking her to sit with him at the ice cream place, and how she orchestrated Priscilla distracting them in time for her to mix ketchup into his drink.

This time, he must have anticipated her, so he bought a raincoat just in case.

"Carter?" His voice cracked through the rumble of the bathroom fan. "Do you mind grabbing my comb? I left it in my drawer in my nightstand."

"No problem."

He almost bumped into a tall lamp on his way over but he easily found the wooden nightstand. Slumping onto the bed, the mattress gave a groan beneath him as he slid open the drawer. A wooden comb sat with its teeth pointed toward the top of the "Wal-Mart" on a receipt.

Wait a second, the receipt. Images flashed through his mind of earlier in the room when he first found Paul in the raincoat. Didn't he stash the proof of purchase in here?

Sure enough next to a $36.54 had the description of a raincoat.

Scanning the list of items, "toothpaste," "detergent," "heating pads for lower back pain." His eyes stopped when they reached the last item on the list. He firmed his jaw, then looked over to stare at the bathroom, letting the whir of the fan drown out his thoughts for a minute.

This doesn't make any sense.

Returning to the receipt, to make sure he didn't need glasses like Priscilla, the last item had smudged from the sweat of his fingerprint pinching it: a 50-count pack of water balloons.

Chapter Nineteen
PRISCILLA

"THAT LOOKS LIKE SOMETHING out of a Dr. Seuss book." Scarlett wrinkled her nose at Priscilla's painting, but she tried to imagine it was because of the reeking paint fumes in the small room covered in paint splotches. "Like the trees from the 'Lorax.' You made all the lines too jagged."

She eyed her friend's painting in all its blue and white glory. *Of course,* Scarlett would be good at both painting and dancing.

Her only flaw seemed to be the times she would get winded or clutch at her chest when they ambled too quickly across the compound. Pity that Scarlett liked to walk fast despite her condition anyway. Reminded her of a certain Grandpa back home.

And if Grandpa keeps pulling what he did on the beach the other day, we might have to check him into a place like this. When she'd run off after she stumbled into her dad, he'd chased after her but lost his breath between the lifeguard stations. He had to dig his phone out of his pocket and shakily text Maria to come pick him up to take him home. Although he'd misspelled every word, unable to see the phone straight, she translated the message and arrived.

When Priscilla found out upon her return, she slammed herself into her room then cried until she couldn't lift her eyelids anymore from the weight of the tears and sorrow. Her stomach burned the whole night. Guilt gnawing its way into her intestines.

Chewing on her tongue, she eyed the sample painting at the front of the "classroom" of sorts. The instructor, a man with a beard and thick, square fingers, showed them step by step how to do the art project for the day: fireworks over a lakeside.

"Well, so-rry, but I don't get to see fireworks all that often, Scar. Mom doesn't let me out at night and draws the curtains close. Thinks it'll keep away anyone who wants to break in. I've only been able to sneak some peeks at shows during New Year's when she's headed to bed." After the ball dropped.

Scarlett brushed a white line to add a pop of light to the offshoot of a blue firework. "I'll kidnap you so you can watch all the fireworks you want and dance with all the boys."

Priscilla giggled, splattering some red paint on the bottom of her wooden easel. "I don't know how my mom would feel about that. She sort of depends on me. I used to go to all her conferences, you know."

"Ay, you're splashing all over me. Stop waving that brush around, or I'll end up more drenched than Paul."

Priscilla plunked her paintbrush into a cup of water stationed at their table, then watched the clear liquid get blurred by blots of rosy. "Sorry." She swirled the end of the brush around to watch the water turn into a Pepto-pink. "Scarlett, don't you think it's weird that he came to your window in a raincoat? There wasn't a cloud in the sky today."

"Eh, he likes to eavesdrop. Maybe he overheard me talking to you about the water balloons when you arrived at my room."

An interesting sight to behold for sure. Scarlett had leaned over her sink in an attempt to stretch the lip of a balloon over the faucet. Water had splattered all over the bathroom and Scarlett's arms before she finally relented to letting her friend fill and tie the balloons.

"I mean, maybe, but Carter and I arrived at the same time. How would they have had time to hear us filling up water balloons, go back to Paul's room to grab a raincoat, and come over here? We barely had enough time to fill up twenty before we heard them knocking at your window."

Scarlett sealed her lips as she continued to dab the edges of the fireworks streams with white. *Why does it feel like she's hiding something?*

Behind her, two women in capri-length pants and plaid talked animatedly with their hands about the upcoming dance held at Country Acres. "Margaret tried to vote for a luau theme again, but we all know what a disaster that turned out to be last year. Remember that, Derinda?"

"Better than the one the year before, 'Earth Angels.' Supposed to be a taste of heaven, but because catering forgot to refrigerate half the food, it ended up being more like the other place." The woman in the pink plaid fanned herself with a glove before returning to her painting.

Hmm, heaven. This place seemed like a slice of it.

She'd read plenty of books her mom had grabbed from various conferences and book fairs on the nature of heaven. In those stories, those who saw glimpses of it early saw twenty-year-old versions of their grandparents or ancestors in the cloud nine skies. Those once old became new again in a never-ending cycle of eternity.

Images from the Bingo Hall flashed through her mind. What had the cursive verse etched on the back wall said?

"People who say such things show that they are looking for a country of their own."

What a strange sentiment when one expected a "live, laugh, love" or some other quote about life taking breaths away instead of measuring breath intake.

But with the way the sunshine always beamed on this place—not to mention the residents had transported back to younger versions of themselves, voices, clothes, and all, as the eye perceived, maybe she had landed in some little sliver of paradise.

Maybe that's what "a country of their own" means. We all want a piece of heaven here with us.

Still, the mysterious gift given to her and Carter made no sense. Why would they need to see the heavenly versions of Paul and Scarlett? For what purpose?

Brain throbbing from all the possibilities, she plucked her paintbrush out of the water, swirled the hairs on a paper towel stationed at her desk, and when the color had disappeared from the poofed out brush, she blotted the ends with a splash of raincoat yellow paint.

Scarlett dipped her brush in the milky liquid, so the blue dye swirled with the pink until the two had together formed a purple.

"Is it a bad time for a casserole?"

How did she find us?

The same woman from the beach, with a boyish haircut, stood at the front stoop with a glass dish cradled in her arms. Accompanied by no man, especially not Priscilla's dad this time, it appeared she'd foregone any flower hair accessories except for a single feather pin, like something plucked it off a peacock from one hundred years back.

Priscilla steadied herself against the doorframe with her hand as the world tilted. She found her balance again. Where was there a Maria or Grandpa to answer the door when you needed one?

"Oh, umm, thank you. I can take that if you want and put it in the fridge."

Anything to get this woman away from this stoop. Much as I don't want to be rude ... I saw her with my dad.

"I wanted to stop by and drop this off for your grandpa. We felt just awful when we saw him collapse on the beach and figured he might like my famous Ritz chicken." She unpeeled part of the tin foil with her free hand. Ritz cracker crumbs decorated a soupy mixture of chicken, sour cream—Priscilla guessed—and something else that smelled warm and savory. "It's not exactly a casserole, but I like to pretend it is for church potlucks."

Priscilla forced a laugh as she knuckled the door tighter. "I'm afraid he's not home, but I can take that off your hands and tell him you stopped by."

The other's penciled eyebrows narrowed then slanted up again when she glanced past Priscilla's shoulder to something behind her.

"My, what a beautiful staircase. I'd love to see the inside of this place. Looks like your grandpa has excellent taste. Mind if I come in?" It didn't come out like a question, more in an expectant tone.

Oh right, Southern hospitality. Probably a rule somewhere that you have to let near-strangers into your house and show them around.

In New York, they had intercoms guests had to buzz to get inside apartments, plus security guards stationed in most buildings to check IDs. What a different world she'd stumbled into, Florida.

She stepped backward, almost tripping on the carpet, and the woman brushed into the house, kicking off her sandals at the door.

"How rude of me not to introduce myself." There came that instructional tone again. Like a teacher walking a student through how to read for the first time. "My name is Elena."

"Priscilla."

Blood boiled underneath her skin, even though Grandpa decided to blast the AC inside today before he left. Her neighbors back home had called her 'so polite, you could be Canadian. You belong in a different decade, dear.' But the rule must not have applied in this state. "Let me show you to the kitchen."

She slid her hands under the dish and lifted it from Elena's arms before the woman could protest. No objections sounded behind her as she rushed to stuff the dish in the fridge. *Maybe she cooked up something so she had an excuse to walk in here.*

"So you followed my Grandpa home? Made sure he made it home okay?" *That how you found us, lady?*

"Well, no." Feet shuffled behind her, a slower pace than before. "I have a friend in the neighborhood who lives close by. You may know her son. He goes to the same church as you."

Besides Carter, she hadn't fraternized with the neighbors or really talked to anyone at youth group. Most of the time she couldn't make the gatherings because they returned from Country Acres too late.

Boy, Florida had changed her. Scarlett had too.

Now she couldn't uphold the promise to her mom. But her abdomen no longer burned when she thought about missing youth group. Maybe her new friend was changing her. "New dogs could learn old tricks," as Scarlett had said during one of her painting sessions.

She swung open the fridge with a whoosh so the cooled scent of something fried hit her nose. Grandpa really needed to watch what he ate. They couldn't have any more scares with him. Nudging a jar of mayonnaise to the side, she shoved the dish onto a clear shelf before she slammed the door shut.

When she spun around, she noticed that everything on Elena had crossed. Her hand grappled her other arm, one leg over the other, until she looked like one big insecure pretzel. Elena didn't meet Priscilla's eyes, then pointed to a hummingbird feeder outside.

"Love looking at this thing. Last time, there were three ruby-throated ones at one time on this."

Pricilla's eyelids narrowed to slits when she glanced at the red feeder with little plastic hibiscuses woven all around it. *Last time.* "So, you *have* been here before."

She dug her nails into her palms as she chewed on her tongue. *Don't be rude in front of your elders. Don't be rude.*

"Oh, dear, did I say I hadn't?"

"I guess that negates the tour. Really sorry, but my mom usually wants me to call around this time, so I should ..." She jabbed a thumb over her shoulder, doubling back to follow the direction she'd pointed.

"Wait, Priscilla."

Shut the eyelids, clench the fists, breathe. She counted three breaths before opening them again. She forced her attention on a metal seahorse sculpture mounted on the wall.

"Do you mind if we sit ... talk?"

The floorboards beneath her groaned when she twisted around to find Elena hovering over a couch in the family room. With a sad lip twitch, the woman patted the cushion next to her. This time, Priscilla couldn't hold back the eye roll.

"No offense." She chewed on her tongue a moment before she unclenched her teeth. Best let the words release this time. "But I don't know if that's the best idea right now."

Half-crouched, Elena parked all the way on the cushion and stooped her neck to glance at her folded hands. "I don't see why we can't just talk." Elena didn't sound all that convinced either.

"Ma'am, I'm not one for being frank, except for when someone threatens or violates boundaries, so please consider this to be a rare circumstance." *Breathe, Priscilla, breathe.* Why were these words coming out of her lips instead of staying in her head? They never exited the mouth. All those times she'd held back retorts when ladies at the knitting club would take on a condescending tone with her. And now? "But I don't appreciate the fact that my dad sent you as a messenger here. Doesn't matter how good that chicken dish is. One meal won't fix seventeen years of silence."

"He didn't send me—"

"I wasn't finished." Sheesh, she hadn't interrupted an adult since, well, ever. "Imagine having never heard from your dad your whole life, your mom having to carry the responsibilities of two parents, only for me to find him on a beach with his arm draped around some other woman. And now that woman wants to make everything A-okay by showing up with a casserole."

She paused to ram a fist against her abdomen. Everything inside of her intestines felt like it had surged up the other way. But nothing came out, nothing physical, anyway.

A word vomit.

That's what Mom called it. When an author wanted to put too many words, held deep inside, into one small paragraph.

Priscilla clung to the entrance that led into the family room for support. Everything spun around like the fan whirring on the ceiling. Cool air wafted down her neck, but everything burned. She glimpsed at the turquoise pool in the backyard. What she wouldn't give to leave this conversation by dunking herself inside until the chlorine fogged her brain as she ran her fingertips over the dark blue tile dolphins engraved on the sides of the pool walls.

"He broke our family apart, in more ways than one. And here you come, trying to fix it with a home-cooked meal."

The last words snagged in her throat, she swallowed, but everything had turned dry.

Elena had sunk so deep into herself that her neck appeared to descend part way into her back, like a turtle shell. The woman rubbed her palms against her flowy pink skirt before they swiped at the corner of eyes that had just begun to sprout crow's feet.

"Priscilla, he doesn't expect everything to get fixed overnight. But after he saw you on that beach, after he saw *her* through you." She hiccuped, then slapped her chest. "He wants to make it up to you. To somehow fix something he broke long ago."

Images of the photograph from Scarlett's wedding flashed through her mind. And then of the pier where she shared alligator bites with Carter. *"Again, I had a picture by my bedside, too. But I just destroyed it, like how you tore up that photo from Scarlett's wedding."*

The more reminders she had of her father, the more she would hinder herself from ever finding friends, ever finding love.

"It's too late, Elena." She pulled herself up on the wall until her back straightened like a yardstick before turning away. "And take that stupid casserole out of this house." With that, she fled down the hall, twisted up the stairs, and slammed herself into her bedroom.

Chapter Twenty
PRISCILLA

"Do you have any dresses that won't make it look like I'm trying to flash everyone at Country Acres?"

Priscilla pinched the hanger of a purple frock that came up high against her thigh when she placed the garment on her bodice.

Acrid perfume and the thrift-store smell she'd known so often from the Goodwill back home punctured her nostrils. Although Grandpa didn't have any vintage shops nearby, he recommended a boutique in the town square that sold secondhand wedding and prom dresses.

The consultant, a woman with a permanent smirk who sported glasses attached to chains that draped behind her ears, flicked through dresses on a rack under dress sizes eight to ten. Most of the gowns would lift high above Priscilla's knees, so she shuffled through the ones that reached closer to the ground.

"What about this one, Prisca?" Grandpa giggled as he held up an outfit covered in faux orange feathers.

"Grandpa"—she reached out in an attempt to hide the dress between two black ball gowns—"don't make me regret taking you here with me."

After the beach incident, she wanted to keep Grandpa close. To spend time with him but also make sure Elena didn't bring any more casseroles. She didn't take her dish home after she left.

And Priscilla didn't want to ask Carter to join her. What a weird outing, her trying on dresses for the upcoming dance at Country Acres. At last, the women in Scarlett's painting class had settled on a theme, Back to the Future. They planned on featuring all songs from the 50s. A local band called Eleanor Rigby offered to impersonate the Beatles, outfits and all, on stage. Never mind that the Beatles didn't make it big until the 60s. None of the residents appeared to mind when they discussed the dance.

Scarlett would hear no nonsense about Priscilla coming in one of her vintage dresses. She wanted her dolled up.

"No visitor of mine is coming in looking like I plucked them out of a library from the 1950s. I've seen your outfits. Let me tell you, they would not have passed for any school dance back in my day. Get a wedding dress if you have to, but come in a gorgeous gown."

"You looking for a dress for prom?" The consultant's chains made a ringing noise when they swung as she plucked out some hangers and threw them on a Z-rack near the dressing rooms, if you could call them those. Really, it was four curtains in a room with one singular full-length mirror.

Not exactly *Say Yes to the Dress* extravagance.

She loved it.

"No, ma'am. I was homeschooled. And I'd heard ... stories about homeschool prom." Horror tales, more like.

"Hmm." The woman had a pen stuck between her teeth as a customer behind her tapped her shoulder with their receipt. "Just thought I'd ask. Some people like to get their prom or homecoming dresses early, shop the sales. Of course, everything in here is always on sale."

After throwing a gown with silver sequins onto the Z-rack, the worker whirled around to sign the receipt. The customer, a man, grinned before throwing his two tuxedos, wrapped in a sheer plastic, on a rack. This place must've operated like a consignment store. People could donate gowns and buy them.

Puffing a sigh of relief, the woman slid open the cash register up front, plunked in the receipt, and continued to sort through the long dresses for Priscilla. "You wouldn't believe the number of customers we've had these past few days. With all the summer weddings, we have so many last-minute brides and bridesmaids looking for cheap, secondhand dresses."

At last, the store had emptied itself of customers, with the exception of herself and Grandpa Silas who was busy giggling at a dress with so many ruffles. Collar up that thing, and it could fit right into the sixteenth century.

Grandpa Silas tapped her on the shoulder, then gestured at the door. "I have a friend who works in a toy shop down the street. Mind if I pop out for a moment?"

Oh, Grandpa, we know you just want to play with the toys.

She eyed the number of dresses on the rack. "By the time I try all of these, Maria will have made dinner. It might even be cold when we get back."

"I know you. You'll spot the right one right away. We might even have time to stop by the library down the street." He chuckled, squeezed her shoulder, and shuffled out the door.

Mmm, but if that Mia girl has a shift at the front desk today, I might have to pass on the library.

Priscilla spied a name tag on the consultant lady's cardigan lapel when the woman placed a lavender-colored dress on the rack—Jennie.

"Jennie, you really don't have to keep pulling dresses for me." By now, she'd almost filled the five-foot rack with ball gowns and longer dresses. "Really, you've picked a lot of good options."

She winced at the strapless tops and spaghetti string straps. After she tried these on, she could scour the shop for some sort of scarf or jacket to throw over her shoulders.

A bell dinged at the front as a woman holding a wedding dress high above her head stumbled in. In tow, two folks trudged behind, an older woman with faint rosy hair and watery eyes and ...

"Carter?"

He halted at the entrance, then shoved his hands into his pockets. Meanwhile the woman with deep scarlet hair, his mom she assumed, tapped the consultant on the back with her wedding dress and asked how much the store would pay to take it off her hands.

By now, Carter had half buried himself behind a row of plus-sized dresses, face matching his hair.

"What are you doing here?" Priscilla wiped her hands on her skirt, to get the grime from the hangers off before she dodged around a poofy skirt toward him.

"Mom doesn't trust me at home alone. Not after a certain incident that happened in my school parking lot. She says I have to 'earn back her trust,' which I guess means going into dress stores, apparently."

"Wow, this is gorgeous!" Jennie lifted the dress out of its plastic casing to run her fingers up and down the lace of the out-of-this-world huge princess sleeves. "Are you sure you want to sell it to us?"

"Gladly."

Carter sunk farther into the rack until bright orange tulle threatened to swallow him whole. She'd heard snippets about his family on their car rides over to Country Acres, but with the way his grandma across the store wiped at her eyelids while feigning interest in some hair accessories with fake pearls, pity tore at her stomach.

She grimaced as she gave his shoulder a squeeze before returning to the Z-rack.

Best leave him alone. He doesn't look like he wants to talk about it.

Instead, a shadow hovered next to her as she filtered through the dresses with her fingers. Carter pulled the skirt of one out to shield his face behind translucent blue fabric. "Sad Mom made Grandma come along though." Lucky for him his non-whisper whisper didn't appear to phase his grandma, who had moved on to racks full of dress shoes, or his mom who was eagerly scribbling on a receipt for the dress. "Our family has a history of broken marriages."

"Yeah?" *Me too, kid.*

"Yeah. I guess Grandma loved another man, but her family didn't approve of him, so she married Grandpa instead. She didn't get her fairy-tale romance. Looks like Mom didn't either."

The woman with the auburn hair stopped her pen short to cast a look toward the lacy bottom of the dress that covered the front counter. A mixture of longing, regret perhaps? So hard to tell with the lines burrowed into her forehead. She wrote again.

Priscilla forced her attention on a blue tea-length gown with a sapphire sash.

"Well, if my dad can find a second chance at romance, I guess everyone can, huh?" Even her mouth tasted bitter at the words. "Maybe your grandma will find someone else."

Soft velvet fabric covered the sash. This one could do for the dance. She didn't like the brightness of the blue, which would make her stand out far too much, but maybe when Scarlett danced, no one would pay any mind to her.

She hoped.

A buzz vibrated nearby; Carter plucked his phone out of his pocket. Out of her periphery, she watched him frown at the screen.

"We can't visit Country Acres tomorrow."

"Why not?" She lifted the dress off the rack.

"Looks like Scarlett's having trouble breathing."

Her heart jolted. "She's what?"

"I guess Pastor says that she has an autoimmune disease, something she's had her whole life, that's been attacking her lungs and heart. Her heart's been running at fifty percent capacity for the past twenty years. Nothing to worry about, according to him, she just needs to rest a few days before spending time with any more visitors."

Her whole life?

"You mean"—she scuffed her flats on the short, green carpet—"she danced, and *still* dances, even though she can't function at one hundred percent?"

He shrugged before whipping his head over his shoulder to see his mom and grandma gathered at the entrance. "I guess you're not old unless you let yourself be."

Silence held the two of them for a moment.

"That means I can't go to Country Acres. But you can still visit Paul."

"I guess you're right. Gotta help him woo her while you aren't there to foil our schemes. I'm sure he's writing love notes and singing songs outside her door until the other ladies start throwing water balloons at him." He winked and jabbed a finger at the dress. "Finally, something almost as beautiful as you."

He tapped his shoes, which showed no socks, then spun around. His mother beckoned him with a wave as the door dinged open.

A grin split her cheeks. She reached up to her face to feel the dimples. Ice cream with him didn't sound so bad anymore. He didn't even hesitate to go visit Paul, like he had when he played hooky from youth group. Did the boy actually follow through on commitments now? *He's not like your dad, running after the next girl who catches his eye.* Both of them were changing, becoming a little less ... opposite.

"Sweetheart, if you wear that thing, I'll have to call the cops. Because someone that beautiful should be illegal."

She didn't hear the ding but shuddered when she spotted the figure in the door frame—Marcus. Her eyes flicked out the window to the town's library. She could have made her escape if he wasn't blocking the door.

Ugh, Grandpa, how long do you plan to spend time in that toy store? He probably was pretending a stuffed rattlesnake was trying to eat him. At least, that's what happened last time she went to a toy store with him as a kid.

Marcus tapped the front counter with a wide grin for Jennie. "Got any blue tuxes?"

She jabbed a finger to the left, grabbed a mug of coffee, and vanished into a back room. Break time, Priscilla guessed.

"Got a prom to go to, Marcus?" Priscilla eyed the door again, but he rushed to the back where a rack full of blue tuxes stood against the window display. Two mannequins posed in short homecoming dresses, each full of sparkles.

Shoot, no luck making a run for the door. He'd block her.

As people passed by the shop, she fought an itch in her arm to wave at them for help.

"A wedding actually." He poked his thumb through the button-hole of a turquoise tux. "I'm someone's plus-one."

"Mia's?"

He didn't respond.

Got 'em.

Her eyebrow shot up, abdomen hardening as a fresh wave of confidence washed over her. She didn't need to make her escape now. He did. "Tell me, Marcus, why on earth would your ex need you to be a plus-one at a wedding? That seems rather embarrassing for both of you."

"What can I say? I'm a nice guy."

But not a good one. "That is awfully nice of you, considering most guys I know hate being dragged to weddings, even while dating their plus-one."

He unplugged his thumb to whirl around with gritted teeth. "Like I said, I'm a nice guy."

Her eyes widened while a pop song played on an overhead speaker. He stepped two paces to the right, directly in front of the door. Clever guy, nice guy, bad guy.

"You know what I think, Marcus? I think no guy, nice or good, would go to a wedding with his ex. I think you lied to me at the coffee shop by saying you two broke up. Why don't you turn around and go back to your girlfriend before I tell her what you said to me when you entered this store?"

She gestured out the window in the direction of the library. If she shoved him into a rack and bolted out the door, she might be able to outrun him. But would Mia believe her? Her hot boyfriend falling all over a bookworm? Yeah, right.

"You know what I think?"

He stalked closer, advancing. No way she could shove him with the momentum now. And with all the racks barricading them in, she couldn't dodge either right or left. She backed into the counter, clutching the dress in front of her like a shield.

"I think you'd be a lot prettier if you shut up."

Marcus lunged forward, grasped at her skirt, and pulled her face toward him. She jerked her head to the side, cringing at his hot breath on her neck. A ding sounded from the door. Relief flooded her as he released the fabric to rush into the men's dressing room toward her right.

At the door, Grandpa stood with a stuffed animal rattlesnake in his hands.

And in the window, a girl with a pixie cut and dark lipstick unpeeled her face from the pane, then fled in the direction of the library: Mia.

Chapter Twenty-One
CARTER

"I DON'T UNDERSTAND. It's not bingo day, so I can't visit anyone *but* Paul."

"Correction, Mr. Carter"—Pat twirled and swung a finger in the air, as if testing the consistency of a drink in a glass—"unless an emergency arises."

"I hardly see how helping the ladies with the dance decorations counts as an emergency."

Pat leered at him over a clipboard as she flipped a sheet.

Behind him a gust of heat kicked at his bare ankles as a couple strode by arm in arm to the left, the woman's white nurse shoes clip clopping on the tile, then muffling when they hit the carpet of the hallway.

"We need all hands on deck. Besides, I already contacted Paul earlier, and he's preoccupied with visitors and personal projects. He said we could borrow you for a couple of hours." She straightened her vest with a stiff tug before motioning for him to follow her in the opposite direction of the couple. "This way, to the Bingo Hall."

He followed her down the hall into the large Jean Rec center. Voices bounced off the walls, the clamor so loud, he struggled to hear his own thoughts. Silver shoestring streamers covered the quote painted on the back wall of the room. Underneath the display, two women were cutting up fish-shaped cardboard cutouts.

Next to them, a man in a khaki suit tore scissors through the head of a jellyfish with streamers attached at its end to make tentacles.

"I thought the theme for the dance was 1950s, Pat."

"Yes, the 1950s prom from *Back to the Future*. It's a movie beyond your time, but it included an 'Under the Sea' themed dance."

"Actually, I've seen it."

He'd noticed that Priscilla often clenched her fists when adults talked down to her. Now he understood.

She directed him to a table where two residents in smocks applied paint to a cardboard cutout of Poseidon. One dabbed black paint on the gray trident to add a three-dimensional texture. They beamed at him as Pat patted an open seat at the table, then handed him a dripping brush.

One of the ladies, who had a gray blotch on her cheek where blush would normally go, tapped an unpainted portion of Poseidon's bicep. He nodded and dabbed his brush into the marble-gray liquid.

"So, Derinda"—the woman without the paint on her cheek spackled the edges of Poseidon's crown—"any idea who you're going to the dance with?"

"Oh, stop acting like that's the most important thing in the world, Ivy." Derinda waved her paintbrush at the other woman. Dots of gray spattered her smock. "We all know it's just a dance."

"True, but we don't have much time left here to find romance, you know."

"Maybe we can take some hints from Scarlett and Paul. Spy them watching movies in the lobby together all the time. Adorable but also infuriating. It's always whenever I want to catch up on *General Hospital*."

He froze, mid-paint dab, on Poseidon's bicep, but not before accidentally sloping the curve too far down. The god of the sea must've done some strange barbell exercises to get them to look that way.

Wait a minute, they watched movies together? Last time I came by, she pelted him with water balloons.

He cleared his throat, "Umm, Derinda. How often have they been in the lobby together watching movies? When did this start?"

She had appeared to have been flirting with Paul outside her window after the water balloon extravaganza. The two may have hit it off after that.

Rubbing her temples, Derinda smeared paint into a curl by her ear. For the first time at Country Acres, one of the residents had sprouted gray hairs. "Oh, why'd you have to go and ask me that? I can't even remember what I had for lunch yesterday." She triangled her elbow on her hip as she tapped her foot. "Hmm."

"Wasn't it after we went to that diner?"

Derinda snapped her fingers. "Thank you, Ivy. Yes, that must've been it. They watched *Singing in the Rain* that night." She stooped over the painting again to stop a drip of gray from forming a stream down the cutout. "I remember because Scarlett wouldn't stop singing that 'Good Morning' song all night long. Got no sleep."

His pulse throbbed in his temples. He plunked the paintbrush in a red solo cup of water, then reached for a paper towel roll on the table to clean up a stream of gray paint dripping down the statue's arm.

They've been together ever since Priscilla and Scarlett pulled the ketchup prank? Then why did he pretend to woo her outside her window in a raincoat?

Soon as he patted away the mess before him, a shriek sounded at the front of the gym, where the bingo caller often stood. A woman in peach pants wielded a newspaper against a man who was occupied with shoveling sugar cookies onto a tray.

Paul.

"Those are for the volunteers!" She punctuated her words with swats.

"Well, I volunteer to take them off your hands." He slipped out the door. The woman unrolled the newspaper with a huff of exasperation.

Carter slid out of his seat and rushed toward the door. He bolted into the hallway, skidding to a halt when he almost ran into Paul, who was busy balancing a tray in his hands. On the maroon plastic sat a steaming bowl of soup—chicken noodle from the scent—a cup of orange-tinted liquid, pureed green something on a small plate, and a little tower of cookies.

"I can see you're preoccupied with your guests." Carter folded his arms.

"Wha-oh. She's not planning on coming for a little while now. Do me a favor and hold this."

Relenting, Carter outstretched his arms for Paul who slid the tray onto them. Then both parked in chairs stationed on the walls of the hallway, the latter puffing out a long breath.

"Just wait till you see what the residents here do when the Girl Scouts drop off cookies."

Carter set the tray on his knees. Warmth from the soup heated his bones. "Paul, why didn't you tell me that you and Scarlett are together now?"

"Together?"

"Yeah, some lady told me the two of you watch movies in the lobby." Flashes of bright yellow raincoats flooded his vision when he stared at the yellow diamond carpet pattern in the hall. "And

I found a receipt in your room that said *you* bought the balloons and the raincoat."

His mother insisting on going to that store to auction off her wedding dress had purged the memory from his mind until now, but everything clicked. Why hadn't he seen it before?

"Did you even need me to help you out? It seems you've been able to snag her all on your own."

"Now, hold on a minute. I was far less confident until you came along. I think my boldness is what was the final clinch."

Carter ignored this. "And she was clearly flirting with you from her window. So why put on a show? Why let her pelt you with water balloons just to make me and Priscilla think that you two have some sort of feud between each other?"

Steamy swirls from the soup clouded his vision for a moment, blocking Paul's expression. Not that he could see it anyway. Paul had craned his neck toward his feet, hiding.

"I'm afraid I cannot say." He kicked his feet underneath the chair. "But as much as I enjoy watching movies with Scarlett, we are not, as you said, 'together.'"

"Come on, man. You're making me hold the woman's soup." Liquid jostled in the tray when he adjusted in his seat. "Also, I'm not an expert on any kind of illness, but any mother would freak out if you gave a sick person six sugar cookies."

A smile tugged at Paul's lips.

"I plan to ask her to be 'together' at the upcoming dance. But she doesn't trust me fully, yet. Thinks I'll run off with some other woman at Country Acres once I find out she's not good. At least, so she told me when we watched *Rebel Without a Cause*."

Yeah, well, two women could play at that game.

He thought back to when Priscilla told him about her dad on the pier, how her mother didn't trust men after him.

"No offense, Paul, but time's ticking. Can't she just relax and be okay with having a boyfriend for a while?"

"I think you misunderstand. Together here works differently than out there." He gestured to nothing in particular. "I suppose we have been dating by your definition. I do have a granddaughter who has explained to me how relationships work for younger generations."

Mia, right. How could two people live in the same family and be so opposite?

"We have watched movies and talked for hours late into the night, long after curfew." He leaned in to whisper. "But between you and me, the workers here appear to be rooting for us too, so they don't tell us to leave."

The chair groaned when he leaned back again.

"But together for us means something a little longer than our dates. We figure since the 'death do us part' part might come sooner for us than a younger couple, that we have to skip ahead a little."

Oh, he wanted to propose. Goodness, they moved fast for being older folks.

Then again, Carter's brain had filled with helium when he was with Mia. He'd gotten some fancy ideas about proposing right after graduation.

"But I figured a little soup can warm up the heart and soul, or so says a famous book series." He groaned as he pulled himself up by the curved wooden armrests. "We need to get her eating. She doesn't take in a whole lot when she has these episodes."

One foot at a time, Carter also rose and followed Paul down the hallway.

Two women untangled blue streamers in their arms on the way to the Bingo Hall. The tail of one of the rolls trailed behind her like a loose string of toilet paper.

Up ahead, next to a painting featuring fireworks signed with a big S in the righthand corner, Elena clutched a white box in her hands. For a split second, he'd forgotten that she had been related to Paul until the two embraced in a hug. After they let go, she held out the white package for him. He took it.

"They had this for you up at the front." She beamed at Carter with a tilt of her chin. "So this is the young man you've been going on and on about. No wonder. He helped me in the relationship sphere as well."

With his free hand, Paul weaved his fingers through his greased hair in a nervous fashion.

"Elena, I wasn't aware that you'd get here early."

"Had to take Mia out for sympathy pies at that cute shop down the road. Had a bad breakup. She wanted to be left alone, and asked to be dropped off at the local shops, so I figured, since I was in the area ... "

Paul glanced at Carter, his daughter, and then the tray in Carter's hands.

"I still have a delivery to make."

"I'll tell her you said hello." Elena shoved her hands under the tray, scooping it away from Carter. "Now you keep that box in a safe place, you hear?"

"Meet us at the fountain?"

"Sure thing, Dad."

She swerved slowly, with the food in hand, then marched down the hallway. The two gentlemen, laden with the new box, carried the package into Paul's room to place it in the drawer, next to the Wal-Mart receipt for the water balloons. Then, they strolled out the lobby toward the fountain. Clouds shielded the sun today, offering a welcome breath of cold air, well, colder by Floridian summer standards.

They parked on the rim of the fountain that acted like a bench, so drips of water sprayed their backs as they listened in silence to the birds and frogs humming and chirping in a summer chorus.

"Let me tell you, Carter"—Paul clapped his palms against the warm fountain stone before he leaned back—"I'm so happy it's summer. Families don't visit as often in cooler seasons. People tend to get busier around that time of year."

Carter bobbled a loose stone back and forth between his toes. "Yeah? What's it like, during the lonelier months?"

"Well"—Paul chuckled—"Like you said, lonely. I think it's really great that you young people are coming to visit. Gives you perspective for later on. Time is more precious than gold here."

Visions of his grandmother flickered in front of his eyes. Even though she lived with them, instead of at a center they had to drive to, how much time had he really spent with her?

How much time would he have left?

"I guess you're right, Paul." He palmed his warm neck. "Time is a dangerous and beautiful thing."

Chapter Twenty-Two
PRISCILLA

"WANT TO KNOW THE SECRET TO ETERNAL LIFE, DEAR?" Scarlett swung open her bathroom door, dressed in a robe with her hair done, and gestured to the tub. "Ta-Da!"

"A bath? Is that how you recovered from your sickness so early?"

"No, dear, look what's on the tub. Just there. On the rim."

She frowned as she picked up colorful snowball-shaped objects caressed in shrink wrap. A pungent whiff of lavender wafted from one.

"Bath bombs?"

Scarlett clapped her hands with a squeal of delight. "That's right! Not just bath bombs, but ones with little gifts inside. Paul's daughter is obsessed with these. That's how I heard about them, before I got sick and all."

Priscilla placed the bomb back on the edge of the tub. A door, half ajar, to the tub caught her attention before she turned out of the bathroom. Many residents with wheelchairs and walkers had trouble with entering and exiting, due to the slippery surfaces, so the tubs came complete with doors and seats inside, like a hot tub.

"I think my mom back home bought a few of those. Don't they have things inside like rings and toys and such?"

"Rings, yes." Scarlett scooped a pile of glittering jewelry off her dresser to show the rings from her bath bombs in a cupped hand. "Don't they look amazing? Couldn't tell some of these apart from some of those ridiculous engagement rings you see now. Diamonds could swallow your finger whole with those things. Let me tell you, diamonds are not a girl's best friend."

"What are, then?"

"Bath bombs and bobby pins."

Scarlett giggled as she returned the rings which dinged against the wood of the dresser. Scarlett then proceeded to her closet then unzipped the plastic casing of a deep green A-line dress, 1950s prom style. She held it up to her bodice; the emerald fabric cut off at her calves.

"You know, Scar, you gotta be careful with those bath bomb rings. Some of them can leave behind a green mark on the skin. My mom's thumb was green for a week, and she can't keep even a succulent alive."

"Depends entirely on the bath bomb." She spun with the dress pressed against her chest, causing the ruffles to swish when she twirled. "Besides, nothing a clear coat of polish can't fix. Help zip me up once I put this thing on, dear?"

"Sure."

While Scarlett had stepped off to the side to shimmy into the dress and haggle with the finicky zipper, Priscilla checked her makeup in the mirror. She didn't wear anything all that often besides foundation for breakouts, so Maria volunteered to help coach her through a 1950s style look, since Maria had worked for a makeup direct sales company for a number of years.

Blue eye shadow was rimmed by a light coat of eyeliner, and bright red lipstick adorned her mouth. She was grateful Maria insisted she keep on her glasses.

"I hate all those movies where the girl at prom suddenly becomes beautiful when she takes her hair out of a ponytail and takes off her glasses. You keep those beauties on, wear your hair as big as possible, and you have fun at that dance."

Her hair didn't have much of a choice. It decided to kink more than usual today, so she wore it natural.

"If we leave this dress unzipped, we might have a few too many men wanting to dance with me, Priscilla."

"Coming."

She rushed over, then pulled up the zipper, but the slider had gotten caught on a change in the fabric. Pulling down on the skirt below with her other hand, she managed to force the thing up. Images from the dress store suddenly darted across her vision. Of how Marcus had tugged at her skirt to pull her in for a kiss. As the memory surfaced, she emitted a quick gasp. Why couldn't she have remembered all that information from the self-defense classes her mother had her take? She could've struck the heel of her palm against his throat or gone for a kick where it counted.

But instead she remained still, petrified.

Good thing Grandpa arrived in time. She hoped Mia, from her spot in the window, also saw her backing into the front desk counter and that Priscilla had panic written all over her expression. Maybe she hadn't read anything else into the gesture.

Yeesh, I knew he wasn't a good guy, but yikes. He really wouldn't take no for an answer, would he? She'd heard plenty of encounters of that type in New York—even had to shuffle away quickly from some seedy characters on subway rides.

But to do so out in the open, in the dress shop ... *Poor Mia. Girl doesn't know what type of guy she's dealing with. Hopefully she saw enough and made the right decision to split.*

Stepping back, she clawed at the zipper of her own dress which she pulled down to catch a breath. The skeleton of the outfit made it too hard to breathe at the moment. She crumpled onto Scarlett's bed and inhaled, held, exhaled.

"You doing all right?"

"Yeah, it's just ... I think I need to follow your lead and swear off all men. You were right. There are no good men left."

Flickering candlelight illuminated Scarlett's face. She'd lit a vanilla-scented candle she claimed was a gift from Paul's daughter. Priscilla bet fifty bucks that the candle also had a ring hidden inside, just like the bath bombs. Some kids in her co-op had shown her videos of similar products.

Scarlett frowned into a vanity on her dresser as she plugged her ears with pearl earrings. "I had passed too quick a judgment. Not all men are evil." Who could she be referring to ...?

Oh. So she did have more feelings for Paul than what she had let on. That could explain why Paul arrived in a raincoat to serenade her at her window, and how Scarlett chattered amicably with him afterwards. They were flirting.

"That may be true, but I met a guy who seemed old-fashioned at first, at a fair. You know, chivalry, doesn't use his cell phone that much, et cetera. But he turned out to be—" She shuddered.

She puffed out a sigh, then ran her fingertips up and down the blue fabric of her dress, catching her nails in the lace.

Scarlett parked beside her. With one hand, she fluffed out her hair sprayed larger-than-usual curls. With the other, she draped it around Priscilla's shoulders.

"The residents here talk a lot about the good ol' days, but they seem to forget a lot of things we're happy to leave in the past. Tensions were high against Puerto Ricans when I was in high school. Paul couldn't be with a woman he loved because his family wanted him to be with a good Korean girl. Yes, we paid fifteen cents for a hamburger, but by adhering to old fashioned values, we also paid the price of potential lives." She gave Priscilla's shoulder a hard squeeze before she rose to the vanity again to apply the rest of the jewelry.

Draping pearls around her neck, she smoothed a wrinkle in the sweetheart neckline of her dress. She spritzed a perfume; the scent of flowers and the woods clogged Priscilla's nose for a moment.

Fresh air, she turned to the side to gasp it in, staring at Scarlett's bookcase. One hardback book with a split spine from being read so many times caught her eye. She pulled it out and felt the texture of the embossed golden letters over a sketch of a ship.

The Odyssey.

Pinching the red ribbon bookmark, she split open the book to a passage Scarlett had underlined in pencil:

"So saying, Athena touched him with her wand. She withered the fair flesh on his supple limbs, and destroyed the flaxen hair from off his head, and about all his limbs she put the skin of an aged old man. And she dimmed his two eyes that were before so beautiful, and clothed him in other raiment, a vile ragged cloak and a tunic, tattered garments and foul, begrimed with filthy smoke. And about him she cast the great skin of a swift hind, stripped of the hair, and she gave him a staff, and a miserable wallet, full of holes, slung by a twisted cord. So when the two had thus taken counsel together, they parted; and thereupon the goddess went to goodly Lacedaemon to fetch the son of Odysseus."

Huh, she had read this for her book club, but the storyline had blended with the *Iliad*. They read too many classic books at once, so she couldn't tell one from the next sometimes.

"Scarlett, in the *Odyssey*, doesn't Athena shroud the hero Odysseus in some sort of mist, so he looks like an old beggar instead of the handsome man he is?"

"Ah, you've stumbled upon one of my favorites." She touched up the rouge on her bottom lip. "Yes, Odysseus wants to see how others will react to him back home if he's unrecognizable. His fellow countrymen treat him like dirt and pay for their lives in the process because of their false judgment, and well"—she smirked—"because the suitors tried to get into bed with his wife. But his wife, Penelope, is hospitable and kind to him, even though he looks like a stranger to her."

Huh, Country Acres, like Athena, had cast some sort of spell over herself and Carter, too.

"So, if everyone, per se, had this mist enchantment over themselves, you'd be able to tell their true character by how they treated strangers?"

"Especially strangers who don't look pleasant to them. Odysseus was a rich man, and Athena made him look like a beggar. All his so-called friends showed they only liked him for his wealth."

That doesn't make sense. The mist here doesn't make anyone look richer or poorer. It just makes them look like teens.

She winced. Back home, she only spent time with retirees because teens were not ... pleasant to her. But after spending time with Scarlett, who appeared *and* acted like a teen, maybe she had passed the Athena test after all and learned to love what she never thought possible.

"Now, put away that book, dear. We have a dance to attend."

Chapter Twenty-Three
CARTER

ALTHOUGH CARTER HADN'T KNOWN WHAT TO EXPECT at the dance that night, almost getting decapitated by an empty fish tank didn't top the list.

He ducked as Derinda, now adorned in a peach-colored dress instead of a smock, apologized before she set the fish tank on the countertop. Pat had disappeared from her normal spot behind the desk, no doubt helping with setting up the decorations. Instead, she had an assistant who liked to scroll on his phone behind the desk today.

"No worries, Derinda. Need help with that?"

"Yes, thank you. It's heavier than it looks. Even though it's empty."

Awkward, the box didn't cradle well in his arms, but he peered through the cloudy glass as they journeyed down the hallway toward the Jean Rec center.

"So, Derinda, what happened to your friend Ivy? You two seemed attached at the hip when you were painting Poseidon the other day."

"Oh." Her voice fell, and from what he could tell through the blur of the glass, so did her expression. Was this what it was like to look through Priscilla's glasses? "Ivy isn't doing all that well. Got sick right after we finished painting that cardboard cutout.

Sounds like a respiratory infection. Hopefully she'll bounce back. So many don't."

Death had almost blipped from his mind in this place.

Had Ethel only passed away a handful of weeks before? All the days had blurred together. Funny, because he actually remembered them. With no late nights grabbing margaritas with his neighborhood friends, he could have a chance at preserving the memory of this summer.

He hoped he could. After all, Priscilla didn't live in Florida. She could disappear forever when they stumbled into August.

They reached the rec center, where men hoisted blue lights on silver beams on the far ends of the room, where those with walkers or wheelchairs couldn't trip over or swerve into them. The tip of his curls brushed against a hanging fish decoration when he placed the tank on a blue tablecloth Derinda patted. Right next to a punch bowl that swirled with orange foam and smelled of pineapple juice.

"Thank you, young man." She gave a pat to his shoulder. Her lips curved upward when she glanced at the boutonniere strapped to his light blue suit.

Here was to hoping Priscilla chose that blue dress in that shop. Otherwise, from the looks of the men in black, khaki, and gray suits in the room, he'd stand out like socks in a no-show crowd.

In the far corner of the room, where the bingo caller usually rolled a cage full of balls, a man stood on a ladder to loop strings around a swordfish cutout. At the other corner of the hall, two men in black suits and ties screwed in lightbulbs to illuminate a large pink clam decoration by a photo booth.

Next to the feather boa props and cartoonishly large glasses, he spotted someone in a green suit. Praise, there'd be someone else in an odd-colored outfit.

Wait a second, was that Paul? If so, he'd slicked his head with so much gel, he might as well have applied oil to his hair. Sure enough, Paul had tangled his fingers in fairy lights to string around a Styrofoam coral decoration. Carter avoided the splash of a hose they'd taken from the kitchen to fill the empty fish tank by ambling over to Paul.

"Need help with those lights, pal?"

He held out twisted fingers. "Sure."

"Paul, you look like a Christmas tree dressed you. Where the heck did you get that suit?"

"Laugh all you want. She happens to like me in this color."

The measures one went for love ...

At last, he managed to unhook the string from Paul's fingers, then looped them around a hump on the coral shaped like a cactus. "Any idea when the dance'll get started? Priscilla told me to come at six."

Paul chuckled as he reached for the other end of the string of lights. "Must've known that you come late to events. It doesn't start for another fifteen minutes."

Paul wound the lights around the base of the coral before jabbing the plug end into an open socket in the wall. Bright white illuminated the dark pink below. Carter scanned the room, realizing how much it reminded him of the set from the *Back to the Future* movies. Throw a couple teen look-alikes in here, and they could film a remake.

This time Pat didn't have a chance to take away his phone. Could snap a pic for Insta.

"Where are all the women?"

"Getting ready. They helped with the majority of the decorations. Without them, we would have a couple hanging fish, and that's about it."

Paul cleared his throat and fell silent for a moment. Then:

"Carter, could you do me a huge favor?"

He turned back to watch Paul scoop up a small white box on the table, the same one Elena had handed him during their last visit.

"I need you to place this at that fountain we like to sit at during our walks. Underneath the ledge, where no one can see it, and where I like to sit next to the small statue of a swan. Make sure it does not get wet."

Carter held the box with shaky hands. Something bumped against the cardboard casing. Was there a ring in there? Paul had said he wanted to ask her tonight. No wonder he didn't want any water splashing in there.

"Got it. Be right back."

Cradling the box to his stomach, he brushed past two men hoisting a cardboard surfboard over their shoulders, rushed into the hallway, and out the doors. He sweltered in his three-piece suit thanks to the warm night breezes. He prayed that everyone else would shed their jackets when the dancing started. At least the suit protected him from the mosquitos and No-See-Ums swarming in clumps around the lampposts.

He wound up the sidewalk.

His heartbeat pounded in his fingertips when he arrived and slid the box underneath the ledge.

"Umm, Carter, what are you doing?"

He spun around to see a bright blue dress that almost caused him to tumble into the fountain. Not the worst of ideas in this suit and summer heat. "Priscilla, why'd you walk up here in heels?"

Instead of flats, today she opted for a white 50s style heel.

She shrugged. "When I was in the lobby, I saw someone in a bright blue suit heading up this way. At first, I thought it was a resident who'd gotten lost on their way to the dance." Many residents did have memory problems or would lose their way to a destination. "But then I spotted that intensely red hair. By the way, isn't the suit a bit presumptuous?"

Priscilla quirked a brow as she gestured at his suit and then back at her dress. They had matched after all.

"I don't know what you're talking about, princess. Who wouldn't want to wear this amazing getup? It's just coincidental that you happened to be wearing the same color. If anything, you copied me."

She tsked, and light from a lamppost nearby twinkled in her eye. "Well"—she looped her arm in his—"I guess we should head to the dance floor. Scarlett wanted to arrive early to get elbow room. Something tells me she'll throw out a hip tonight."

Electricity surged through his arm. Besides the shoulder squeeze she'd given him in the dress store, they hadn't grazed skin that much. A far cry from Mia who wanted to touch. All. The. Time.

When they reentered the building, he gasped at the AC that breathed down the color of his oxford. Praying he didn't sweat too much in the heat, they ambled toward the hall which seemed to puff heat from the number of bodies inside. He'd never been to a school dance (Mia didn't like the crowds and how everyone made a big deal about the events), but he had heard from some of his other classmates that the gym had sweltered because of the hundreds of students dancing at once.

A man with a mop-top haircut tuned a guitar on stage. He, along with four others, wore matching hairstyles plus black suits and ties. Why they decided to have a Beatles cover band when the Beatles definitely did not play in *Back to the Future*, Carter couldn't tell. He just praised his lucky stars they didn't recruit him for the planning committee.

Priscilla tensed. "Oh man," she breathed. "Look at all the people." Not even bingo day had drawn this large of a crowd.

Her shoulders scrunched, but the fabric of her dress restricted them from going up more than an inch. Elbows still interlaced, he tugged her toward the back where pockets of space existed between a table with assorted bowls of popcorn flavors and a jellyfish decoration whose tentacles reached the tips of Priscilla's hair. The corners of her lips tugged upwards.

"Thanks. Probably better we're back here so Scarlett can't watch me fail at dancing."

She squinted at the crowd in the dim lighting of the room. Probably not the best idea to have a room full of people, who mostly didn't have perfect vision but maybe the lack of lights helped with the electricity budget of the whole event anyway.

"Don't worry, Priscilla, I don't have much experience dancing either. I think you just hobble back and forth like you're on hot sand or something."

He swung his arms around, demonstrating, hopping from one foot to the next. "It's important that you get some windmill action with the arms, see?"

Nose scrunched, she hid a giggle behind her palms while the guitarist on stage greeted those closest in the crowd. "You know what, I'm not so worried about Scarlett seeing *me* dance anymore."

Up front, the four Beatles impersonators strummed to a song about twisting and shouting, all of which the residents appeared to be doing. Flashes of green, a dress and a suit, earned a bubble of space in the middle as Scarlett spun in circles around Paul. Wow, Priscilla hadn't exaggerated. She could dance.

Priscilla imitated his dance of bouncing from one foot to the other until the two of them had to gasp for air from laughing too much.

They drew together when the band strummed a slow song about a guy named "Jude." She grabbed his hand to place it on her hip.

"I don't know much about dancing, but I do know you don't have to hold your arm out inches away from me. I don't *always* bite you know."

He smirked. "Just leaving room for the Holy Spirit. He wants to dance with us too." At least, that's what Pastor Timothy told them during homecoming and prom season.

Whites of her eyes showed for a moment before she grasped his shoulder and pulled herself closer. They swayed in a small circle; Priscilla's chin nuzzled on his shoulder. Electricity surged through him. He wondered if she could feel how his heart was beating so fast it sounded like he had left his phone on vibrate in his jacket pocket.

A picture for Insta seemed pointless now. None of the filters could do this scene justice.

Priscilla froze the sway as she twisted her chin to the door. He followed her gaze to watch Scarlett tug Paul out the doors and down the hallway. The buzz died when Priscilla dropped her hands from his shoulders.

"Where on earth are they going?"

Good question. They angled to the left, disappearing into the lobby. Wait, shoot, he knew the answer. But why was Scarlett tugging at him and not the other way around? Did she know about the proposal?

No way she'll handle that well if she's been trying to keep them apart.

"Ha ha, maybe to get fresh air."

He winced at how his voice squeaked when he lied. Well, he wasn't supposed to tell Priscilla, or anyone for that matter. And he hadn't settled on the answer yet as to whether she approved of the Paul and Scarlett ship yet.

Priscilla fiddled with a flower on her dark blue sash. "I don't know. It's pretty dark out there. Shouldn't we check to make sure they don't get lost?"

Carter unclenched and then clenched his jaw. What on earth could he say in response to that?

Ha ha, no, they'll follow the stars back home. Just like they had in the olden days.

Yeah, that would go over well.

By the time he'd mulled over the possibilities in his head, Priscilla had already begun a march toward the green exit sign, covered by fishnets. Through the hallway into the outdoors, he followed her, shedding his jacket which he offered to her. He had to race ahead because not even a semi barreling down the parking lot could stop her, but she did halt when a jacket blocked her vision of the fountain.

"Lots of mosquitos out here." He grimaced. "Don't ever listen to those books or movies that describe love like a summer evening down South."

She smirked as she wound the jacket around her shoulders. Seconds after, she proceeded with full strides up to the fountain. Two figures ahead sat on the ledge in the blur of lights coming from the illuminated jets of water. Priscilla's heels paused in their clopping halfway up the sidewalk when Paul leaned over and grabbed the box underneath his feet. Per his instructions, Carter had placed it near the statue of a swan.

"What is he doing?" Her voice came out in a warning tone more than in a question.

Paul popped off the lid of the box. She advanced a few steps closer, Carter close behind. Not noticing them, Paul struggled with some shrink wrap covering a ball of some sort. Scarlett chuckled, took it from him, and dug her long nails into it. She tore off the plastic, then tossed the ball into the fountain.

Okay, not what he expected at all. Maybe he'd read the whole "together" conversation wrong from the hallway the other day.

Red fizz swirled in the blue lights from the fountain. Priscilla paused in the dancing shadows casted by the lamppost above her head. "Is that a bath bomb?"

"A what?" Some scent, floral and powerful, caught his nose as he turned back. Most of the "bomb" had already dissolved into the waters.

Scarlett bent over to pluck out a small ball, a plastic one, and jiggled the contents inside.

Taking the sphere from her fingertips, Paul had to use the ledge on the fountain to guide his knee to the ground. And then:

"Scarlett, would you do the honor of marrying me?"

Priscilla didn't say anything. In his periphery, Carter saw her clap a hand to her mouth, eyes wide.

"Oh, Paul, you ridiculous man. It's about time you asked."

Chapter Twenty-Four
PRISCILLA

WHAT?

She clenched her jaw, then swallowed, breath still minty from a Listerine spray Scarlett had given her before they left the room. Claimed she bought it at a drug store near Country Acres.

Scarlett. Now she had her hand outstretched, tears forming mascara rivers down her cheeks, and nodding. Paul slid the ring onto her finger.

What? She said yes?

Rustling her skirt a moment created a soft wind to cool down her legs. Then she advanced forward into the light where the happy couple could spot her. "Scarlett, what?"

Scarlett lifted her chin as she swiped away some of the mascara rivers. "Oh, Priscilla, isn't it wonderful? How do you feel about being my maid of honor?"

Had Scarlett gotten heat stroke from the gym? Was she temporarily loopy?

The heat from the gym had certainly caused Priscilla's brain to bubble like liquid as that was the only explanation for what she was seeing. "Scarlett, he proposed to you with a ring from a bath bomb."

"I know." She showed off the new addition to her finger in the light. A blue and green jewel, like a fake opal, glimmered in the lamppost's beams. "Isn't it just darling? I would've hated it if he'd spent thousands of dollars on a ring. After all, who knows how much time I would have to wear it before—" She stuck out her tongue to indicate an impending death.

"Scar, it's going to turn your finger green."

"Well, at least it'll match my dress then."

"No, this isn't part of the deal. You wanted my help to *prevent* exactly this from happening." What was the other part of the deal, anyway? Scarlett had never told her, and she hadn't dedicated much thought to it past the first two weeks together.

Her friend didn't answer. With a twirl of her emerald dress, she returned to the fountain, cupped Paul's face, and planted a long sweet one on him. Something wriggled in Priscilla's gut. Disgust? Pity? Confusion? Envy? She couldn't identify the emotion.

Instead, she forced her attention away from the kissing couple to the white box cracked open at Paul's feet.

Hold on a second. Hadn't she seen a certain boy in a blue suit placing that box at the fountain earlier? He had whipped around, surprised when he called out to her.

Because he didn't want you to see.

She turned to him, shoulders burning under the suit jacket draped over her shoulders. "How long have you known?"

"I'll explain on the way."

"The way to where?" She said this through gritted teeth.

"Let's leave these two alone for a while and make a loop around the compound, okay? I'll explain what I know." He glanced over his shoulder at the couple who had just torn themselves apart from the embrace. "Congratulations, you two. Come on, Priscilla."

Arching her back away from his hand, she marched inches ahead, every part of her ignited.

He waited until they had reached the parking lot before speaking. "I only found out a few days ago. Paul wanted to keep it a secret until he proposed."

"So she went from pelting balloons at him one day to marrying him the next? That doesn't make sense."

"Well, I guess the two hit it off after the ketchup incident."

"They what?"

Carter slumped his hands into his pants pockets and explained what he'd learned from Paul the day Scarlett had gotten sick when Priscilla couldn't visit Country Acres. They talked as they wound their way around some bushes at the women's end of the building complex. She repeatedly gripped the edges of her skirt to catch the moisture from her palms.

"So after the diner, they just pretended to have a feud, but really, they were madly in love with each other? They still got together fast, though."

"Yeah, well, they don't exactly have a whole lot of time to, as Timothy calls it, court. I guess once you know, you know."

Her lips sagged until she could almost feel her dimples disappear. "But why on earth would they fake it for us? Did they just like pretending or are we missing something?"

A row of floor length windows caught the light of a nearby lamppost, spotlighting the green scuffs on her white shoes in the reflection. She should've followed his advice earlier to not walk on the sidewalk with those heels. Mowers *had* just cut the grass that day, after all. Green. Like Scarlett's dress and what some of those bath bomb rings did to fingers if they were made of bad metal.

Appearances meant nothing.

Apparently, she couldn't clearly see the budding relationship between Paul and Scarlett, or the dangers of Marcus who looked more relatable at first glance. *He was like those bath bomb rings that weren't made right. Pretty, but turns your fingers green.*

Her breath caught in her chest at the memory of Marcus in the dress shop. Would she ever be able to pump oxygen correctly again around men?

She remembered what Scarlett had said back at her room. Not all of them greened the skin, just the bad ones, the "nice" ones.

"You know, Priscilla, I've been trying to figure out the same thing. I had once dated a girl back in my sophomore year and tried to keep it a secret from Mom. Mom didn't want me dating anyone until I graduated. The girl's dad was the same way. Big scary guy, with a gun."

Carter sighed as he kicked a loose rock into a bush with flowers. She couldn't tell their color in the darkness.

"Fun as it was to sneak out my window at nights to go on dates with her, we both got tired of the charade after a month or so. Although I wanted to stay together, she just wanted her dad's approval. When you love someone, you just want to tell everyone."

"And it seems like they love each other."

"Exactly. So why wouldn't they tell us?"

Green grass confetti littered the sidewalk as the throbs of guitar pulsed from the building. The guitarists must've cranked up the volume to appeal to those with failing hearing aids. Green. Scarlett's dress. Scarlett's deal. What was the second half of the deal?

Did Scarlett want to make her more confident? More bold? Check.

She'd stormed out on Elena the other day in the house. At the beginning of the summer, she would have cringed but nodded her way through small talk and a tour until the woman left.

Did she want Priscilla to be more accepting of younger folks? Check.

She even kind of had fun pelting Paul with those water balloons and gathering the boys at the jukebox so Scarlett could pull a prank. A year back, she would've trembled at the idea of ever engaging in a shenanigan. Scarlett had aged her down at least ten years.

But that wouldn't make Scarlett hide her love for Paul.

What if she wanted Priscilla to take down the photograph from her own bedside? Just like she had done for Scarlett's ex-husband. Then she could open up her chances at happiness, and … she hadn't realized that she'd weaved her fingers between Carter's now. Pale lamp light showed the beet red flush that had crawled up his cheeks.

"Well, obviously, I didn't approve, so maybe she wanted to be like you and wait to tell 'Mom.'" She meant to unclasp his hand but couldn't. Didn't want to.

"Yeah, ha ha, that must be it."

No, it wasn't.

Because he fully approved, like a dad who had never heard of the idea of grounding or sitting in a time-out. And from what she gathered from his story, he coerced whatever information from Paul he could when he found out about the receipt from Wal-Mart and about their movie dates.

A mosquito buzzed a high-pitched note by her ear. She swatted the insect away.

They looped around to the men's side of the compound toward the tennis courts off in the distance. Beyond the courts, in the darkness, a flag waved on a golf course, hills shrouded in shadow. A worker must've forgotten to take the pole down.

Then the idea hit her. Like a golf ball aimed straight between where her eyebrows narrowed.

"Carter, Scarlett and I made a deal when I first met her to keep her and Paul as far away from each other as possible. But she never explained to me the other half of the deal. What she'd do for me."

A nervous laugh bobbled in his throat. "Yeah, haha, umm." His free hand tugged at his collar. "So anyway, you were saying?"

"Well, once I removed the photograph from her nightstand, things changed. I guess she watched movies with him and had heart to hearts, opened up to him. So I'd failed my end of the deal, but I don't know if she failed hers."

"What do you mean?"

"I mean." She winced but clasped his hand tighter. "What if she didn't want to end up with someone, but she didn't want me to end up like her?" She couldn't meet his eyes, forcing her gaze to the cracks in the sidewalk. "In the Bingo Hall, she saw I was like her. Closed off, distrustful, hurt by past circumstances, and she wanted a vicarious experience through me."

She noticed his eyelids narrowed at the word vicarious.

"Oh, honestly, read more. It means she wanted to live her experience through me."

"Gotcha, gotcha, like all those movies where the dad says to the boy, 'Why are you giving up on your dream?' and the boy is all like, 'No, Dad. It's your dream I'm giving up on.'"

Her eyes rolled. "Yeah, like that."

They roamed in silence until they reached the parking lot again. Their arms had begun to glide back and forth like the swings on the playground. She hid a smirk, amused.

"So, when you say Scarlett wanted to vi-vica—that word experience through you, I'm assuming she didn't mean with any of the residents. It's pretty slim pickings in there for a guy your age. Unless she wanted you to be a gold digger."

She squeezed his hand hard until his fingers jutted in odd directions. "Oh my word, Carter, she didn't want me with some eighty-year-old."

"She's unpredictable. You never know."

There was that stupid, goofy grin.

"So maybe they pretended to have a feud and all that to bring us together." She chewed on her bottom lip. "So we'd spend more time together to find out what the next person was planning. And so we could drive together, not stuffed into a friend-zoning church van."

"I don't know, princess. I've heard that van is quite the aphrodisiac."

"Ugh, so you know the word aphrodisiac but not vicarious?"

She nudged him with her hip, then tugged him toward the sidewalk where a white bus had parked underneath the pavilion to the front entrance. The fountain now sat empty. Maybe the happy couple had returned to the dance.

After a few seconds during a pause from the guitar strums, Carter cleared his throat.

"Well, did it work?"

"What?"

"Scarlett's half of the deal for you."

Her heels scuffed on a broken slab in the sidewalk, throwing her off-balance. But something told her without that torn off corner, she would have still tripped.

He held her hand tight to help keep her upright.

"You know what, lover boy? Ice cream doesn't sound too bad on a night like this. What say we get out of these ridiculous outfits and head over to that 50s diner? I think they're open for another hour."

"Gonna let me pay this time?"

As they locked eyes, she squeezed his hand before letting go. "Maybe just this once."

She patted the sides of her dress. Wait, no pockets with this one.

"I need to call Maria to let her know she doesn't have to pick me up." Priscilla had asked to be dropped off, so that Carter didn't get to see her in her dress until the event. Sure, it wasn't a wedding, but some sort of bad luck would surely have happened if he had caught a glimpse beforehand. "Meet you back out here in ten?"

"Make it five. I want ice cream."

She grinned at the Big Dipper constellation on his nose before spinning around to rush through the lobby doors. Good thing this dress came with a zipper and not the ridiculous weaving corsets some prom dresses featured. Then she *really* wouldn't make that five-minute deadline.

Praise, Scarlett hadn't locked her door. Probably too anxious about the proposal. She jostled open the doorknob, unzipped her dress, and dialed Maria. Clicking the speakerphone button, she squatted on the bed to undo the buckles on her heels.

"Priscilla? I've been trying to get a hold of you."

She kicked off one shoe, which landed on a reclining chair. "Sorry, Maria, didn't see the notifications. Are you okay?"

"I'm with your grandpa at the hospital."

Her fingers shook, halfway through undoing the buckle on the second shoe. "What?" Electricity jolted in her rib cage. "Do you— do you need me to have a friend drive me to the hospital?" She frowned. It would be a lot to ask him to take her to the hospital when he'd expected a date. "Or I can get an Uber. I've tricked the app into thinking I'm eighteen." Since they wouldn't let anyone under that age get a ride.

"No, dear, he's stabilized now. Another breathing scare. Shouldn't be more than an overnight stay."

"Are you sure?"

"Yes, we just wanted to keep you updated. Enjoy your night. Grandpa says to kiss all the boys."

The receiver beeped, indicating Maria had hung up. Priscilla collapsed on the bed. It was all she could do to remind herself how to inhale.

Chapter Twenty-Five
CARTER

SHE SAID YES TO ICE CREAM!

Carter kicked off his shoes in Paul's room, then unpeeled his no-show socks.

After Priscilla had bolted inside, he ran to his car to grab his civilian clothes from the trunk before dashing to Paul's room. Although his friend was often meticulous about locking the doors, he'd forgotten today, so Carter scored a free entry into the abode. Even if he couldn't manage to get in, they had guest bathrooms by the front. But he winced at the thought of the funny odor from those closet-style restrooms getting on his dress clothes.

Popping his head through a t-shirt, he reached for his sandals and slid them onto his feet. After he had shimmied into shorts, of course.

Once finished, he relaxed on the bed to check his phone for the time. How on earth did he do all of that in two minutes? He hadn't realized how fast he'd run from the car to Paul's room.

And girls took a while to change into new clothes.

Scanning Paul's bookshelf, he found a yearbook with Manchester High School on the spine, an old yearbook. He shot a glance at the door and then shrugged. Eh, he had a little time. Anything to keep himself from scrolling on social media.

Even after he'd deleted Mia, she still showed up in his feed. She had a lot of friends plus she played hooky on a lot of shifts at the library. Several shots of her in bikinis on beaches or posing with friends next to downtown art pieces had filled his screen whenever he clicked on any app. Much as he loved to keep up the TikTok numbers, he needed a break until all her friends went back to school and didn't have as much to post about.

Signatures and mementos from classmates filled the first page of the yearbook.

Because of Paul's shyness, he'd assumed this page would be a little sparser of names, but then again, images from his last day at school flashed through his mind. Even seniors in his class he'd never talked to had shoved a Sharpie marker into the hands of anyone in the hallway to get another name in their books. Seniors in high school had a weird habit of wanting to preserve every moment.

Thumbing through the pages, he landed on a dog-eared one of a black and white photo of Paul posing in a football jersey with his arm wrapped around a girl in a fancy dress, wearing a crown. Beneath, the attribution read, "This year's Homecoming King and Queen."

Huh, so Paul did have a little boldness in him during his younger days.

After all, only the most popular of students landed the coveted roles of Homecoming King or Queen. He wondered what mellowed him over the years. Maybe age. But at least he and Scarlett must have more in common than he thought. They maybe discussed their high school days during their late-night talks.

Not so opposite after all. Like him and Priscilla.

He wouldn't have to buy any bath bombs for her soon, but ice cream was a good start.

Right before he turned the page, the nose of the girl in the photograph caught his eye. Where had he seen that long nose before?

He scanned his memory for anyone at Country Acres who shared that feature, but his brain failed him. Where on earth did this deja vu come from then?

His phone buzzed, a text message from his mom reminding him to put on bug spray, then he noticed the time.

Shoot, seven minutes had passed from when he talked to Priscilla at the front entrance. By now, she must be waiting at the meeting spot. Tapping her foot and muttering something about how he never showed up on time. He did, after all, come fifteen minutes late to the dance, or really, the time she'd given him to come to the event.

Bundling his dress clothes in his arms, he shoved them into a grocery bag and vowed to work on his punctuality.

He tied the bag's handles into a knot before flying out the door toward the main entrance. When he sprung out the sliding doors, he spied no one outside except for a car's red lights sliding into an open parking spot. Huh, she was still changing.

He spun the keys in a circle around his index finger after putting his clothes in the trunk of the car. As he threw them in, he found a can of Spring Fresh Febreze to spray the seats and bag. Hopefully the stench of sweat wouldn't overpower their drive to the diner.

Deed done, he shut the doors to march back toward the main entrance.

He stopped when he spotted a figure with a pixie cut. She locked eyes with him, then folded her arms as she tapped her foot.

Ugh, no, Mia. Not now.

Every inch of his skin prickled, as if begging him to dive into his car, lock the doors, and text Priscilla a new meeting spot. But then he noticed the streams of mascara cascading down Mia's cheeks; her nose rimmed with red. Pity tore away at his abdomen.

Stupid, stupid. Go back to your car now. There's nothing but trouble for you here.

Images from the fair flashed through his mind, as one of the few times he'd bumped into her since their breakup.

But still, she looked awful crying like that.

"What happened, Mi?"

She sniffled as she glanced up at the overhead lights strung on the pavilion to try blocking out any more tears. "I caught Marcus ch-cheating on me. We broke up, and-and I thought I would come visit Grandpa to check up on him. He always helps keep my mind off of th-things. Plus, I needed to get away from home."

Carter had never seen her stop by to visit in all his days here. Then again, he didn't spend 24/7 here. "Why'd you need to leave home?"

"Mom's all over her new boyfriend. I didn't need the reminder."

The doors to the entrance slid open for a couple who brushed past them to stride arm in arm down the path he and Priscilla had followed minutes ago. A fresh batch of tears started again for Mia. Pity boiled again in his stomach. After she and him had broken up, every other post in his feed appeared to be couples kissing, going on dates, or getting engaged.

He hated those reminders too.

"I'm sorry to hear that, Mia. Your grandpa's a bit preoccupied right now with the dance. But I have a feeling they might end the event sometime soon."

The music inside had quieted to a slow strumming. From what he could recall from movies, they saved the slow dances for last.

He wouldn't know, thanks to Mia.

"Th-that's okay. I'm just happy to have someone to talk to who understands."

A breeze rustled his shorts when the doors slid open again. Another couple, each adorned in gray outfits, turned to the right, then began the loop around the compound. He wondered how soon they would bump into the other pair who'd gone the other direction.

"Yeah, I do understand, Mia. But that's because you didn't tell me that we broke up and started dating Marcus in the first place." He folded his arms. "I'm sorry to hear that this happened, but I'm not exactly the best person for you to unload this on."

Mia tilted her head to observe something in the lobby, then brought her attention back to him. She advanced two steps, brushing the heel of her hand against her cheek. "I know. I didn't know your parents took away your phone until a friend told me later. That was stupid of me."

Another two steps.

"You know what else would be stupid of me?"

Another two, now a mere foot away from him. Alarm bells whirred inside his skull.

"If I didn't kiss you right now with how handsome you look."

Before he could react, she lunged at him and yanked at his t-shirt, pulling him in for a kiss. He flailed his arms attempting to wave himself back, but it didn't matter. She gripped tighter until she twisted the fabric in circles around her fingers as she continued to kiss long, hard, wet.

Then she released. Shame prickled his cheeks. She ... just took advantage of him again.

He tried to focus on anything else. The breeze from the automatic doors caught his ankles. He stared over his shoulder to look away from Mia, directly at the person walking out of the building.

Dressed in a tank top, shorts, and socks that went up to her calves stood Priscilla. She cradled what looked like a garbage bag in her arms, containing something blue inside, her dress. Her glance flitted back and forth from Mia to Carter.

Her eyelids and eyebrows narrowed; she flared her nostrils once, then retreated inside.

"Mom, I don't understand you. One minute you're all like 'nursing homes are evil,' and the next you're like 'let's check my mom into Country Acres.'"

His mother pinched the bridge of her nose while they waited for his grandma to emerge from the Wendy's bathroom to get back in the car for her first tour of the place.

"For your information, she *requested* we check her in. Said the stress from home got to be too much for her, and she wants a temporary break where people can look after her."

The thick scent of fries and savory burgers filled the back of the car. He crumpled the Wendy's bag, then rolled down his window to let in some fresh air.

His parents had been shouting at each other more than usual. And no matter how many walks in the neighborhood Grandma asked him to accompany her on, when they returned, they could hear the yelling from down the street. Carter had half a mind to check himself into Country Acres.

Grandma returned minutes later, smoothing down her flowery sundress.

Wonder what she'll look like when she checks into the place as a resident. Grandma as a teen. Images from her photo books at her house flashed across his mind. She was a cheerleader with a long, narrow nose that she still sported. Like his mom, she probably had deep red curls. The black and white photos would never tell.

Mom clicked the radio onto a country station as they drove to Country Acres but flipped the station when one of the gravelly-voiced singers mentioned beer too much.

At last they arrived, and he could've imagined it, but Grandma clicked open the door before Mom had even finished parking.

His stomach twisted when he saw the pavilion again. The dance had just happened last night, and he still couldn't fight the images of Mia pulling him in for a kiss. He should've shoved her away. Pulled back more. But how could he when she gripped his shirt so tight? She would've simply yanked him back in for another make out round.

Heat seared his cheeks at the memory. No wonder Priscilla had a hard time trusting guys.

No wonder he put up his own fun house mirror version of himself. Because when he let girls like Mia Patel see the real version ...

He slid his phone out of his pocket, then clicked on the messages to Priscilla. Pastor had given them each other's phone numbers back when they first signed up, in case they needed to get a hold of someone.

But he hadn't risked sending her a message until last night.

CARTER: It's me, Carter. What you saw at the pavilion isn't what you think.

CARTER: She came onto me.

CARTER: I know you probably don't trust me because I have a history of playing hooky and giving up on commitments, but I've changed. I'm not the guy you met at the beginning of summer.

CARTER: Please let me know somewhere we can meet so I can explain more.

No response. Not exactly surprising, even if she'd read it (she didn't use read receipts) she didn't respond to most notifications on her phone.

Puffing a sigh, he slid the device back into his pocket to follow his mom through the front entrance. There Pat gave each of them name tags in addition to handing Mom a folder full of information about the assisted living home. Mom flipped it open, there he spotted a brochure with the tagline: Country Acres, a slice of heaven.

"Carter didn't tell me he had such a wonderful grandmother." Pat lifted a brow.

Yeah, because you spend half the time scolding me for touching your potpourri. I don't have time for backstory, lady.

"If you'll follow me, I'd love to show you around. We'll first head toward the Jean Rec center. Today, because we're tearing down from an event that happened last night, we don't have any current activities. But you'll be able to see most of the decorations. Although some of our male residents have volunteered to begin tearing down right around this time."

Great. Another reminder of a night that could've gone right but went oh so wrong at the end.

They passed by a couple cuddled on a couch in the lobby. He half expected it to be the Paul and Scarlett power team, but the woman's blonde hair gathered into a poof dissuaded that theory.

Pat swung open the gym door, and sure enough, most of the decorations still hung from the ceiling and walls. With the exception of some low-hanging fish cutouts and an empty Beatles-less stage, the dance hall remained as is, though now a few ladders were scattered throughout. Younger men, in non-50s era clothing, maybe sons or other volunteers, scaled the ladders. Someone got smart about lawsuits the other day, likely banning the male residents from climbing them.

"Although we have many rooms dedicated to activities, this is by far the largest one. Here we'll hold various events from auctions, to bingo, to Grandkids' Night, to, as you can see, dances."

Mom and Grandma pointed with an "ooh" at a life-sized mermaid decoration on the far left.

Next to it, Paul, decked in all white instead of green today, had gotten his fingers intertwined in something again. This time, fishnets.

Carter stepped toward him, then offered to help detangle while Pat chattered away to one of the women about how Carter was a "really big help" here. The words stung his ears. No wonder Priscilla hated it when people treated her like a little kid.

Ah, Priscilla. *Don't think about her now, dude.*

Sorrow filled his lungs until breaths became labored. He focused on unplugging the nets from Paul's thumbs and dropped them on the floor.

"Thank you." Paul gave him a firm tap on the back, but then something caused him to freeze. Carter mirrored him, following his stare to Grandma.

"Irene?" Her name crackled in his throat.

His grandma had frozen too. Moisture brimmed in the bottom of her eyelids. Even though they usually appeared watery, a tear slipped down her cheek to indicate that more was going on. It caught on her nose. Her long, narrow nose. Wait a second, he'd seen that nose before.

The only un-wrinkled feature on her face. He spotted it last night in Paul's yearbook in the picture where he had his arm draped around a young lady, Grandma. They had a thing for each other in high school.

Memories flashed across his mind of his conversation with Grandma in the family room about past relationships. She had stopped him when he asked if she loved Grandpa. She had loved, yes, but someone else.

Paul.

Arms outstretched, the two of them ran together in a hug, her arms curled around his shoulders. She planted a kiss on his cheek and whispered, loud enough for Carter to hear (no one in their family could truly whisper, old voice or young), "I never stopped loving you, you know."

They released their embrace, although Grandma held on a little longer than Paul. A blush had crawled up his cheeks when a huff sounded from the gym door. No one had heard it open.

At the entrance, Scarlett held a cupcake from, Carter guessed, the cafeteria. Face as red as her new fiancé's, she dropped the pastry on the floor. Frosting splattered the light blue tarps meant to imitate the ocean floor.

Then, she stormed out the exit, doors slamming behind her.

Chapter Twenty-Six
PRISCILLA

"DID YOU KISS ALL THE BOYS, PRISCA?"

She grinned at him through a blur of tears as she lifted her glasses to swipe at her eyelids. "Yeah, Grandpa. All the boys."

Grandpa mirrored her expression as best he could with a plastic oxygen tube plugged into his nostrils. Above his bed, a heart monitor beeped, various numbers displayed in orange on the screen. She wished she'd spent more time reading medical books versus history ones. Half the numbers meant nothing to her.

After the dance, Maria had said he'd be out of the hospital by morning, but here they were, two days later. He hadn't downed more than a cup of juice his whole stay. She squeezed his fingers that had gone cold while a doctor at the door snapped on some gloves.

She was pushing it on time. They'd already wanted to operate on him, something about leaking fluid out, when she arrived, but Maria's somber expression managed to convince them to hold off for five minutes.

"I'll be downstairs, okay, Grandpa? Want me to get you anything at the gift shop?"

"Do they have any stuffed animal snakes?"

Nothing said 'Congratulations, you had a baby!' quite like a stuffed rattlesnake, but maybe she could convince him that the teddy bears she saw in the display window would serve as a decent substitute.

With one more squeeze, she glanced at the IV dripping water into the crook of Grandpa's elbow before meeting Maria at the entrance of the room. She couldn't bear to glance at his sunken face again. Even though he still had his laugh, some sort of Athena's mist had fallen over Grandpa. He didn't look like himself. They headed for the elevators, then journeyed down two floors in silence.

When they landed on the ground floor, Maria suggested they stop by Au Bon Pain, a French bakery with cafeteria foods. She'd seen those in airports before.

Priscilla shrugged. It felt like someone had dropped forty pounds onto her shoulders. Gravity, perhaps. In the restaurant, they each ladled broccoli cheese soup into a bowl. Maria bagged a chocolate croissant and paid for the both of them. Priscilla promised to spot her back, but Maria would hear none of it.

They snagged a red table by the windows of the food shop; Priscilla split a pile of napkins between the two of them.

"Maria, what happened?"

Soon as she got home from the dance, she'd crashed on her bed, sunken into a stupor. She hoped, when she woke up the next morning, that she'd find Grandpa in his usual family room chair with a cup of coffee in hand, but no such luck. She went the whole day without hearing from anyone. Finally, last night, Maria texted her that she could drive the two of them to the hospital the next day.

"It's worse than last time. I called your mother this morning to see if she could cancel her appointments at a conference. Just in case."

Those three words caused a cold shudder to run up and down her spine.

Just in case.

She stirred her soup before ladling a spoonful onto her tongue. Although cheesy and warm, she didn't feel much like eating the rest. "I thought you said he'd be back home by today."

"We can hope he'll make a recovery in the next few days."

"And if he doesn't?"

Maria didn't reply, but bit into her chocolate croissant instead. Flakes spiraled down onto the table like fresh winter snow. She swallowed. "They could be operating for a while. Why don't you and I stop by downtown and try to distract ourselves for a little while?"

Priscilla nudged her backpack lying on the ground with her toes. She'd brought along some library books to read in case they got stuck downstairs.

"I should probably return these." She reached down to pull out a book with a green spine. "Don't want to get a late fee."

That would mean she would have to confront Mia. Ugh, that was the last thing she wanted, especially after what happened after the dance between Mia and Carter. But who knew? Last time she'd checked out some new titles, a middle-aged man with large glasses met her at the front counter, so she could strike lucky in terms of library shifts today.

"Sounds like a good idea. We could also stop for ice cream at that diner you mentioned afterward."

Soup burned her throat when she swallowed. She put the spoon in the bowl and shoved it forward. "No thanks, Maria. I don't think I'm in the mood for anything sweet."

They rose, then plunked their bowls in the trash before heading to the parking deck across the road. On the drive, Maria played an audiobook of some murder mystery set in France. Priscilla glimpsed at the title of the CD case Maria had left in the front seat: *Let the Ghosts Speak.*

At last, they arrived at the library to pull into a spot near the fountain at the entrance.

Priscilla clicked her seatbelt off, motioning for Maria to stay put. "I won't be long."

In case she found Mia at the front desk, she didn't want Maria there to catch her reaction. She flew in through the front doors. Her heart hammered against the books she had pressed against her rib cage.

Through the heavy doors she shot a glance at the front desk. Whew. No one. She made a beeline for the book deposit bin and slid her books through the hole. They made a dunk sound when they hit the metal on the other side.

In her periphery, she watched someone spring up at the noise.

Mia twisted around to collect the books from the bin but froze when she spotted Priscilla backing up toward the door. Wrinkles formed on her forehead, as Mia folded her arms to cover her name badge.

"Glad to see you're just dropping off instead of checking out."

She couldn't help herself. "What's that supposed to mean?"

"You seem to be a fan of checking out things." She tallied the list on her fingers. "Books, my ex-boyfriend Marcus ..."

Priscilla rolled her fists, blinking away tears as the memories from the dress shop resurged. "He came onto me."

"Yeah, right." Mia slammed her palms on the counter, leaning over the computer like an incensed book dragon. "I saw you two at the fair. You were flirting."

Uh huh, moments before I found out he was dating someone.

Priscilla weaved her fingers through her curls. "So you broke up with him and decided to make out with Carter to make things all better, huh?"

The whites of her eyes showed. "Yeah, like that 'made things better.'" She threw up air quotes. "He wasn't even into it. Didn't you see him trying to pull away? Arms like windmills. It was like doing a stage kiss." She swore. "He used to be able to kiss, too."

"What do you mean like a stage kiss?"

"I don't have to explain myself to you." She ran a book from a pile on the counter over a metal slab. "But if you must know, I do a bit of theater, and most guys who I've had to kiss on stage didn't fully commit. There was one who had a girlfriend when we were in a show together, and every stage kiss felt like I was making out with a dead fish."

Oof, yeah, she was sorry she'd asked. Didn't like that imagery.

But wait, that would mean that Carter didn't like the kiss at the front entrance. Now that she thought of it, he had tried to back away. And Mia *really* had her hands wound tight into that t-shirt fabric.

Like how Marcus came onto me in the dress store. That's what happened to Carter last night.

Had Carter also felt his blood drain when he thought about the kiss with Mia? How she took advantage of him, then stole something from him that she shouldn't have?

Did it also make him mistrust everyone all over again?

So he wasn't like her dad—a nice guy. He turned out to be a good one.

She jabbed a finger at Mia as she adjusted the strap of her bag on her shoulder. "Speaking of last night, you spotted me in the lobby. You were waiting for the right opportunity for me to exit, so I could see you two kissing."

"Look who decided to turn her brain on." She clacked away at the huge computer. "Heard about the dance from Grandpa and all about Carter and you. Figured he'd have to come out the front entrance eventually. When I saw him go to his car, I bolted out of mine."

Mia huffed before going back to the book pile on the front desk.

"But clearly I didn't get what I'd hoped for. It doesn't make

Marcus any less of a cheater. And it didn't make Carter any less of a prude. So you can have him back. Happy?"

Sparks dimmed in Priscilla's chest.

Although she didn't like Mia all that much, no one deserved a Marcus.

Prickles filled her cheeks when she thought about the incident at the dress shop. A mixture of anger ... and hurt.

"I'm sorry, Mia."

"For what? Making out with my boyfriend?"

Heat flared in her face again. She tried to blink away the memories with Marcus. Would she ever get over these? "That you can't seem to destroy that photograph by your bedside."

With that, she spun around, then bolted out the heavy doors to the library entrance, the bag and weight on her shoulders far lighter. She raced to the car, diving into the front seat. Maria was holding up Priscilla's phone.

"This thing won't stop buzzing. I think you better answer it."

"Carter."

She opened her phone. A shaky thumb tapped the green messages app, but instead of a new message from Carter, several from Pastor Timothy blinked in bold on the screen.

PASTOR TIMOTHY: Scarlett was taken to the hospital this morning. Her nurse found her on her bed, unresponsive. They think it might be that autoimmune disease acting up again. Please don't visit Country Acres. They've already taken her to the hospital in an ambulance.

PASTOR TIMOTHY: And be praying.

PASTOR TIMOTHY: It's looking grim.

Chapter Twenty-Seven
CARTER

"Don't you think I feel just terrible about what happened at Country Acres?" Carter's grandma placed a green puzzle piece next to one of the corners. She liked to start with the edges and work her way in. "It's been eating me alive. I didn't know he'd been engaged the day before."

She exhaled as she tried to fit two blue pieces together. They didn't.

"All I know is as soon as I saw Paul ... I don't know what came over me, but he looked like how I remembered him. Emotions came over me and ... I feel just terrible."

Carter pinched a puzzle piece with a pink spark drawn on the edge.

"Sorry, Grandma. I would've warned you, but I didn't put two and two together that *he* was your high school sweetheart." He flipped up the box to glimpse at the completed picture again, fireworks over a sunset and field. "Does this mean you won't check into Country Acres?" He set the lid back down.

Grandma leaned back into her chair with a shrug, fanning herself with the box lid.

"I wouldn't want to cause either of them more pain than necessary. Just"—she placed the lid next to a pile of napkins on the kitchen table—"at my age, you never expect anyone to get engaged or married. All the movies portray young couples, so you think you hit your expiration date past thirty."

Lip sagging, she pushed her seat back to shuffle over to the oven. She clicked a button on the oven that beeped as a light inside beamed on a pastry. She and Mom had decided to bake a pecan pie today. Sweet and nutty scents overwhelmed the kitchen, so they had to place box fans all around the room to cool down the room. Carter had said key lime would be easier, but apparently pecans went for cheaper at Trader Joe's.

"Still could use five more minutes." She clicked off the light to shuffle back to the table. "And to answer your question, I don't intend to stay there. There are plenty of assisted living homes in the area. Country Acres can get along fine without me."

She hmphed back into her seat, tearing her gaze over to a yellow folder on the table. The packet Pat had given Mom at Country Acres.

Last night, on his way downstairs to get a glass of water, he spied her flipping through its pages in the dim light of a family room lamp. Something told him Grandma liked that home a lot.

"Although I'm not disagreeing that Scarlett wouldn't like seeing you there, you sound hesitant."

The round edge of a puzzle piece rested against her chin before she found its brother, another corner piece. "I don't know, Carter. Something about that place made me feel, well, ten years younger. None of the others I've researched made me feel quite the same way."

"Felt like a slice of heaven?"

Her eyes flicked back to the oven. Cinnamon overpowered the kitchen now. "Something like that." She cleared her throat as she piled some napkins on the folder, to bury it. "As beautiful as that place was, I couldn't stay there while his fiancée lives at that home. Wouldn't want to break up a happy couple."

If she hadn't *already* caused a rift between Scarlett and Paul. Scarlett had stormed off, just like Priscilla at the entrance of the pavilion.

Even though Paul didn't text Scarlett, Carter imagined his attempts to knock at her door had gone in vain. Could a serenade of "Singing in the Rain" outside her window even salvage them now? From what he'd heard from Priscilla, Scarlett didn't trust men because her last husband cheated on her. If she caught Paul, the next day, cradling his high school sweetheart on the dance floor right after he proposed ... no wonder she fled in a fury.

And no wonder Priscilla did the same when she spotted him and Mia at the entrance doing a little more than just hugging.

He blinked away the memory, fist clenching. What if the genders were reversed between him and Mia? What would that be called—Mia forcing a kiss on him?

Just like she'd heavily influenced him to go farther than he wanted a few months back in that parking lot.

Carter blew out a long breath. This was a lot to take in.

He checked his phone again. Several new messages from Pastor blinked on the screen. Tapping on them, he read a moment, then visibly paled. He grabbed the keys from the wicker basket.

"Sorry, Grandma, I think you're going to have to eat that pie without me." With that, he swung open the front door and dashed to the car in the driveway.

Of all the things to find in the gift shop—among the "New Mom" t-shirts, emergency packs of deodorant, and toothbrushes for family members who waited in the lobby to hear news, good or terrible—Carter didn't expect to find Paul cradling a bouquet of red roses.

"Paul, they let you leave Country Acres?"

Startled, he jumped, knocking over a teddy bear off a display shelf. Carter bent to pick the toy up.

"I thought they didn't let people out unless they traveled in groups?" He thought back to the white bus they'd traveled in to get to the diner. And he'd overheard conversations about group trips to Wal-Mart or to the local fairs and art galleries in town.

"They made an exception."

Paul jerked his head over his shoulder at a woman in navy scrubs. Because he had seen so many nurses, he couldn't tell if she worked here or at Country Acres.

"Have you seen her yet?" Carter had arrived minutes ago, yet he thought about perusing the items in here to find something to bring up to Scarlett. No bath bombs adorned the shelves, not that they would let her take a bath anyway, but a stuffed elephant in a green dress tempted his fingers to snatch it up for the impulse buy. "Pastor hasn't texted me the room number yet."

"3870, I'm waiting to go in with someone. I have a feeling she hasn't forgiven me."

Stones plummeted from his heart into his intestines. That must've been the last time Paul saw her, over his grandma's shoulder when they hugged. If she passed from this world before he had a chance to reconcile …

Carter grabbed the elephant off the shelf and set it on the checkout counter. Handing the woman a twenty, he gave the gift to Paul. "Have a feeling she'll warm up to you when you give her this." He grimaced. "At least, it can prompt a discussion about talking about the elephant in the room."

The plastic encasing the roses crinkled when Paul set the elephant on top of it. He cast a wary glance at the elevators right by the Au Bon Pain.

"Follow me to her room, will you?"

"No problem, Paul. But once you two start kissing, I'm hightailing it out of there."

The elevators dinged and a man with a walker stepped off, accompanied by a younger woman. His daughter, Carter assumed. They stepped on before the doors slid shut. He counted the floors until they reached number three.

They followed the signs down the hallway until they approached a set of closed doors. Paul clicked a silver button connected to a camera that scanned them in the hallway before the entrance swung open.

Two doors down, a yellow curtain separated them from Scarlett's room. Behind a round nurse's desk, a woman typed at a laptop. They'd entered the ICU unit. At least, that's what he could tell from the dark blue signs they followed.

Each visitor pumped a fistful of hand sanitizer onto their palms to rub in before they stepped into her room.

A polka dot hospital gown and nostril oxygen tubes adorned her, but otherwise, she still appeared as a teen. Albeit a sunken-eyed teen with wires jutting every which direction.

The heart monitor above her bed beeped. Everything in the room smelled ... yellow. He remembered back in English class they'd read a short story called "The Yellow Wallpaper." Although he had skimmed most of the story, he remembered the author had described the room as having a yellow smell. He didn't understand that until now.

Yellow smelled like sickness. Green like grass and health. How two colors so close together could smell so different, he couldn't tell why.

Scarlett's closed eyelids peered open in slits. With shaking arms, Paul produced the gifts, then placed them on the white blanket on her lap. Carter wished they would turn on the lights in this room. Beams from the blinds stopped by the bedside, rendering Scarlett's expression indiscernible.

"Scar"—Paul wrung his hands—"what you saw in the Bingo Hall. I want you to know that—I would never. No one could—"

"Oh, you ridiculous man." She sat up in her angled bed as she scrunched the pillow underneath her neck. "Hours after I returned to my room, I knew that something felt off about your face. When I'd asked my husband why he cheated when I found him out, he looked panicked. Cornered. You. You looked concerned, confused, hurt."

She winced and bunched her pillow more.

"I knew I'd seen her face before in a yearbook of yours from when I watched a movie with you in your room. Face had no wrinkles and no back hunched over, obviously, but you could tell it was her." She jabbed her nose. "This part of her was the same."

Why didn't I see it before? All those years, scanning those old photo books in her basement.

"But I knew that she must've hugged you because you weren't completely embracing her back. Looked like an awkward chicken. I'd half a mind to get out of bed to go talk to you, but I couldn't move. Everything was on fire. Tried to hit the call button but couldn't muster the strength to even lift my arm. My nurse found me the next morning and rushed me here."

Well, her tongue certainly hadn't stopped working.

"You-you're not—?"

"*Dios mio.* No. I'm not angry at you. And it's about time you got here. The nurses haven't given me any more juice, so I'm dying of thirst. That lady at the front desk keeps ignoring me when I hit the call button. Something tells me she is jealous of my looks."

She lifted a hand to bounce a curl before dropping it back on the bed.

Carter snickered. "Glad to see you're recovering, Scar."

Shadows fell over her face as she laced her fingers together on her lap. Did he say something wrong? Sure, a wan hue had dyed her skin and eye bags hung from her eyelids, but most patients at hospitals typically looked like that.

He clapped Paul's back, then gestured toward the door. "I think I'll leave you two lovebirds alone."

Marching into the hallway, he wondered why it felt like someone had dropped a weight on his shoulders. And why he was struggling to breathe. Something about that yellow smell.

Chapter Twenty-Eight
PRISCILLA

PRISCILLA FOUND HERSELF CAUGHT in the hallway between rooms. Down the hall, Grandpa was eating Jell-O on a tray table. He wanted her to leave the room because he kept laughing, subsequently spraying the contents all over his hospital gown.

Or so he claimed. She couldn't help but notice however his lips and arms kept trembling when he held the spoon.

Down the other end of the hall, Scarlett's room was shrouded by a yellow curtain. The nurses usually put that up when they wanted to prep someone for an operation, but also some patients wanted their privacy in ICU.

She didn't want to venture back into the hallway again for fear that she would bother the front nurse by having to click the button, so they could catch her on camera to let her in.

So she pressed herself against the wall, next to a painting of a purple flower, and waited. All the rooms in the ICU were curtained, including Grandpa's.

The doors ahead clicked as a nurse rushed past her, pushing a cart of some kind.

She folded her arms, then glanced at the Purell stationed next to her. Well, had to do something to pass the time. She stuck her hands underneath for a glop of foamy hand sanitizer to fall onto her palms. Rubbing, she glanced at the doors which clicked again.

And let in Elena.

Elena cradled a bouquet of yellow roses in her arms, to match the flower in her hair. Battling the squirmy sensation in her intestines, Priscilla glanced left and right before she realized that she couldn't duck and hide behind anything. Like when she found Mia in the library, she had to confront this one too.

"You never took your casserole home."

The other froze by a tissue box set on the counter of the nurse's desk. Elena brushed off a hair on her skirt, then stepped toward Priscilla, a pitiable expression stamped onto her face. "How is he doing?"

Priscilla sighed as she leaned against the wall again. So she'd play the game this way. Fine. Her shoulders relaxed. She didn't feel much like putting up a fight either.

"Fine, from what we can tell. I think it's possible that he can make a recovery if he promises to take better care of himself at home." She pinched the bridge of her nose. "Might have to check him into Country Acres soon, since Maria can't provide round-the-clock care." The yellow flowers caught her eye. "Also, congratulations."

Elena reached for her empty ring finger before clasping her hands. "For what?"

"Your dad got engaged." Carter had mentioned the connection between the families to her a while back. When? She couldn't remember. Not now. All her memories held static in her brain right now.

She said this deadpan, then went on to explain the story of their engagement when she was met with a confused expression from Elena. Setting the flowers on the welcome desk, Elena wrapped herself in a hug, hobbling from one heel to the next.

"I didn't know he was planning to do it so soon. He'd spoken about the next month or so, but not the moment he received that package at the front desk."

"Well, the wedding might have to be cancelled anyway."

With a thumb jab, she gestured to the yellow curtain that barricaded Scarlett's room. To think, she could lose her grandpa and friend in a matter of days.

No, not to think. Not now.

"I'm sorry to hear that." Wrinkles formed frowny faces on Elena's forehead. "I brought these for your grandpa when he opens the room again. And"—plastic casing crinkled—"I was hoping that maybe we could pick up our conversation where we left it at the house."

Air puffed out her nostrils when Priscilla flared them.

Just what she needed with two close companions checked into a hospital. But weakness drained at her muscles and pulled down on her eyelids. Much as she wanted to fight Elena, like she had Mia, something told her it wasn't worth it.

Not now with shadows looming under the yellow curtains.

"Let's find a place to sit." Priscilla massaged her calf muscles that had grown stiff, then gestured at two chairs stationed in a hallway with a water cooler. "I've been standing nonstop since when I got here."

Elena appeared to like the idea, so they parked on the chairs. Beeps from nearby heart monitors filled the silence. Priscilla drew her knees up to her chest with a sigh.

"Listen, Elena, I know it's not your fault that my dad ran off or that he chose to take a liking to you." A nurse rushed down the hallway with a clipboard in hand. "I just don't know what to say to him. We haven't talked my whole life, and it wasn't the best introduction finding him with his arms wrapped around someone … who wasn't my mom on the beach."

In her periphery, Elena nodded, then rubbed her forehead. "I know, also it wasn't fair for me to barge into your house and try to force a conversation. He does want to talk with you, but only when you're ready."

Priscilla drew her knees tighter until her air almost constricted. "I don't know if I'll ever be."

"No, dear, I suppose no one ever is. I thought my father would be with his wife forever, but now he has found someone else. Give yourself time. Here's his number." She reached into her purse to pull out a black and white business card. "No rush or pressure, but give him a ring when you feel most ready to do so."

Another nurse in blue scrubs brushed past them on the march toward Grandpa's room. Moments later, she pulled back the curtain. The chained strings holding it gave a ding as she slid them.

Elena pressed on her knees as she lifted herself, armed with roses. They perfumed the hallway with a wet, green scent.

"Be right back. Going to deliver these to the champ."

She raised her hand to give Priscilla's shoulder a squeeze, thought better of it, then marched toward the room. Behind the half of the yellow curtain remaining, she vanished.

Guess that answered the question on what room to visit first. She rose from the chair, by habit sticking her hand underneath the hand sanitizer machine.

Her ears tickled when she heard another curtain slide open. Scarlett's.

She turned on her heel, expecting to find a family member or maybe even Paul, if Country Acres would let him out. Instead, Carter trudged out with his hands slammed into his shorts pockets. He looked funny with his flip flops in a hospital, but everyone in Florida wore sandals everywhere.

His face flushed as he caught her eye, bright lights all around him highlighting every freckle.

"Priscilla, I—"

She rushed toward him and snagged him in a hug. They tumbled backwards, almost ramming into a wall with a pull-down fire alarm. Good thing they protected that in glass.

"I ran into Mia at the library." Against his chest she rested her head, tilted to the right to prevent her voice being muffled. He smelled like a pine tree. Too much cologne, but still, nice. "She came onto you. I know that now." His cheeks flushed again. So he must've felt the same way about Mia ... that she had about Marcus.

How long would it take for them to trust other people again?

She firmed her jaw. No, couldn't think about that now. Too many other weights on her shoulders ...

They pulled apart as Priscilla crumpled the business card in her palms. She shoved it into her pocket, and the two of them, hand in hand, returned to the seats from earlier.

"So we're still on for that ice cream date?" He sounded hesitant. No wonder he had spent so much of summer underneath a filter, with how much Mia had hurt him.

"As soon as my grandpa and Scarlett make a miraculous recovery, yeah."

"Your grandpa?"

As she explained, shadows covered his features.

"Oh gosh, Priscilla, I'm sorry. I didn't know you were here for both of them. I assumed—"

"It's fine. Trying not to think too much. Is she at least doing all right?"

His teeth clenched but his cheeks bubbled when he blew a breath out. A man in a ponytail handed pamphlets to a family standing outside a room. He stopped by each of their chairs to give them.

On the cover, an illustration of Jesus with children at his feet said "Jesus Loves You." Carter waited until the man disappeared behind double doors. He thumbed the sunglasses strapped to his chest.

Good thing the sunglasses held on for dear life when Mia had kissed him. With the way she'd twisted her fingers around his shirt, they could've fallen and cracked on the concrete below.

"I'm not sure. Scarlett seems to be chatty, like usual, but she looked different. Something tells me I'm glad I can still see her as a teen. If she looked like her normal self, I might lose hope."

The curtain to her room swished open for Paul to shuffle out. Immediately, she and Carter sprung to their feet to offer their chairs, but he held up his hand with a jerk of his chin.

"Been sitting all day. Please."

As they sank back into their chairs, Priscilla watched his expression, hoping she could read something into the lines that had formed under his eyes. Even though he looked seventeen, in this lighting, he aged at least twenty years.

"They've already issued a DNR for her."

Priscilla squinted her eyes while hurt and moisture filled them. In her periphery, Carter rubbed his chin. "What does that mean?"

"If her heart fails, they won't resuscitate her." Priscilla swallowed then hunched over her knees, attempting to digest the new information. "This doesn't make any sense. At the dance, she was doing just fine. Why did this happen all of a sudden?"

Paul leaned against the wall and traced a crack he found.

"She's been fighting this for years. Had a number of medical scares throughout the past decade. With her not eating as much as she should, and overexerting herself at the dance, her body decided it was time to quit." He sighed as he rubbed red-rimmed eyelids. "Kidneys are failing, and the nurses are giving her a couple days at most."

"Can't she get someone to donate?"

"Not enough time, doesn't qualify, and other organs are shutting down too. We have days. Maybe even just today."

She pulled her knees against her chest again, clamping her eyelids shut. Dizziness overcame her. For a moment, she couldn't fight the sensation of spinning, falling, and floating at the same time.

When the room stopped turning, she released her knees and tried to breathe. No luck.

"So what do we do now?"

"Stay by her side. Ask her for last wishes." His voice cracked. "Say goodbye."

Carter's thumbs chased each other around in a circle. He stopped to glance up, eyes bright.

"Did she ever have something she wanted to do that she didn't? Maybe we could make that happen."

He was looking at Priscilla for the answers, but how could she summon any? She had only known Scarlett for a handful of weeks. Sure, she learned plenty over Pinochle and painting, but enough to recall any dying wishes?

She glanced at her ring finger which displayed the purity ring her mom had bought her for her twelfth birthday. She twisted it around staring at the single amethyst gem that adorned it.

"I know she wanted to get married. Like, actually married. Her last husband basically made them do a fake wedding and never signed any court papers. But." She stopped twisting the jewelry. The amethyst against her palm. "I don't know if we could pull that off in less than a day." She leaned forward to glance at a clock over the nurse's desk. "It's almost noon already."

"Sure we can."

Carter had risen in his chair and pulled out his phone. He typed something into a search engine, then waved an article in front of her eyes. The brightness of the screen burned her retinas.

"See? This couple managed to pull off a hospital wedding in seven hours. When they found out a woman had a terminal illness, they got to work that day and pulled everything together. I remember watching a YouTuber talk about it."

Seven hours? Was that possible?

Maria emerged from Grandpa's room with a large cup full of sweet tea from Au Bon Pain. No way she could leave the hospital now with both her grandpa and Scarlett ill.

"They may have pulled it off, Carter, but I don't know if we can."

Elena trailed right behind Maria. She pinched a leaf that had fallen onto her skirt before she binned it in a wastebasket by the nurse's desk. Carter waved the two over to explain the idea for a wedding-in-a-day. Priscilla chewed on her cheek, listening, until he reached the part about the court documents.

"See, that might be a problem. Most states require you to wait three days after you sign those. I'd read a book on this, and the only exceptions are if you do a premarital course. And they just got engaged." She squeezed her eyelids to prevent an onslaught of tears. Not now. Crying could come later. "We don't have three days."

"They can make an exception." Elena brushed some loose strands of hair behind her ear in a nervous fashion. "I work in the Planning and Development department and know the office manager of the City Clerk's office. He owes me a few favors. Especially when it involves my dad getting married." She squeezed her dad in a side hug, resting her head on his shoulder.

Whoa. Would they bend the law to make this happen?

She didn't care. Crazier requests happened on deathbeds. And they owed Scarlett a real wedding after the disaster with the last one.

A nurse in scrubs yanked a plastic smock out of a bin, drew it over her head, and headed to Grandpa's curtained room.

"I don't know if I can help you with Grandpa Silas also being in the ICU."

Maria sidled next to her to pat her on the back. "You go and keep your phone on you. I'll let you know if anything happens, but I'll give him a stern talking to. Not allowed to get any sicker."

Her arms formed triangles on her hips. Priscilla's lips titled.

"Okay, so what all do we have to do to make a wedding happen?"

Elena pulled out a pen she had nestled in her pocket before twisting around to find a sheet of paper. Carter found a "Jesus Loves You" booklet on a side table and handed it to her. Ponytail guy must've deposited this. Elena found a blank page meant for a "Gratitude Journal."

Upside down, the notes read:

Wedding Dress
Wedding Documents (Elena)
Pastor to officiate
Decorations (if possible)
Flowers?
Cake or a dessert?

Carter snapped a picture of the list with his phone, then reached for Priscilla's hand. "We can take most of these items. While Elena gets the documents, we'll swing by Country Acres to enlist the help of the residents. Get them to salvage whatever decorations we had from the dance and create some more if they can." He squeezed her hand. "Then we'll work on the dress, pastor, and flowers if we have time."

"Don't worry about flowers." Elena unclipped the flower from her hair. "I have dozens of these at home. I could just glue them together and wrap them in parchment. No one can tell the difference in that dark lighting in that room."

"Okay, so the pastor, decorations, and the dress. We can do this."

He ordered Paul to stay put and give Scarlett as much company as possible, before marching down the hallway hand in hand with Priscilla.

They would make this wedding happen if it killed them.

Chapter Twenty-Nine
CARTER

"I'M AFRAID YOU CAUGHT ME AT A BAD TIME." In his church office, Pastor Timothy rubbed a greasy spot on his forehead. "I've been called to officiate a funeral this evening, and don't know if I could swing both events at the same time. You said six or seven o'clock at night?"

Carter's foot nudged the wooden desk in Pastor Timothy's office.

Six or seven hours is what they'd planned. And although several churches lined the downtown square, none of them knew Priscilla or Carter. Or the two lovebirds getting hitched that day. And Scarlett would want a pastor ... she didn't get a traditional wedding the first time around.

"What if we made the wedding earlier? Say, five o'clock?"

Priscilla cut him a glance from her chair before settling her gaze on an oval paperweight on the desk. Inside the glass, a silver cross gleamed in the dim lighting of the office.

I know, I know. We're already cutting it short if we go with six hours. But we don't have much of a choice.

Pastor Timothy's eyes roamed the bookshelves, the ceiling fan, the floor, anything to avoid their stare.

"'Fraid that I have at least an hour's drive to the funeral. And it starts at six. Latest I could officiate a ceremony, without running late to the funeral, would be four o'clock."

The couple's eyes met across the seats. Carter slid his phone an inch out of his pocket to check the time. They'd already lost half an hour on the drive over here from the hospital. Gotta love small-town Florida, where the medical centers kept a safe, introverted distance.

Priscilla tilted her chin, then jerked it over her shoulder. "Would you give us a few minutes, Pastor?"

She didn't wait for a response before rising and stepping into the hallway. Carter followed her several paces down the hall to where she deemed the distance far enough away from the office.

"There isn't any other pastor who is in the office today?"

"I think they're all out on some pastor's retreat. Didn't you hear the announcement on Sunday? Plus, I know he's officiated weddings before, even in a pinch. He's our only hope at the moment."

With a sigh, she lifted the corner of a picture hanging in the hallway to get a better look at it. This one was Jonah about to be swallowed by a whale.

"Listen, I wish we had other options, too, but we don't have time to explore anything else. If we want a pastor, we need to bump the time of the wedding to four."

"But that only gives us a little more than three hours. If they pitched all the decorations from the dance ..."

"We'll cut up gloves and disposable aprons to look like snowflakes. If Scarlett's mom ate onions mixed with peanut butter during the Depression, we'll use what we have, okay?"

She cupped his chin, giving his cheek a squeeze.

"Okay." She dropped her arm to take a swipe at her lip. Once again, the church had decided against AC today. Lucky for them, their next stop, Country Acres, liked to blast the cool air to seventy-something degrees inside.

Priscilla blew out a breath before marching back to the office. "Room 3870 at four o'clock. Do not be late."

She popped her head out of the doorframe, then slammed the door before they could catch wind of Pastor's reaction to the bluntness held in her voice. Sure, she'd talked to Carter that way but never an adult. Goodness, what had Scarlett done to her?

And why did she suddenly become twice as attractive now?

He slid the phone out of his pocket to message the group text to let them know about the new deadline for the wedding. Here was hoping that Elena found her friend at city hall and nabbed the documents. She could hopefully pick up a cake or some other treat in addition to getting the flowers.

A quick scroll through the chat indicated no one had any more updates. That was both good and terrible. Good because that meant Scarlett hadn't deteriorated any more, but bad because no one else had managed to check another item off the list.

The lights burned his eyes when Priscilla swung open the doors in the church foyer to the outside. He tapped on his keyboard once more to change the name of the group text:

A MARRIAGE MADE IN HEAVEN

"If we have any decorations left over from the dance, we would have put them in here."

Pat jammed the keys into a knob. The doors stood near where the bingo caller would roll the cage. No wonder they hadn't noticed these doors before. They painted them the same color as the walls.

With a creak, the doors swung open, and she flicked on a light switch. A single bulb buzzed over a pile of various large rolls of colored paper, cans of sparkles, and pipe cleaners that jutted in every direction. Pat swung the keys around her finger before turning to leave them with a wave. "Hope the ceremony is beautiful."

"Think you can make it, Pat?" Priscilla had begun plucking up white pipe cleaners with silver sparkles, very wedding-esque. "Maybe you could drive some of the residents in the van. We could always use a congregation."

Huh, they hadn't added people to the list. But he supposed he, Priscilla, Maria, and Elena didn't make that big of a wedding party. Even in a hospital bed, she probably would love to see some more people there.

"I don't know if they let more than three visitors at a time into those ICU rooms. Germs and all that." Pat clasped her hands. "But I can see what I can do."

Brilliant. With three hours to go, they might actually pull this thing off.

He kicked past a fallen-over stack of orange papers to fish through a shiny netting roll for the contents beneath it. Priscilla grabbed the roll from him, placing it in a stack outside the doors. She paused, then glanced at the back wall, at the quote, which silver streamers no longer covered.

"People who say such things show that they are looking for a country of their own."

She shoved the stack to the side, rubbed her forehead with the back of her arm, and returned to the hodge-podge closet. "Is it just me, or do you think the quote says something different without the mist?"

"The mist?"

Priscilla explained how in stories like *The Odyssey* gods and goddesses would cover something or someone with a mist to disguise their true form from the naked eye. He saw something like that in a Percy Jackson movie once.

"So I feel like that quote back there has to be something else like, 'Live, Laugh, Love,' or 'Keep Calm and Carry On.'" Her knees cracked as she squatted to retrieve a bundle of fairy lights. "Something you'd see on a t-shirt."

"Yeah. I've also wondered why they look like teens when we leave this place, too. Figured the sunglasses or fun mirrors theories somehow played into that. Ever figure out why we were given the gift in the first place?"

"I thought it was to challenge my thinking. I wasn't a fan of people in our generation until I had to spend time with someone who looked *and* acted like a teen."

Strings coiled around her arm.

"Right, but I don't have a problem with young people." He stretched his arm to reach a giant string of pearls from the dance. It fell underneath a poster board. "But maybe it challenged me too. Before this, I couldn't even have a conversation with Grandma. After Paul, well, today she and I were baking pies and doing puzzles."

He lunged, managing to snag the string to pull them up.

"Priscilla, do you think it'll ever wear off? The gift?"

She reached for her glasses which had almost slid off her nose. "If it hasn't by now, I don't see why it would."

Both of their phones vibrated on the gym floor, one after the other. The group text must've gone off. He tossed his pearls onto her pile, then scooped up his phone. Elena had messaged.

ELENA: My friend at the office has gone out to lunch and isn't answering his phone. I might not see him for another hour. He takes LONG lunches. His office seems to be rather dead, everyone's on vacation right now, trying to get away from the Florida sun. Shouldn't be long once he's back, but don't know if I can grab the cake and flowers in time, since they're in opposite directions. Will keep you posted.

After Priscilla threw some blue and white streamers onto the pile, she scanned his expression.

"What went wrong?"

"We might have to end up getting flowers or cake."

She weaved her fingers through her hair. Her hands started at the bottom and worked her way to the top before she spoke.

"This is a disaster."

Tears streamed from the corners of her eyes as she crumpled to the ground. He rushed over to place a hand on her back.

"Hey, hey, it's fine. She'll enjoy the wedding if there's a cake or not. I don't even know if she can eat cake at this—"

Her sobs intensified.

He waited in silence. She muffled her cries with her palms as she rocked back and forth. When the noises quieted, she unrolled herself and tore off her glasses to wipe down her face.

"It's not—it's not the flowers or the cake. It's, well, everything. Last I saw her, she was dancing with Paul, and now she has tubes trying to keep her alive. So now we have to scramble to get her the per-perfect wedding. She deserves so much better."

"Listen to me, I'm a hopeless romantic. Would I love her to have a huge wedding in Italy, surrounded by four hundred of her closest friends? Yes." He squeezed her shoulder into his. "But right now, she has her closest friends and a man she loves. And that's enough."

She trembled in his arm, using the corner of her shirt to clean her glasses.

"You're right." She shoved the glasses back on to squint through a blur of wiped tears. "So let's make enough count."

Chapter Thirty
PRISCILLA

SHE FROWNED AT THE DRESS RACKS, finger pointed at the size listings above the wedding dresses.

Although she'd seen the teen version of Scarlett and could hazard a guess as to her dress size by what she remembered, she didn't know the dimensions of the older Scarlett. Grandpa Silas's wife, before she passed away, had lost so much weight that she would drown in a size four dress. But other women she'd seen at her knitting club, the grandmothers of the group, had earned a full-bellied stomach pouch.

Lips sagging, she filtered her way through the price tags on the dresses. Even though the store owners sold them between $100-$150, she hoped they wouldn't stray much beyond that. Even with her checkbook on her in the bag strung over her shoulder, most of the funds in that account were meant to go toward college.

Eh, she could splurge for Scarlett. She deserved a nice dress anyway.

Now for sizing.

She turned to Carter who was standing off to the side, awkwardly grasping at his arm. Men.

"Any idea what size she is in real life?"

"Your guess is as good as mine."

Jennie, the shop owner, quirked a brow over a nail file at the front desk. She shoved the file into a drawer and blew on the nail shavings.

"Can I help you two find anything?"

"A wedding dress for my ... friend. Shotgun wedding, you know?"

"Sure, no judgment here. We get all kinds of customers. Retirees who want to finally tie the knot. Teens who just graduated. Any idea what size range we're talking about?" She slid a dress with gaudy beads to the side. "Or if she can stop by here to try something on?"

"Oh, well, I'm not sure if she can."

Priscilla winced but explained the situation in the hospital. Jennie's face fell. She chewed on a hangnail as she turned her chin to avoid meeting their eyes.

"Gosh, real sorry to hear about that. You know what, take whatever dress you want. On the house. We get all these from donations anyway."

With that, she slid one more garment to the side, one that seemed to magnetize feathers from every white fowl on earth, then disappeared behind a curtain that led to a back room. Warmth filled Priscilla's chest like a glow.

What a good person.

"I guess we can splurge more on the cake." She slid the feather dress to the right. "If we can even fit a cake with all the decorations we threw into your trunk and back seat. But we don't even know remotely what size to pick."

Carter shrugged with a motion to his phone. "We can text Maria to find out."

A second later, her bag buzzed. He had sent the text. He read the content of it to her.

CARTER: Maria, any chance you can slip out of Silas's room and guess what size dress Scarlett might be?

Metal hangers slid to the right in a rapid motion. A ball gown with cheap-looking sequins. Some slim fitting lacy thing that could constrict even the skinniest of Minnies. A plain white dress with no frills, nothing, far too simple for Scarlett.

Her bag buzzed again. Bright light stunned her periphery when Carter checked.

"You might want to take a look at your phone, Priscilla."

A thunderclap beat against her rib cage when she fished her phone out of her bag.

MARIA: She's deteriorating, not sure if she can do much except move her neck a little. Says her back and hips kill. Probably because her kidneys won't function much anymore. We had to bring in two nurses to help her adjust to a more comfortable position in the bed.

Rocks plummeted in her chest. She slammed her eyelids shut to prevent any more tears from leaking out.

"Do you think we should just get a fancy one and drape it over her?"

"Like a blanket? I don't know, that seems a little odd." Carter feigned interest in a sparkly belt on a circular display. "But I suppose it doesn't hurt to ask Maria."

Before his three dots in the group text could say anything, her phone buzzed again with a new message from Maria.

MARIA: She says she wants Priscilla to wear it for her.

So she knew about the wedding. Between two poofy dresses, she hunched her neck over to clamp her teeth down hard on her bottom lip. Why her? She'd sworn off wedding gowns for herself ever since she watched her mom refuse to go on dates with men, but now ...

"I don't know if I can do that, Carter. It's her wedding."

"Who knows? She might see part of herself in you. You saw the text from Maria, she can't use her arms and legs anymore. So we just have to be those things for her."

She breathed in the acrid perfume from the fabrics. Then pulled her head out and tilted her chin to him.

She nodded.

"Help me pick one out, please."

They ventured to the sizes eight through ten, filtering through dresses full of brown and yellow stains, not to mention torn lace. Ordinarily, if she had to pick one, for say a costume party or themed event at the library back home, she would've chosen the one with the most holes or frayed seams, to give someone else a chance at finding their dream gown.

But she couldn't risk that. This time, they had to pick something Scarlett would love. Something bold, beautiful, unafraid of anything ... even now.

"Got one."

He swung a dress out from the rack, then drew the fabric close to his chest. If not for the time crunch or gravity of the situation, she would've giggled at the sight. She scanned the garment up and down. Ball gown skirt, silver beads and lace running down the bodice to the skirt with lace statement sleeves running all the way down to the elbows of the dress. When he spun the garment around, she felt the heat rise to her cheeks. The back plunged all the way to the hips in a V.

Ridiculous, loud, and proud. Priscilla would never be caught dead in a thing like that in a million years.

"It's perfect. Let's go try it on."

Elena had sent two text messages on their way to get the cake. The first, to the group text.

ELENA: Got the documents (finally). Should've known Lewis would come back late when talking with his rugby teammates at a sports bar. Racing home now to concoct the bouquet. Thank you two so much for volunteering to get the cake. Sorry I dropped the ball on that one.

Then she'd sent one to Priscilla in a private message.

ELENA: I hope you don't mind, but your father wanted to attend the wedding as well. He's been playing guitar for well over a decade and can play some of her favorite songs. Have any requests?

She threaded her fingers into her hair with a groan. Carter, in the middle of a highway merge, waited to speak until they swerved into the right lane.

"Please tell me that they didn't bump up the time of the ceremony." His engine chugged, giving her notice to a Christmas tree of lights illuminated on the dashboard. It looked like he needed an oil change, tire pump, and a dozen other repairs. "Because we only have an hour and a half left to get the cake, get the decorations set up, and get started."

A lot of gets and not a lot of gives. Yeah, they'd cut it close.

"No, we're fine on time. She wants my dad to play guitar at the ceremony."

"That seems ... complicated."

"She of all people should know that this is a *horrible* time to do this. With my grandpa and Scarlett at death's door, the last thing I need is for my dad, who I haven't seen my whole life, showing up to play an instrument. Doesn't help that Scarlett had married *his* father either."

Yeah, "complicated" appeared to fit that description. She leaned back in her seat, trying to let the lyrics from Carter's indie playlist drown out her thoughts. But a beep from his phone indicated he had shut off the music.

Her eyelids flew open in time to watch an ibis soar overhead. Gray clouds shrouded the skies. In time for a typical summer thunderstorm in Florida.

"Priscilla, I'm not going to pretend like I have a solution for this. Not that I get along great with my own folks, but if anything, it adds one more body to the room. Knowing her, if we could stuff in all the people from the hospital, she would love that."

Her lips curved toward her nose at the thought. She imagined grabbing family members off couches and chairs in the lobby to go to a wedding of a random hospital patient. Who knew? It could come to that.

"Yeah, I guess so."

"And there's no rule that you have to talk with him at the ceremony. If you want, I can stare him down. Give *him* the talk. 'If you hurt my girl, I'll come after you, kill you, and make it look like an accident, you hear?'"

Laughter bubbled in her throat. She'd never imagined anyone could reverse *the talk*.

"You're a good guy, Carter. You know that?"

Scarlet covered his cheeks, but he refocused to jab a finger at a green highway sign. Their exit.

Time for cake.

Puffing out a sigh, as they approached a stoplight, she tapped a quick message to Elena.

PRISCILLA: She loves "Singing in the Rain." But so help me, if he gets one note wrong, I'm throwing his guitar out the window.

Three dots preceded the next message.

ELENA: He won't miss a note. See you soon <3

They rolled into a parking spot at Publix and slammed the doors. Wind kicked up at her skirt; the temperatures had already cooled by ten degrees or so. Even though she never thought she'd adjust to the Florida heat, now she could tell to some degree why they would wear winter coats in fifty-degree weather.

She dashed toward a navy sign with "Bakery" etched in a light brown font. Cakes and cream-based pastries decorated small display windows near a silver checkout counter. They reached the case, smacking palms against the glass. A quick scan of each cake. The one with strawberries that formed a star looked nice but didn't scream "wedding." One had chocolate dripping down the sides, but that felt more like something for a birthday.

Carter eyed her in her periphery.

"Priscilla."

"Mmm?"

"You're making the same face you did in the dress shop."

"What face?"

"It's all scrunched up like you smelled something bad. Which, of course, is impossible in a bakery." He gestured to cases of pies in a stack on a table nearby. "We both would love to make this perfect. And in a perfect world, she could wear the dress, we'd have it in a huge church packed to the brim, and Charlie Puth would play the music."

"Yeah, umm, scratch that last part, weirdo."

"What I'm saying is, get that strawberry cake. Or the chocolate one. No one cares, and in that dark room, you can't tell the difference anyway."

She rested her chin on her thumb before giving the white cake another scan. The strawberries did look festive in the star arrangement. They matched some dresses she'd seen Scarlett wear. She approached the man at the counter and motioned at the cake. He left to find a lid to encase it.

Once again, her bag vibrated. They pulled out their phones at the same time.

One after another the texts came, causing the devices to buzz so much that her palms felt numb.

ELENA: The hot glue gun got jammed might have to start over on this flower bouquet.

MARIA: No time for that. She's in a lot of pain right now. I think we need to rush the ceremony.

ELENA: By how much?

MARIA: Just get over here when you can. They're trying to hold off on morphine for now. Soon as she gets that, she may not be lucid again.

ELENA: Grabbing the court documents. Does anyone have a hold of the pastor officiating? Can he come sooner?

Shallow breaths trailed off her lips as she read each text again and again. Over her shoulder, Carter mentioned something about a twenty-dollar bill before handing something to the man behind the counter. Then, he clapped a hand on her shoulder.

"I'll call Pastor Timothy. He's not doing anything earth-shattering until that funeral later, anyway. Don't worry about anything. Just get there, get in the dress, and I'll handle everything else, okay?"

Sounds of shopping carts whirring around the aisles and beeps from the checkout stations blurred into one ringing note in her ears. All of this was happening so fast. Her eyes darted back to meet his. Warmth crawled onto her bones where he touched.

They could do this. She could do this. She had to.

"Okay."

Chapter Thirty-One
CARTER

SOMEHOW, HE MANAGED TO FIND a parking spot on the first level of the deck. Score, considering this afternoon he had to venture up at least three levels. It paid to arrive around three o'clock at a hospital.

He popped open the trunk, then reached over the back seat to toss the dress into her outstretched arms. "Lucky that Pastor can make it, huh? If he runs late, we can have your dad play an extra song or something." He ignored the glare. "Now go put this on and run upstairs. The groom isn't supposed to see you in it until the ceremony starts."

"Carter, the groom is Paul."

"For now." He winked as he gathered as many pipe cleaners, sheer sheets, and fairy lights into his arms as he could.

Footsteps echoed down the parking deck walls as Priscilla charged down the slope to the left toward the parking lot. The train of the wedding dress flapped like a parasail in her arms.

Some pipe cleaners dropped onto the ground, but he followed while saying a quick prayer that he could race back and forth between room and trunk enough times before the ceremony started. Maybe Maria would be willing to throw up some of the decorations.

Hopefully no one felt like stealing items out of his trunk, since he left it open. No time or arm flexibility to close it right now.

When he reached the outside, sparse raindrops tickled the pavement. He'd have to hurry.

A white bus swung around the emergency pickup entrance, so he read the cursive "Country Acres" stamped onto the side. Pat climbed out first and gave him a curt jerk of the chin.

"Room 3870, Pat."

"You need help, young man?"

"Don't you need to escort the residents?"

"I meant, they also wanted to help with whatever they could."

"Really?" He squinted at the tinted windows. Every seat appeared to have a head by the window. They must've brought a full house to her wedding. "Do you think they can?"

Pat frowned.

"You'd think, by now, Mr. Carter that you wouldn't make assumptions based on someone's age. They're willing and able, also stronger than you think." She outstretched her arms and scooped up the materials in his. "We'll help set these up. Go get the rest of the materials."

He saluted her with two fingers, then dashed back into the parking deck to the open truck. No pilferers yet.

Cake, more sheets, and lights in arm, he barreled down the slope but had to skitter his heel to prevent himself from slipping on the puddles that had formed on the sidewalk. Weddings were dangerous things. Ahead, under the roofed entrance, a flash of white caught his eye. The last of the residents hobbled off the bus to where Priscilla waited with her arms outstretched in a wedding dress.

"Wow, beautiful." Only two words slipped off his tongue, but they seemed to suffice.

Meanwhile, his skin prickled in irritation when the rain dewed his arms.

"Priscilla, go upstairs. You're going to get the dress wet."

"There's a horde of people already heading up there to decorate."

She pulled up on the bodice. The dress didn't fit her everywhere, but for the most part, it squeezed her in the right places, flaunting everything else that needed it. He especially liked the way the lace caressed her arms, like it was part of her.

"I'm able to help get things set up. Now, give, lover boy."

He did so, and she spun around with an armload of decorations. The train of her dress mopped the sidewalk leading up to the entrance, but thank God they covered that area with a roof. She vanished behind two sliding doors, then he raced to his trunk to grab what was left.

For the last load, he had to stuff all the streamers underneath his shirt.

By now, the rain was slapping against the pavement. Even though ten- or fifteen-feet's distance stood between the parking deck and the hospital entrance, he didn't want to risk soggy paper. He hunched forward into a sprint toward the doors. Beads of water pelted his cheeks, and then, at last, he reached the dry space. He stood a moment to listen to the rain drum on the sloped roof where it slid off onto the flower bushes below.

Hold on, flower bushes.

Elena hadn't managed to complete that hair-flower bouquet. With a free arm, he plucked a few handfuls of pink blooms for a makeshift hairpiece. He whipped his head over his shoulder to make sure no hospital worker had caught him in the act, but if they had, they might understand. Like the woman at the dress shop, maybe they wouldn't worry.

Fragrant blossoms in hand, he darted inside, while wet petals rained all around him.

He scuffed his wet shoes on the carpet in the entrance, shivering from the blast of AC.

Cheesy soup scents caught his nose as he passed by the cafeteria headed toward the elevators. On, up three floors, ding. His breath hitched when the double doors to the ICU opened. A cluster of people swarmed outside her room.

Oh yeah, they'd definitely broken the "only three people in the room at a time" rule.

People in poofy skirts and suits, as if dressed for the occasion, found him in the hallway to take the various items out of his arms. He teetered on the outer edge until he spotted a familiar face. Pat, next to the yellow curtain, instructed a man with a Beatles mop of brown hair to wrap the bouquet in streamers, since they'd run out of paper.

"Pat"—he had to shout this above the din of the crowd—"how'd you get them to come here so early on such short notice?"

"Oh, you know people of their age. Always arriving at places half an hour before events start. And we've been waiting on this wedding for a while."

True, his grandma did like to eat dinner at four. If they ever went to restaurants, they would arrive at the same time as the other seniors in the area. He scanned the crowd for Pastor Timothy, but no sign of him yet. Instead, he landed on a man next to a hand sanitizer station, who gripped the neck of a guitar. Dimples. That must be Priscilla's dad.

Feeling useless and needing something to occupy his thoughts before they went too dark, he marched over to the man, then extended a hand.

"Are you Priscilla's dad?"

"You her boyfriend?"

"Hopefully." They shook, and then he shoved his hand back in his pocket. "Sorry for the quick notice, but we're glad Elena invited you to play guitar."

A laugh blew through white teeth. No, her dad didn't believe the lie either. "Happy to help." He laughed, bobbled on his heels, and then his face fell. A finger swiped at his eyes before he also shoved them into his jean pockets. "I hadn't seen her my whole life, and today she was in a wedding dress." His deep voice crackled like glass. "I've missed out on so much."

His guitar echoed when he placed it on the ground to wipe at his face with both palms.

Carter shifted his weight from his heels to his toes. What could he say? Another lie? *"Oh, it's really not that bad. She only didn't trust men until this summer because of you."*

"Sir, I won't downplay how much your being absent hurt your daughter. But look around." He gestured at the crowd by the door. Two women were busy making braids out of three colors of streamers: blue, white, and pink. "We're having a wedding during someone's last days on earth. If Scarlett and Paul get a happy ending, I don't see why anyone else can't."

A white dress in a sea of black suits weaved through the cluster of people. Priscilla bent down to help two men with creating paper flowers that looked like half-moons with spikes.

A curtain swung open, Maria peeped out at the crowd, then glanced at her watch. She made a sweeping motion to Carter with a clap of her hands. "All right, people, stop what you're doing and hang up those last-minute decorations. The pastor is getting here in five minutes."

He checked his phone, and sure enough, Pastor had sent him and Priscilla a message with his ETA. The crowd passed along the almost-done streamers and flowers before they faded into the darkness.

Maria gave him another frantic wave, motioning him inside.

"I don't know"—he sidestepped two men—"Maria, is there room in the room for us?"

"Don't be ridiculous. You're Paul's best man. Now, get in here, you two."

Best man? He hadn't realized Paul considered them to be that close. His Adam's apple bobbed, as he breathed. Best not to think too much about anything until later.

Behind him, Priscilla's father loomed two inches above him. She didn't get her height from him, to be sure. They skittered around until they found a pocket of air by the girl in the wedding dress and Paul by the bed.

It appeared someone at Country Acres had fished out Paul's suit jacket from the dance, which he wore now. The decorations scattered around the room screamed baby shower with all the pinks and blues, but the fairy lights did bring a warm glow to the dark place.

Stationed by the closed blinds on the window, Priscilla's father strummed. Slants of light lit up his fingers as they shifted cords.

"I'm singing in the rain."

Although a little gruff, his voice carried nicely in the room. The rest joined in the lyrics. Tears sparkled in Scarlett's eyes as she clutched at the bouquet of flowers placed on her lap. No, not clutched. She didn't have much control of her ligaments now. Maybe someone put the flowers on her belly, then stuck her hands on top of the arrangement.

A greasy man parted the crowd mid-chorus. Pastor Timothy swiped at his forehead as he stationed himself by an open space near the heart monitor.

Scarlett opened and shut her mouth again and again. To sing along to the lyrics, perhaps. By now, according to the frantic texts from Elena and Maria on their way to the hospital, she couldn't raise her voice in more than a whisper. Thanks to the oxygen pumping through her nose, she could get a few words out every couple minutes. At least, she'd manage an "I do."

They finished the song after two rounds of the chorus. At the conclusion, Pat flashed pictures on her camera. They would all want to keep these ones by their bedside.

Pastor began his "dearly beloved" bit, while Carter rocked back and forth on his feet. Heat sweltered in the room from the number of bodies. He wondered how long the residents could last standing with walkers and canes, but even though legs shook, no one spoke a word of complaint. Paul clasped Scarlett's hands. She tilted her chin to look at him, cheeks wet from tears.

A hand popped up from the crowd while the pastor went on and on about some passage in 1 Corinthians; it was Elena who waved a stack of papers. "Sorry, Pastor, but I think the nurses outside might be getting antsy about all these people. Is it possible that we can sign these first?"

Light had overtaken all of Scarlett.

Elena brandished a pen from her pocket, sliding the papers into Paul's hands. "Don't worry, Scarlett. I filled out most of your information on the sheet. Pat can help me with the rest from the documents you provided at Country Acres. All we need is your signatures."

Scarlett opened and shut her mouth five times before she managed to whisper. "So this is real?"

"Yes, dear." Water rimmed Paul's eyes when he squeezed her hand again. "We're actually getting married."

Laughter bounced off the walls of the room. Paul placed the papers on her lap, then helped guide her hand on the signature line, since she could hardly grip the pen. Once signed, she gave a gasp, the oxygen part of the heart monitor beeping and turning red for a moment. But she inhaled, exhaled, and the machine stopped its whines.

The ventilator hummed in the near-dead silence when Pastor moved to the next part about the exchanging of the rings.

Pangs filled Carter's chest for a moment. They'd forgotten the rings.

Somehow, though, Elena slid two rings into the Pastor's hand, which he gave over to Paul. One to put on himself, and the other to slip onto his wife. Priscilla leaned over to whisper, "Some of the residents kept their rings from their late husbands and wives. We had to try them on her fingers before to see which ones fit, but everyone figured they'd donate since they didn't need them anymore."

A mixture of joy and sadness swirled in his chest at once.

How did everyone manage to pull this off in three hours? His hand itched for his phone in his pocket, but he thought better of it. TikTok didn't need to know about the miraculous three-hour set up for a wedding. This time, they could keep this memory all to themselves.

"Do you, Scarlett, take this man—"

"I do."

He could've imagined it, but the whites of her eyes showed for a moment as if to say: Oh, you ridiculous man. Shut up and get me married already.

"And do you Paul—"

"You know I do."

Power vested, kiss the bride.

Paul leaned over the bedside, gripped the railing that flanked the sides of the mattress, and planted a kiss. Applause rang throughout the room along with some whoops and whistles.

When the couple pulled apart, she opened and shut her mouth again, oxygen levels lower than normal.

Then: "Oh, Paul. I could die happy now."

Chapter Thirty-Two
PRISCILLA

PRISCILLA BREATHED AGAIN once people leaked out of the room.

They had squeezed Scarlett's hand to say a mixture of "congratulations" and "goodbye." Then they headed downstairs to attempt to split the cake amongst all of them. Someone promised to steal paper plates from Au Bon Pain. Everyone else volunteered to help tear down the room and take a decoration with them. They left behind the flowers on her bedside.

Priscilla fanned out the train behind her because the space had grown far too hot. Not just from the bodies. No wonder Scarlett had such a hard time breathing without an oxygen tube in here.

At long last, she, Pat, Carter, and Paul were the only ones who loitered in the room. A woman in blue scrubs hung by the door, fingers half in a box for a disposable smock. The nurses had to wear those at all times in this room, then throw it away once they left.

Pat gave Scarlett's hand a squeeze before motioning Priscilla into the hallway. Following after her, she had to lean down to receive Pat's whispered message.

"The nurses want to administer morphine soon. She held out for the ceremony but is in a lot of pain. You might want to say your goodbyes now."

Her breath caught in her throat until she choked it down. She blinked hot tears away as she smoothed down the dress. Into the darkness again, she forced a smile up her cheeks and hiked her voice high.

"What a beautiful ceremony, Scarlett. I'm so happy for you two."

She flicked a glance at Paul who now sat in a chair by a table, which held a box of tissues. Boy, she would need to grab more than a dozen of those on her way out. Just like the residents had. She'd be lucky if they left behind at least three in the little box with cartoon flowers printed all over it.

Scarlett didn't answer. Instead, she winced and whimpered through her nostrils.

"I know it hurts. But it'll be over soon. I promise."

Pastor had spoken to her before he left about her personal relationship with Jesus Christ. Far as anyone was concerned, she'd earn a place in a country of her own soon. But for right now, her back hurt, her hips hurt, her chest hurt. From the failing kidneys, failing lungs, failing body.

How to say goodbye?

Priscilla didn't have much practice. Because she lived in New York, she didn't have time to make it down for the passing of Grandpa Silas's wife. Her mom didn't hear about what happened until she managed to get out of a writing conference. They attended the funeral, but never said a proper goodbye.

Where to even start? She stared at the slants of light from the blinds for inspiration, then the blank TV mounted onto the wall. Rasping sounds from the ventilator echoed off the walls.

"Scar, I dreaded the day you called me into that hair salon." She reached up to grab her curls, but the tight lace from the dress pulled her arm down. "We were so opposite, and I worried those two hours together would take forever to pass. Now." She swallowed. "I would give anything for two more."

Her knees wobbled underneath the dress. She gripped the banister on the side of the bed, avoiding Scarlett's eyes. Scared of what she would find in them. Scared a glance would make her burst into tears.

"You convinced me to do pranks, to stand up for myself, to fall in love."

She stopped to reach for the lace that cut at her collarbone.

Everything in her skull exploded like a light. Like a water balloon that hit a patch of thirsty grass and burst.

"That was the other half of the deal, wasn't it? You wanted to bring me and Carter together. You saw us glancing at each other in the Bingo Hall, and you decided to find a way to force us to spend time with one another. Even though you had a tough go at love, you wanted me to have a chance at it. But you knew that if you told me that half of the deal, I would refuse."

Scarlett didn't answer but nuzzled her neck into the hospital pillow with a grin at the ceiling. Yes. Priscilla caught Carter staring from across the room. She almost forgot he, too, had been in here, wedged between the ventilator and another chair. For the past few seconds, she thought only she and Scarlett shared this space.

"You'll be happy to know it worked, you ridiculous woman."

She mirrored Scarlett's expression and reached for her hand. Icy cold fingers intertwined with hers. Inhale, hold it, exhale.

"Goodbye, dear friend. You better dance like nobody's business up there."

Rain splattered against the windowpane as she gave the hand a tight squeeze. Finally, she let go ... hugged herself, and then trudged into the hallway, dress train weighing down her steps.

She had to give Carter and Paul a chance to say goodbye before Scarlett received morphine.

Her shoes skittered to a halt when she turned to almost run into a man holding a guitar, her father. She released a breath, then relaxed her shoulders. Well, she dealt with one goodbye. Maybe she could use a hello.

The corners of his eyes crinkled in a wince. He clutched at the guitar. "Listen, I—"

She held up a hand. "I'm just going to skip right over the awkward, polite small talk. I think we learned today that the past doesn't have to determine everything about someone's future." She sighed. "And that it's never too late for second chances. Now, why don't you save me a spot at Au Bon Pain downstairs, and I'll catch you up on the last seventeen years?"

Like Scarlett, his jaw opened and shut several times. Before, at last, "I'd like that."

Her lips curved up into a smile. She gave his back one pat before plowing her way toward her grandpa's curtained room in the dress.

The yellow curtain swished under her arm to reveal Grandpa Silas setting down a spoon in an applesauce cup. He placed it on a tray and beamed at her. Maria hid a laugh behind her hand when Grandpa Silas cocked his head.

"Great, when your grandpa gets sick, you decide to run off and get married."

She rolled her eyes, before coming over to clasp his bedside. Color had returned to his cheeks, plus it appeared that he'd almost emptied the applesauce cup.

"Just found this in my closet, Gramps, don't worry." She found some flaky crumbs from another snack on his sheets and brushed them off. Then she stepped back to take in Grandpa again.

The wanness had disappeared from his skin now while he sat up in bed. Lights from a baseball game on the television flickered in his cognac eyes. No doubt he'd get better soon, ultimately leaving the ICU if he kept up this progress.

"Told your mom to hold off cancelling her writing conference." Maria grabbed a tissue from a nearby stand to swipe at her nose. "She'd almost booked a flight, not wanting the same thing that happened to her mother to happen to Silas."

She had missed saying goodbye.

A weight tugged at her chest, but she was happy she did have a chance this time.

"But stubbornness runs in your blood, and he's refusing to receive any goodbyes today. So she's staying put in New York for now." She crumpled the tissue, then stuffed it in her shorts pocket. "I'm off to get a panini downstairs, anyone want anything?"

They didn't.

Chains rattled when Maria swished the curtain to amble past the nurse's desk. Priscilla bunched the train around a seat before she parked on the soft cushion.

"Grandpa, we need to talk."

"I know, I know, business as always. Maria already spoke to me about care options. Don't want you and your mother worried up in New York."

Oh, right. She had to go home in a few weeks. Yet another goodbye that she had to give to Carter. Never had she entered a relationship before, and now, she had to navigate a long-distance one.

"We think assisted living is a good route to go, Prisca. From your recommendations, I think I might try out Country Acres, starting this fall."

She rose in her seat until she felt the squeeze of the boning in her dress when she breathed. She couldn't wait to get back into her normal clothes she'd left in a pile in the women's restroom below. Twisting her fingers, she hoped no one scooped them up to dump them in a trash bin or lost and found. That would make the ride home in Carter's car an interesting endeavor.

"Country Acres, huh?" Carter had mentioned his grandma was interested in staying there as well. Maybe Silas could meet a new friend there.

"Yes, ma'am."

"Grandpa." She untwisted her fingers as she rose to her feet. "What did you look like as a teen?"

She hated the waiting part the most.

While she and her dad sat across each other, wisps from steaming soups blurring their faces, she kept jerking her head over her shoulder. Waiting. For Pat to emerge from the elevators, laden with news. She made sure to board the elevator before the nurse injected Scarlett with morphine. She didn't want to see her asleep or any more sunken.

No, she would rather remember her dancing on a blue tarp with a man in a green suit.

"So, you have an interest in library sciences?"

Her dad's voice yanked her back. She grimaced, then stirred her spoon in the thick broth. "Yeah, with mom working as an editor, I grew up loving books. Besides, I hear Florida State has a nice library science program. Might investigate that when I graduate this next year."

"Tallahassee's thirty minutes away from here. You going to visit your old man?"

She paused.

He swallowed. "I—I understand the hesitation. I spent too much time with a bottle instead of family. This doesn't heal any past hurt, but I am clean now. Two years sober."

This filled her abdomen with a mixture of relief and hurt.

Her eyelids squinched. *Well, I meant more for Carter, but,* "Yeah. Of course I'd like to visit once in a while."

Tightness constricted her abdomen. Even though she had managed to put back on her civilian clothes and buy a small container of deodorant at the gift shop, used wedding dresses carried a foul, yet perfumed stench. She distracted herself by watching a family out in the waiting area play a game of UNO. No doubt, they awaited some news. But the balloons anchored to a bright pink gift bag indicated they came here for news on the other spectrum of life.

How strange, she mused, that the same building could give life and death sentences on the same day.

She caught Carter's eye in the waiting area. He was busy scrolling on a social media app before dropping his shoulder in a sigh and shoving his phone back in his pocket. Might as well wait with him too. She scooped up her tray, then dumped the remains of her soup in the trash. Before she ambled off, she told her dad they'd continue the conversation at another time. Reaching the couch where Carter sat, she nestled herself between Carter and his arm draped over the cushion.

"Hey."

"Hey, yourself, princess."

"You get to say goodbye?"

"Yeah. Asked her if I could name one of my future kids after her. She nodded for me to lean close and whispered, 'As long as you don't name them after Paul.'" He chuckled as he nudged the legs of a square table with his feet. On it, models with stethoscopes posed on medical magazines. "Took her a minute to get it out, but she thought it was worth it."

"That ridiculous woman."

"Indeed." Shadows fell over his features. "The world could use a bit of ridiculous."

"I know." She cushioned her head with his chest. "How else could we survive our short time here without a Scarlett in our lives?"

They waited in silence while a young boy from the cluster of UNO players cried when his sister next to him placed yet another +4 card down. When the elevator doors slid open, the whole hospital appeared to draw in a breath. Two figures trudged out, Pat and Paul.

No need to deliver the news. Their sunken faces said everything.

She buried her nose into Carter's chest and shook from her sobs. Oxygen refused to flow to her lungs until ten short breaths later darkness had begun to cover her eyes. Breathe in. She realized he'd belted her in with his arm; his fresh tears wetted the back of her t-shirt. Just like Mia had outside Country Acres, she clawed at his shirt, hoping to grasp at something, anything.

They'd held back tears until now.

Her abdomen bobbed back and forth from her hyperventilating breaths. She counted them until her chest slowed when she noticed how more bodies had surrounded them in a hug. Pat, Derinda, Elena, and some residents whose names escaped her now. Why didn't Pat have name tags on her when you needed them? The women's perfumes caused her brain to bobble, already dehydrated from the tears lost. Her mouth and eyelids had gone dry. Her eyes opened only a fraction, unable to stay open because of the weight placed upon them.

Everyone stayed suspended in silence for an eternity. A hush sounded from outside the huddle, no doubt from the family playing UNO.

Then, arms released until she saw the light of the waiting room again. Nurses in navy scrubs carried trays of food from the cafeteria to nearby tables. A woman in a bun answered a phone call at the circular front desk.

Oh-La-Di, how the life goes on.

Two women bunched tissues they'd grabbed from the room to dab at their noses. She sniffled, wishing she'd snagged some fistfuls when she left. Settling for the corner of her shirt instead, she smeared her nose, face, and glasses until they dried. Who cared? She could wear the wedding dress home if she really wanted to.

She didn't.

Pat clapped her palms together and announced that "sadly" the residents' group had to accompany her back on the bus. She punched some numbers into a cell phone, draped her arm around a hunched over Paul, and glued the phone to her ear. Calling the bus driver, Priscilla assumed.

Across the room, the clock's hour hand strained for the number five. They'd waited for over an hour since the ceremony to hear the news, and now it had arrived. She stared at the oval-shaped leaves of a fake plant stationed at the corner of the room, wishing for two more hours that could never come.

Carter coiled his arm around her again, then gave a light squeeze. She understood. Time to go. Knees crackled as they rose. She chewed on her tongue to hold back a joke about herself being an old woman.

Hands wet from tears, their fingers interlaced as they headed toward the automatic doors. Gray skies filled the windows with a black and white haze, but the rain had stopped falling. Sunshine would fight its way through the clouds soon.

"I guess we'll have to work out plans for a wedding and a funeral on the same day, huh?" He dug into his pocket. A jingle indicated he'd managed to fish out his keys.

"Right." She puffed out a breath as she cradled the dress she'd put on a brown chair in the waiting room with her free arm. The train dragged on the floor. "But this time, let's spend a little more than three hours pulling together the next event, okay?"

"Deal."

Chapter Thirty-Three
CARTER

HE ALWAYS THOUGHT HE HATED OPEN CASKET CALLING HOURS.

After his grandpa had passed this year, he remembered staring at his grandfather in a wooden box. How his waxed skin gleamed in the dark lighting of the funeral home's room. He'd first spotted the thing across the room when his family arrived early to form a receiving line. A certain haunting aura surrounded it. Like looking at the body sucked all the air out of his lungs.

Carter always thought he hated calling hours ... until he gazed at Scarlett's casket today.

Curly gray hairs curtained the sides of her wrinkled face. Even in death, she wore a red-lipstick smile and thin eyebrows raised close to her lined forehead. He did hate that they had dressed her in a suit with a ruffled collar that went up to her neck. Old or young, she would never be caught alive in that outfit.

Priscilla rested her head on his shoulder as they gazed at their friend.

"You know, she's still beautiful like that. Wrinkles and all."

"Agreed. Always the movie star. Why do you think the gift wore off on her but no one else?" He craned his neck at Paul who was receiving the next guest in line, a woman with a round collared dress and black veil hat who just hugged him. But he still looked like the teen version of himself.

She lifted her head before placing it back down again. "Well, I suppose she's technically not a resident of Country Acres anymore. She's found a different country now. A country of her own."

They gazed on in silence for five more seconds before she tugged his arm.

"We should let the next person pay their respects. She drew a huge crowd."

Behind Paul, a line snaked out the doors of the large room and into the foyer. Guests had to clump together to avoid getting stuck outside in the hot Florida sun. Good thing the funeral home liked to chill everything to sixty-something degrees. If not for the number of bodies in the room, he'd throw a hoodie on.

She pulled him to a table with photo books. They turned the glossy pages and grinned at the baby pictures of Scarlett frowning in a Halloween costume as her mother buttoned her up in a large winter coat. Scarlett never did like covering up.

"You know, she reminds me of this one painter I'd read about in a book." Priscilla turned a page to see Scarlett in torn up ballet slippers. "Most of the time he would paint his subjects with their faces turned to the side, as if those who he'd painted had something to hide. But on rare occasions, he would create someone with a full face, showing that that person was bold, unafraid, and always true to themselves."

"Like Scarlett."

"Exactly"—the next page featured her on the first day of school in a plaid dress—"Scarlett was a full-faced person."

Priscilla tugged at the bodice of her black dress and then clawed at the lace which covered her throat. Spying a table with cups of punch, she wandered over to it, and Carter trailed behind. She scooped up a clear glass in her hand, ladling herself a cup of red liquid. The foam in the bowl smelled like Sprite. He grabbed a glass for himself to drink the cherry-flavored liquid.

"How's your grandpa doing?"

Bubbles swirled in her glass before she took another sip.

"Better. He's home now and resting. But Maria did have to throw out the ingredients for sangria so he wouldn't be tempted."

His lips twitched into a small smile that fell again when he gazed at the line across the room.

Muted conversations filled the airless space as people passed by glowing orange lamps on small tables. It was like they wanted to make a depressing atmosphere. This place would have given Scarlett's hospital room a run for its money on lack of lighting alone.

"What I don't understand is why these people never visited her. Paul had his daughter, sometimes his granddaughter, stop by. I even had one of her former dance pupils behind me in line."

He drained the rest of the glass before pitching it in a recycling container by the window.

Priscilla frowned. "So how come we were the only ones who stopped by Country Acres for her, Carter?"

"I wish I knew. People get busy. Don't realize that the last time you say goodbye is truly the last time. It's not an excuse ... but it's probably a reason."

A greasy forehead reflected the glow from the lamplight. Pastor Timothy clutched a program they'd handed out at the door with a picture of Scarlett, from her middle-aged years, on the front. He spotted Carter, asked his wife, a woman with mousy hair, to hold his place in line, and beelined toward the punch table.

"I had my doubts about you." He waved a finger like a wand before fishing through a bowl of Chex mix on the table. Swallowed.

"You skipped youth group every chance you got and hung around a questionable crowd."

He paused and scooped another palmful of mix into his mouth.

"But after the wedding, on my way out, countless residents told me about how you went above and beyond to make that day special for the couple, in a matter of hours. You granted a dying wish and blessed lives in more ways than you know." He rubbed the crumbs from his palms onto his shorts. "Whenever you decide to enroll in college, let me know. I'll write the world's best recommendation letter."

Tightness fled from his chest. For some reason, he'd expected another lecture.

"I appreciate it, sir. But I'm taking a gap year. Might have to hit you up after that."

With a curt nod, Pastor bounded back to his place in line. His wife gestured to him before pointing at something in the program. He overheard something to do with a typo.

Priscilla fanned herself, then jerked her chin toward the doors. "Outside?"

"It's not going to be any colder out there."

"Maybe we could sit in your car?"

He agreed, so they weaved their way around the crowd of people, avoiding eye contact. If spotted, that would mean getting trapped in another conversation. They already had forced their way through five of those on the way up to the casket. Much as he loved discussions, he was starting to understand why Priscilla preferred to stay inside, cuddled up with a cat and book.

They slid into his car, using the fabric of their shirts to touch the handles, and he blasted the AC.

"Gap year, huh?" She shouted this.

"Yeah, much as I'd love to get out of the house with my parents at each other's throats every day, I figure I need time to re-plan."

"That's wise."

"And with my grandma talking about going to Country Acres, I should probably stick around to visit her often." He smiled at the thought. Plenty of puzzles in store awaited the two of them. "I've spent so much of my life screwing around. And if Scarlett taught me anything, anyone can get a second chance. Don't want to blow mine."

"You won't. And if you do, you'll get another one. That's the beauty of life."

Silence hovered over the shwoooom of the AC. Minutes later, head aching from the cold, he dialed the knob down two notches.

"Well, you're always welcome in New York, lover boy. It's cold, crowded, and everything costs three times the amount it should."

"Man, you're really talking me into it."

She chewed on her lip with a grin. "You know, we never did get ice cream."

"You think we should? On today of all days?"

"Oh, come on." She flashed the program. Scarlett's slight smirk stared him down. "She's practically begging us from heaven to get some. She even sent rain this morning. It's a sign."

True, she would've hated the calling hours display. The moody lighting, white flowers placed on her chest, tissue-dabbing of eyes all around. Scarlett liked a party, and she loved that ice cream shop.

After all, she fell in love there.

"Fine, but you're letting me pay. Paul told me to watch out for you. Said you might try to slip some ones into my wallet without me looking."

"Ugh, fine, you can pay for it this time."

He kicked the gear stick into reverse, peering over his shoulder to make sure he wouldn't run into some passerby from inside the home. A group had huddled outside with plates in hand. Guess they were handing out cake somewhere inside. Images from the room inside flashed across his mind, as he remembered a table with various foods piled high. Deviled egg arrangements and slices of key lime pie. Now that Scarlett would've liked.

"And whatever you do, princess, you can't convince me to get a strawberry malt."

The funeral happened two days after calling hours. Enough time for Carter and Priscilla to grab ice cream together.

But not enough time for Carter to take in Paul's latest development on funeral plans.

"Paul, are you absolutely certain she wanted *me* to read a speech?"

He had the pile of papers in his hand. They'd gone over this when he, Pat, Paul, and Priscilla helped plan the funeral, but he still couldn't believe that Scarlett would choose him over Priscilla to give the speech. After all, he hadn't spent nearly enough time with her.

Wincing, Paul thanked someone as they entered the dimly lit sanctuary before returning to Carter. "She said, and I quote, 'Don't have Priscilla say my speech. She'll cry too much and tell no jokes. Carter must do it.'"

"Why didn't she pick you?"

"She also said, 'Your voice is so quiet. The back row can't hear you. Carter must do it.'"

With a frown, he watched Pat place tissue boxes on the remaining open pews.

A line snaked through the door, underneath a wooden cross stationed above it. A man in white robes, the pastor of the Lutheran church, shook hands with one of the guests before ducking underneath the low entrance. Tassels swung from a cord tied around his robe.

When Pat finished zigzagging through the rows, she bustled to the door, then waved for Priscilla and Carter to follow her.

"We saved you both two seats up front. She didn't have much family left alive, so you two'll fill in for today."

She parked them at a rickety row, right where multicolored light from the stained glass windows left colorful fingerprints behind. They sat, and a blue light danced across Priscilla's magnificent curls. Ahead of the congregation, on a PowerPoint, a slideshow displayed photographs of Scarlett from baby pictures to her eightieth birthday. She almost looked like a stranger blowing out those candles, but no one could mistake the curve of her lips. Always twisted up in some knowing smile.

When the sanctuary had filled, the pastor lifted his hands, and all the rows rose. They sang a hymn to start off the service. Priscilla broke down in the first verse. Carter dug his nails into his palms to try and focus on the pain instead of the tears. He had to hold those back until after the speech.

But as her sobs continued, he stopped singing, wrapped his arm around her, and listened to the last verse.

I'd stay in the garden with him
Tho the night around me be falling;
But he bids me go; thro' the voice of woe,
His voice to me is calling.
And he walks with me, and he talks with me,
And he tells me I am his own,
And the joy we share as we tarry there,
None other has ever known.

Warm tears spilled from his eyelids, as he reached for the tissues Pat had placed in the row. He fought visions of the gardens around Country Acres, of the so-called fountain of youth where Paul proposed. *What are the gardens like in heaven?*

The last note from the organ absorbed the silence in the sanctuary which queued the pastor to motion for them to sit. Carter bobbed his leg up and down, squinting at his speech in the dark sanctuary. All these words felt wrong now. They didn't seem like her.

Priscilla nudged him and whispered over the prayer of the pastor. "What are you nervous about? You've done crazy stunts for social media. This is nothing."

Still, she swiped a clumped tissue under her nose before relaxing her shoulders. She didn't have to give the speech after all.

"Right, but those are dumb things like spray painting math homework and accidentally getting some of the green on my mom's car. But this is different. This is something real. Heavy."

"She chose you for a reason, now go up."

He hadn't realized the pastor had finished talking and had returned to his pew at the front. Knees a-wobble, he left his speech behind on his seat as he ascended the steps to a mic podium. He blurred his eyes to avoid seeing the crowd but couldn't fail to miss Priscilla brandishing the speech with a furious movement. Like a newsie waving the latest edition to make a sale.

"Hi, everyone."

The greeting echoed throughout the congregation. Every seat had filled, plus some folks had stationed themselves out in the foyer just outside. He exhaled, glanced at a purple banner on the wall that read "Let there be peace on earth," and continued his speech.

"A few months back, if you'd told me that I would become friends with someone who was over the age of twenty-one, I would've laughed. I shut myself in my room to avoid my parents and even came to church a half hour early, because I didn't want to be stuck inside one on one with my grandma."

His words hitched at the back of his throat.

"Until I met Scarlett."

He gripped the edges of the podium to steady himself.

"See, Scarlett had this ability. This gift, if you will, to make everyone around her a teen again. She pulled pranks." He told the story of the diner, unblurring his vision to watch the congregation double over with laughter and swipe tissues on the corners of their eyes. "And even at eighty-something years old, she could dance like someone set the floor on fire."

The PowerPoint in his periphery flashed a photograph of her leading a line of her majorette troupe in band.

"But most importantly, she believed in second chances. Because of Scarlett, I managed to have a wonderful ice cream date with a beautiful girl I didn't have a chance with. And Scarlett got to marry a truly *good* man, even if for just one day."

The multicolored beams disappeared from the windows. At their absence, rain tapped the glass outside.

"She showed me that everyone is young at heart, and wise beyond their years."

The roar of raindrops against the wooden roof echoed in the sanctuary now.

"And that you can witness heaven on earth right at this moment."

He rubbed at his eyes. Moisture filled them. Then he clutched at his chest to tug on his tie. He'd forgotten to strap something to the collar of his shirt today. Good. Didn't need it anymore.

"If only you take off your sunglasses and see."

Author's Note

I started this book because I saw Mountain Brook Fire was kicking off their speculative line with a contest. For the first round, they only required the first ten pages to be written.

"Ten pages? No problem."

The idea had come to me after I saw a series of photos on Facebook of elderly people glancing into the mirror to see younger versions of themselves. This made me think of the phrase that I believe so encapsulates this book: Everyone is young at heart and wise beyond their years. The photo series is by Tom Hussey titled "Reflections of the Past." Give it a Google search; I highly recommend taking a look.

I felt a special urge to write it as tensions escalated between Gen Z/Millennials and Boomers/The Greatest Generation. Neither seems to understand or respect one another.

And a society's best measure comes by how we treat the most vulnerable. Although many assisted living facilities and families can provide great care for seniors, we have miles to go in treating every human being with respect and dignity, especially those older than us.

So I wanted to level the playing field. To help both generations see eye to eye and the humanity in one another. Also to show that marriage can happen at twenty years old or eighty. True love has no expiration date.

Nothing could have prepared me for how personal this project would get until a mere handful of days after I had submitted the first ten pages to the contest my grandma was rushed to the hospital. Having battled an autonomic disease in her lungs that had attacked her heart over the span of three decades, all her organs had started to shut down.

Days later, she passed away. Unexpectedly.

My grandma exemplified a young-at-heart spirit and a wise-beyond-her-years intellect. She tap danced into her eighties, explored the world, and gave back in so many ways to her community. Her selflessness knew no bounds. This woman attended so many of my athletic competitions, theatrical performances, and came to my first book release party. She and Grandpa had run a bookstore several decades back, and I firmly believe she played an integral role for my love of writing.

Even on the day of her passing, she worried that we paid too much for the parking garage near the hospital.

I wanted to write this for her.

Grief and I don't handle each other well, and I have a feeling I won't be able to write this as fast as I hope to. I can expect a lot out of myself, even when my body forces me to slow down and reflect.

But I do hope I can choose all the right words to say.

This is for all the teenagers trapped in elderly bodies, and old souls trapped in a teenage mind. We're all looking for a little bit of heaven on earth, and at last, we'll find a country of our own and reunite with the Grandma Jeans who came before us.

About My Grandma

A number of my family members gave beautiful tributes at my grandma's funeral, including a poem by my sister that I believe deserves publication in every journal out there. I don't say that lightly.

Poetry is almost impossible to get right.

After the service, which was packed to the brim, a few days before the governor of Ohio issued a ban on gatherings of more than one hundred people in one place because of the COVID-19 virus, one of my aunts pulled me aside and tearfully said she wished I had said something during the service. I was the writer of the family, so why hadn't I written something?

I explained to her that I was already 15,000 words into this story, that I'd started a few days before. I told the family I was writing a book dedicated to Grandma, but some of them took it to mean it was about Grandma, as in a biography of sorts.

In some ways it is. I did try to throw in Easter eggs for the family to find and say, "There is Jean. Living on in a book." She did absolutely love books.

One of her favorite songs was "Singing in the Rain." For her Senior Follies group, they planned to dance to that song for their next performance. On her last rehearsal with them, she danced but got winded fast and had to take breaks off to the side frequently at practice. Her dance instructor could tell she was frustrated because everything within her wanted to dance, but her body said no.

At the funeral he said, "We all thought Jean would come back again. She always rebounded. This time ... she didn't."

But no, Jean was not at all like Scarlett personality-wise. If anything, you couldn't find two people more opposite. Much as I love Scarlett, I do love Grandma more.

I'll shed some light on some of the ways she inspired this book. My grandma was an extremely talented woman who enjoyed dance from an early age. She participated in her high school band as a majorette and tap danced until her final days here on earth.

Like Scarlett, she hit it off with my grandpa over a date at an ice cream place in Akron known as Mary Coyle's (still around to this day), but no, she didn't stir any ketchup into his strawberry malt.

They stayed together for sixty plus years ever since they married, being able to take a picture on their sixtieth at Mary Coyle's together.

Although I can't do a tribute justice like my dad has on Crosswalk. com in an article titled "3 Life Lessons My Mom Taught Me at Her Life's End," I do know she had a heart for service her whole life. From adopting a family from war-torn Laos to visiting the elderly in nursing homes when she had moved to a new state, she never spent a moment without thinking about how to take care of someone else. She cared deeply about family and drew together as many relatives as she could for every family gathering imaginable, even though we lived in different states, had become broken by divorce, or any other reason why a normal family would avoid joining together over a meal.

Unlike Scarlett, she never enjoyed the spotlight.

Everyone at her funeral said she would've hated that day because it was all about her.

She loved deeply and was deeply loved in return. And most importantly, she loved Christ. She wanted to share His joy and love with anyone who would venture down the same pathway as her.

Dear Grandma, I am deeply sorry that this isn't even close to being a biography or memoir. I know you spent years helping Grandpa compile his and not enough time on yours. I hope the snippets of you throughout this book: the love of dance, love of reading, and seeing everyone as worthy of loving—did a small inkling of justice as a tribute to you.

I know it's not perfect, but I hope it helps others to see the legacy you left behind: to love others and leave this world a little more beautiful than how you'd found it.

Acknowledgments

To my Lord and Savior Jesus Christ who "was there to hear (our) borning cry (and will) be there when (we) are old."

That comes from my favorite hymn because You walk along beside us in our youth and old age. May we find pieces of heaven on earth as we seek a country of our own. And when we finally find that country, may we be filled with joy as we reunite with loved ones.

To Grandma Jean to whom I dedicated this book. I do hope they have books in heaven. You certainly loved them.

To my other grandparents: Grandpa Clyde, Grandpa Bill, and Grandma Joyce. I have learned so much from you and am always listening to your stories. Even though we have differences, that makes us unique and able to bring a piece of heaven down to earth with us. I know you are all young at heart, and I'll never be able to tell you I love you enough.

To Grandpa Clyde, who unfortunately, passed away during the editing process of this book.

To my other family members who have supported me throughout the writing process. I give up easily and forget how tough publishing really is. Thanks for sticking it through with me.

To my ceaseless encouragers Sonya, Alyssa, James, Carlee, Jess, whatever the Cyle Group Chat is called now, and all those in the writing community for your nonstop support. You make it hard to quit and easier to write.

To Miralee for creating the contest that inspired me to finally write this book like I'd wanted to for years. I'm so glad you gave me an opportunity to write this story I'd sat on for more than two years.

To Victoria who found a beautiful home for this book. I'm sorry if this book made you cry. It makes me do so every time I edit it. Today, for instance, my mom is over at my house painting, and I'm a tearful mess. It's a fun, awkward situation.

To Nikki, Alice, Erin, Kandi, and the other editors on this project. Thank you for the grace you had with me in the edits and for handling such a personal book so well.

To Tessa and Cyle, so sorry. I know I'm tenacious, ridiculous, and send way too many projects your way. Thank you for bearing with the crazy and enduring with me in the difficult, often-thankless job of agenting my books.

To all the old souls, I understand you and hear you. I've often been told I never fit in with my generation. This might explain my inability to find a man my age. Publishing has forced me to be a bit of a Carter. Platform, platform, platform, but even back in high school I'd given speeches about how I was wary about smartphones. I guess some part of me would still love to bring back elements of different periods of history: the fashion, the music, neighbors knowing each other's names, and cooking meals for each other. But as Scarlett had said, there are many old-fashioned things I am so happy we no longer participate in. Everyone deserves a seat at the table and deserves to be loved and valued.

And to everyone from every generation, I see your beauty, your humanity, and that you all have something important to contribute. Let's listen to each other, challenge each other, and most importantly, love one another.

About the Author

Hope Bolinger is a Managing & Acquisitions Editor at End Game Press and the Founder of Generation Hope Books.

More than 1300 of her works have been featured in various publications ranging from Writer's Digest to Keys for Kids to HOOKED to Crosswalk.com.

She has worked for various publishing companies, magazines, newspapers, and literary agencies and has edited the work of authors such as Jerry B. Jenkins and Michelle Medlock Adams.

Twenty of her books are under contract or out now with traditional publishers, and she hopes more of her stories will find a home soon. She has also contributed to ten other books.

When she isn't accidentally writing a book in a week, you can find her on local runways, acting in plays, hiking in Ohio's national parks, or petting her ridiculous cats—Odin and Freya.